First Run

two firefighting novels past and present

by

Barry Roberts Greer

Cover photo by Kaitlin Greer copyright 2018

ISBN-13: 978-1720790037
ISBN-10: 1720790035

Author's Note

First Run brings my two firefighting novels together under one cover with one change in structure. The third part of Seven Two has been dropped for reprint here although it remains part of the original Seven Two novel. That makes both short novels included in First Run pure firefighting narratives.

But "pure" means the stories are embedded in the political and social reality of both the past as in Seven Two and in the present as with Engine 10. But strong similarities exist across time. Rookie firefighters appear in both stories and the risks of the profession remain the same even as the equipment improves, because natural disaster and human ignorance and stupidity remain the same.

The critical importance of fire suppression and other emergency services therefore also remain as a stabilizing force that keeps communities from burning to the ground literally and metaphorically. No matter what the politics or the weather, when someone dials 9-1-1, firefighters respond.

Contents

Seven Two

1 first run

It was a still alarm and that one long ring allowed Tommy Beck and John Gary to get down to the carriage floor during the half minute it took the lieutenant to pick up the phone and get the location. By the time short, round Lt Marco was down the stairs, Beck had the overhead door up, the driver had the Seagrave started, and the vollys were lined up on the tailgate. The 1954 Seagrave had a split hose bed with a catwalk between and a rear-facing jump seat just behind the cab at the front of the hose bed, but nobody road there. They kept the foam nozzle, the resuscitator, and the Scott pack on the jump seat. Everybody just climbed on the wide rear step and hung on, remembering to duck as they left the station, which had been built originally for much smaller apparatus. The overhead door was actually too low, so the rotating red emergency light on top of the Seagrave cab had to be placed on a bracket that hung out over the windshield to lower it rather than on top of the cab. And when the front wheels of the Seagrave dropped onto the ramp as the pumper left the station, the tailgate rose up high enough to plant the head of a firefighter into the overhead door if he didn't duck. So they ducked.

In the middle of the night, the rule was that the siren on top of the firehouse would not be triggered to avoid waking the neighbors, and that time of night they didn't even need to use the siren in the nose of the Seagrave because no traffic was around at 2:33 am when the call came in, but the real reason was that New London FD was in transition to a fully paid department with a union that did not want volunteers around. Free labor threatened union jobs, according to IAFF logic, so slowly but surely volunteer fire department practices and traditions, such as rooftop sirens or bells or air horns to alert the community of an emergency, were being phased out. So be it.

They rolled up to home where the small wooden storage shed was fully involved, and the Marco stepped out of the cab to order the booster line pulled, but Beck had already pulled the nozzle with Gary on backup, and the third volly, Joey Pazolli, a welder at the Waterford nuke plant construction site, pulled the line off the reel. It was all very old fashion back in the late 60s. Firefighters wore quick hitches at night only. They never used air masks at small outside fires and never at structure fires in New London, not on initial attack anyway. Putting air on slowed down a quick attack because the Scott pack was carried in the case, and the case was in the jump seat, so somebody had to go get it, had to open the case, and had to open the tank valve, put the tank on, the mask put on, and then the firefighter entered the building behind somebody who was already there on the nozzle. And it was the only Scott in the entire department. The bad old days. So for this little shed fire, they just cracked the nozzle and went to work.

Beck was a good foreman who led but also knew when to allow newer volunteers to take a turn on the nozzle to gain experience, so after the initial knockdown, he turned the nozzle over to the Gary who finished the job of dousing the flames while Beck went back to the Seagrave to get a pike pole for overhaul. He pulled the burned boards of the shed apart while Gary soaked the ashes. Joey took an ax and cut and smashed larger boards into splinters to make sure they had it all out. Nobody wanted to be called out again that night for a rekindle if they could avoid it, and nobody wanted to spend the rest of the night on fire watch at a shed fire when they could soak it good in a half hour and return to the bunk room.

And they did it as quietly as possible with Marco not having to do much other than observe, because until the first paid lieutenants had been added to each fire company, the volunteers ran the show. The driver got the rig to the scene, ran the pump, and the vollys did the rest. But now the lieutenant had the last word, and he gave the nod in a half hour, and they started to take up with Joey connecting the booster reel crank under the tailgate, then turning it slowly so Beck and Gary could guide the hose carefully and evenly back onto the reel to be damned certain it could be pulled out again without jamming.

Back at the station, Lt Marco nicely decided that they didn't need to wash down the Seagrave. After they filled the booster tank using the overhead line and Marco made his entry into the log for the run, they all trudged back up to the bunk room, except for Gary. His job at a bus company started at 4:00 am when, being the junior mechanic, he had to arrive first and open the doors, pull the school buses out, fuel them, and get the drivers off on their morning runs. If one of the drivers was a no show, he had to drive the route. But it was a job, one he got through a connection in the volunteer fire company, and one that offered the opportunity to work around truck engines, even if they were mounted in a school bus or coach chassis. To be blunt about it, he liked machines, and couldn't understand why any firefighter wouldn't spend more time understanding engines, pumps, and hydraulics. Like Beck, he was gung ho, but unlike Beck, he hoped someday to be a full time firefighter, although he had days when he wanted to punch out the New London paid men for the way they treated the vollys, especially given that most if not all of them had started where he was as a volunteer bunkman.

He stayed down in the day room after he went up to put on his work clothes and told Marco he'd turn out the lights when he left for work.

The day room was part lounge with a couch and television on one side and part kitchen with sink, stove, refrigerator, and a table for meals on the other. Gary kept sandwich meat and bread in the fridge for his lunches and milk for his morning cereal. He also started a pot of coffee, and after eating, while he waited for the coffee to brew, he did his unappointed rounds, quietly going through the screen door out to the carriage floor to slowly walk around the Seagrave, the sacred if aging 1954 Seagrave Class A 750 GPM pumper. One of the finest fire engines made from the ground up with the smoothest running gas engine he'd ever heard operate. A near perfectly balanced V-12 flathead that started without fail and never flooded.

Yes indeed, he wanted to learn how to operate the pump. Hell, he wanted to learn how to overhaul pumps, figuring that the more he knew, the better pump operator he'd become. Same for operating fire equipment from booster lines to pre-connects to the large hand lines, the 2.5 that required at least two people to control. He needed to know how to use a hose clamp, a hose strap, a double female, a double male. He needed to know how to connect a hydrant and charge the line, he needed to know how to get control of an out-of-control nozzle. He needed to know how to operate the foam applicator, the fog nozzle applicator, how to use the pike pole, the Halligan bar, the bayonet nozzle, the hand lights, the axes, spanners, the resuscitator, and even the wheel chocks. And he needed to know where all that stuff was so when someone called for the equipment or he just needed to find it himself, he knew without hesitation which compartment to open. Beck had given him the tour the night he joined the vollys at Pequot Engine Company No 8, but he didn't remember it all, so his morning routine was a quiet walk around the Seagrave until he did remember it all.

The Seagrave also carried a wooden ground ladder, hard suction for drafting, and soft suction for the large 4.5 inch connection to the main port on the hydrant. And yes the Seagrave was red, the color of the VW Beatle he drove to work that morning through the dark after he turned out the light and left the station through the backdoor of the day room to the parking lot. Off to the dirty, greasy, smelly job of bus maintenance, but going in early meant he would be done by early afternoon unless he had to work overtime. He'd be free again to chase fires, which was damned near as important as chasing women, and unlike most vollys, he could make runs during the day.

2 Car fire

Beck made sure new vollys attended fire school. He told Gary after he'd been voted in as a member to stick close to him until he'd been up to Willimantic and had taken a few classes. The Eastern Connecticut State Fire School ran during the summer because most of the classes were held outside in good weather. The school had a Christmas tree to teach new people how to fight gasoline fires, three oil pits for oil firefighting, the smokehouse for learning how to use the Scott pack, and a three story building where they learned ladder use and rappelling. They also ran classes on extrication, forced entry, but nothing on courage. That was always on the job training and nothing people talked about unless you were seen as lacking in that particular skill.

Luckily that first summer Gary bunked at Engine 8 they had no serious workers, so Gary got away with basic skills like showing up at the firehouse, getting up on box alarms at night. When a box came in anywhere in the city, it rang into each firehouse, and every firefighter on duty, paid or not, even if they did not have to go out, had to get up and go down to the apparatus floor until the box was cleared. The reasoning was simple. With only four engine companies and two ladders, every piece of apparatus would be needed on a second, which meant the entire department would respond. So if everyone was up, then they could all get out the door faster. They also had a smoky dumpster fire one afternoon behind a restaurant and Gary, being the only volly hanging around the station, pulled the nozzle on the booster line and did the wet down after the lieutenant flipped the lid up. Luckily, B-Line was on duty, and he happened to be one of the old timers who dated back to the time when the only paid man on duty was the driver who depended day and night on volunteers, and B-Line wasn't getting any younger, so he was happy to let Gary take the line and douse the dumpster fire while he stepped back after flipping the lid up and chewed on his cigar, chuckling every once in a while at the young gung-ho volly and growling "Good job" past the cigar.

And they had one standby on the 4th of July at Ocean Beach Park where they did nothing but show up on Engine 8 for fire watch at the fireworks display that evening wearing their volunteer dress uniform, which was dark pants, white shirt, dark tie. Easy duty. But even then he had the new man jitters, wondering always what to do if, and wondering if he'd measure up, and wondering when the next run would be, and wondering what it would be. The older guys like B-Line found some way long ago to not worry, or they didn't seem to worry.

Fire school helped calm Gary down a bit. Beck was a tough teacher on the Christmas tree, and barked instructions at the two four-man hose crews before he lit the gasoline. "You open your nozzle and wet me down," and the man on the nozzle did, then Beck opened the valve outside the seven foot tall metal shack that was open on the side facing the rookie firefighters and occupied only by a six-foot vertical pipe with short horizontal pipes sticking out the side, each 45 degrees from the next, each with a right angle in it so when the gasoline was turned on, it sprayed out of the short, horizontal pipes and spun the whole contraption around. Then a wet Beck lit it off and stepped away just as a rolling, roiling, roaring small tornado of flame shot up and out. Yes, the word "diabolical" is appropriate, because the roof of the metal shed made the flames roll out toward anyone approaching and fried their faces. Nobody wore a Scott. Air masks were for inside fires only. They faced the Hell with nozzle only.

Over the roar, Beck yelled at one crew with an 1.5 line to open up and keep a steady fog spray on the attack crew. Then he yelled at the attack crew: "Do not open your nozzle until I tell you to. Remember, you have to smother the fire, and the only way you can do that is to get close enough to open a fog pattern that covers the flame. You've got to get close before you crack the nozzle. Do not open it until I tell you to."

Gary had backup position just behind the nozzle man on the attack line, but they'd each get a turn on the nozzle, each get a turn to feel the pain of the heat right through the skin on their faces to their bones. No PPE used then other than turnout coat, gloves, helmet, and boots. No hood. No mask. No bunker gear. So with Beck backing in to one side of the satanic tornado, yelling "Not yet, not yet," the attack crew, soaked and protected by the fog spray of the backup crew inched closer and closer, hoping Beck would let them open up because it was starting to hurt. When it seemed they were close enough to spit on the fire, Beck, yelled, "Now. Fog pattern. Do not sweep. Smother." The firefighter on the nozzle opened up and it seemed a miracle had occurred. It worked. The wide fog pattern of fine water particles covered the fire, cut off the air supply, and put it out. Thank you Navy for developing the fog nozzle and the shipboard firefighting tactics Beck taught, though Gary did notice, especially after his turn on the nozzle, that he had a sunburn.

It paid off later that summer.

One long ring at 1:53 am, the time recorded later in the log. Beck was up, in his hitches and out the door first, as usual, with Gary second, Joey third, then Seigel, who was driving that night, and finally B-Line after he hung up the phone. The door was up, Engine 8 running, the lights on, and the vollys on the tailgate ready to go by the time B-Line got down the stairs and climbed into the cab. But Seigel made up for B-Line's lack of speed. He was the fastest driver---maybe too fast---at Engine 8. Though he seemed like a lazy, lanky slob most of the time, Seigel was quick when the bells went off and out the door they went and took a left turn at the bottom of the ramp, then another left onto Montauk a block later to race toward downtown, and with no traffic that time of night, Seigel put his foot to the floorboard and had the Seagrave all the way up into fourth gear.

Maybe three minutes later there it was. Through the flames, It looked like a new Shelby Cobra or some sort of Mustang built for extra speed that was too much engine for the driver to handle. He'd survived, somehow, even after the car climbed a lawn and smacked a five-foot diameter oak tree with enough force to snap the gas line and start the fire. Nobody on Engine 8, anyway, seemed concerned about extrication because nobody appeared to be in the car and no civilian screamed to get someone out. The car was fully involved when Seigel stopped the Seagrave about ten yards back from the fire. B-Line radioed for backup. Normally one engine was assigned on a car fire, but he knew from decades of experience that they didn't have enough water in the tank to last five minutes if they used two pre-connects, but he didn't want to take the time to make a hydrant, so the tactic would be to let Beck and his crew pull the pre-connects and use the tank while Engine 5 arrived and dropped a single 2.5 line from Engine 8 down the street to a corner hydrant.

Beck and Joey pulled one pre-connect and stretched to a safe place behind another tree 20 feet from the tree the car smacked while Gary pulled the second pre-connect and stretched it down the street side of the fire. "Hit it together," Beck yelled at Gary, who nodded and gritted his teeth. "But don't get too close." That seemed like odd advice given the way Beck taught at fire school, but here in the street, Beck knew the car's tank could blow even though the volume of the fire was in the front of the car where the gas line had snapped. The Christmas Tree did not blow up; gasoline tanks did.

"Charge the lines," Beck yelled to Seigel, who pulled the valves to run water from the 500 gallon tank to both pre-connects just as Engine 5 arrived. "Open up," Beck yelled, and they both opened the fog nozzles at the same time and waited until the popping ended as the air cleared the line and nothing but a steady stream of water flowed. "Move in," Beck yelled, and they moved the nozzles in toward the car, hitting the fire from right angles. And there was another kind of popping as the metal cooled under the water, and hissing as steam rose, and screaming. Some woman, Gary noticed for the first time, was screaming from somewhere, but he never did find out where she stood or why she was screaming. "Oh my God!" People did that, he learned over time. Some people would just lose it at fires---maybe a primordial, instinctive fear. He had the advantage of knowing he could do something about a fire. Maybe feeling helpless combined with the innate fear made people scream even when no one sat trapped in the flames.

"Don't get too close," Beck yelled, still behind the tree with Joey as the car cooled, but Gary was already five feet from the car, blasting it with water, killing the fire, daring it almost to try to return. Stupid, maybe, but the adrenaline short circuited thought. Some people screamed, others got aggressive, and, of course, being young and new to it all, he had something to prove to himself, to Tommy Beck, Tony "B-Line" Basilica, to the New London Fire Department, until he started to shake. Not much, but he noticed he was coming off that adrenaline rush as the last smoke turned to steam. Beck walked over and sort of smiled at him and told him to keep the water on the car while they finished overhaul. Beck went back to the engine and brought the bayonet nozzle for his line, snapped it in place, then rammed the steel point through the top of the hood and opened the valve. After the engine cooled for a couple of minutes, while Beck held the nozzle in place, Joey took the crow bar end of a Halligan and jammed it under the hood to pop it open, then he and Beck shut down their line and set the Halligan aside and lifted the hood while Gary turned his water onto the engine compartment to make sure it was out, dead out.

And it was over when B-Line said, "Pick up. Let's go home" after the wrecker arrived and hauled off one burned out Mustang soon to be scrap. Just the pick up, then they could leave. Each hose line had to be disconnected into 50 foot sections, each section drained by walking the length of it while running it over a shoulder, then rolled. The rolls were stacked on the tailgate for the return trip. Then back at the station, the wet hose had to be hung and replaced on the engine with dry pre-connect and the nozzles screwed back into place.

It was over an hour after the call before they crawled back up stairs to the bunk room, but again Gary stayed up because he had to go to his job, the one that paid, and he also had those thoughts of the fire still roaring in his head. What a rush. It was his first working fire of any consequence, car or not, and he'd never imagined a car could burn that hot and the flames could get so big. And he never imagined he could face something like that, but he knew he did only because he hadn't stopped to think about it. He just did it and did not freeze and stayed coordinated with Beck and his line, more or less followed orders, and they'd done a good thing.

Who needed Woodstock when you had fires to face. What a rush, man.

3 dead man

Autumn in New England means fall color, long country drives to find that color on Sunday afternoons, the October fire safety ritual at local schools, and burning leaves, sometimes legally, sometimes by accident, so Engine 8 had its share of routine runs to douse burning leaves. Autumn also meant Gary had his first run in with Damon Pasquale, Lt. Marco's driver. Beck told him to stay away from the guy, which meant don't let him push you around or goad you into doing something stupid so Marco could kick you out of the firehouse even though vollys had as much claim to being there as any man paid.

Pasquale, though he started as a volunteer like most of the paid men, flipped a switch mentally when he put on a dress uniform to go to and from work and started working on assigned shifts for a paycheck. A lot of them did that the minute they joined the union as paid men. The IAFF line was purely and simply that the volunteers had to go. They were volunteer labor who took jobs away from people. Besides that, the more paid men, the fewer volunteers, the more the city depended on the paid people, and the stronger the union. The vollys couldn't be used as leverage in contract negotiations any longer. Pasquale flipped to the union position overnight and didn't give a damn if it meant giving the shaft to former friends; it was all about the paycheck. Simple as that. Protect the job. And Gary could understand that at one level, knowing that he would jump at the chance to become a paid firefighter, especially since he seemed to be gaining more knowledge day by day and had completed six fire school courses that summer. But, for Chrissake, until the day the city decided to get rid of the vollys, why not try to get along?

"What are you doing here." Pasquale said, more a statement than a question, when Gary walked into the day room after work.

"I live here," said Gary.

Pasquale laughed. "Don't you have anywhere to go after work?"

"This is where I go after work."

"Someday you want to be a fireman."

"I am a firefighter. What's your problem?"

"So when are you people moving out?"

"So when are you going to get off that couch to get a real job?" Gary started to push back hard knowing he was twice Pasquale's size. "This place gets 125 runs a year. That's 30 a shift a year. So how often do you get off you ass in one year?"

Marco, who was sitting at the table sucking on a cigarette as usual, and as usual not saying much, finally stepped in. "Okay, that's enough."

Pasquale smirked and mumbled something about "vollys" and Marco said nothing. Gary thought it was a good time to exit the day room before Beck's warning became reality. Maybe he'd run into Pasquale when he was off duty and beat the shit out of him. But no, that wouldn't be a good idea. He'd get kicked out of the volunteer company and ruin any chance he had of becoming a paid firefighter.

In the meantime, Pasquale or not, Gary kept showing up at as many fires as he could and kept gaining experience. One evening they had a sports car burn, a Triumph, and he had the booster line nozzle and attacked as usual, and the third shift lieutenant stationed at Engine 8, who people just called Albe, got along with the vollys and had, like B-Line, a sense of humor, although unlike B-Line, Albe's humor had an edge to it. "You looked like a real fireman," he said to Gary after the car fire. One day when four volunteers were at the station during shift change, they all stood in the parking lot behind Engine 8 and offered Albe a mock salute when he drove in. Albe jammed on the brakes in response, put his car in reverse, and started to back out. Everyone laughed and Albe returned and kept his usual deadpan expression, parked, and walked into the station with one comment as he passed the vollys, a comment drawn out by his speech impediment: "Aaaaall you people need to go home." Unlike Pasquale, Albe was kidding. NLFD needed more than a driver and a lieutenant at fires--until the IAFF forced a third man onto each crew.

So they'd hang out at the station, set their boots behind the   tailgate, select a coat and helmet from the wall rack at the back of the carriage floor, and wait. It was the season of burning leaves at first, which moved into the colder months of lighting up oil furnaces or flipping the breakers on electric heat, and in old New England homes, that meant fire that occasionally did more than heat the house and required a smoke investigation. At dusk one chilled early November day, the still phone rang, and Gary followed Albe out of the day room and hustled to the front of the station while Albe picked up the phone and got the location and type of call. Gary punched the button for the automatic overhead door opener, then jogged back to get his boots on and throw his coat and helmet into the catwalk just before he stepped on board as Albe got into the cab and they left the station. The drivers never looked back to make sure people were on the back step. When the lieutenant got in the cab, they went, so all the vollys knew they had to get gear on and step up before the lieutenant got into the cab.

Left turn, then another left a block later onto Montauk for a run toward Sherman Street, a neighborhood with old, wood frame homes with wooden plank siding, wood porches, woods beams, and wiring that should have been replaced decades before. Or, as Beck said, "It's not the wiring. Copper doesn't wear out. It's the insulation." On Montauk, they accelerated and Albe hit the siren, which meant the call was serious. Even though the November chill numbed his hands and made him wish he'd been able to get the turnout coat on before leaving the station, Gary gripped the rail with both hands and hung on tight until they reached the house. He learned that when the Seagrave was in a hurry and hit a bump in the road and the tailgate bounced, that he'd become airborne. His feet would leave the back of the engine for a second. Maybe he should have been riding in the jump seat or the catwalk, but nobody did that, the tactical logic being that if a firefighter road on the tailgate, he could step off faster on arrival to make the hydrant or pull either the pre-connect or booster. No cross lays. Everything came off the back of the engine.

The house was full of light smoke with no visible fire when they arrived. Engine 5 was first due, so it parked in front of the yellow, three-story house while second due Engine 8 parked up the street a block next to the corner hydrant. Always bring something when you leave the pumper was the standing order, so Gary took a Halligan and a battery lamp from Engine 8 and followed Albe into the house where the duty officer, the Captain from headquarters, told Albe to send a man to the third floor, which was really a converted attic with a steep sloped ceiling. Standard procedure during a smoke investigation. Since the fire was unseen, firefighters on each floor checked for fire and, if none were found, waited there until ordered down.

The duty officer and the lieutenants from Engines 5 and 8 stayed in the kitchen with the two men from Truck 1, stationed with Engine 5, who hacked at the floor with an ax when Gary walked through and went up to the third floor to squat in the smoke with another firefighter from Engine 5. The guy didn't say much. He just squatted there in the room as if it were a competition to see who could take the most smoke before puking. No Scott packs. Real New London firefighters used air packs only in heavy smoke and only if the option was passing out or wearing the tank. Both the rigs and the tactics in New London dated from the turn of the century. NLFD still, in late 1969, used four antiquated Seagraves at Engines 5, 7, 8 and Truck 2. Slowly things were changing. Slowly. Headquarters had a 1966 Mac diesel, cab forward 1000 GPM pumper. Truck 1 was also a diesel, a cab forward American LaFrance, and Gary suddenly felt nausea. Squatting in the smoke trying to tough it out like the other firefighter was like having his face in front of a fireplace when someone forgot to open the flue.

Luckily, the attic room had a small window that worked, so he opened it, took his helmet off, and stuck his head outside for real air to stop the nausea.

The other firefighter just squatted there. Some could handle it better than others, Gary supposed. He was one of the others and kept his head out the window until he heard Albe yelling from below. The principle fireground communication technology of the day was yelling. "Get the heeeell down here." He didn't have to be asked twice, but the lower they went on the stairs, the thicker the smoke got and the lights in the house were out because the power had been cut. The ladder men had opened the floor and found the fire on the 8x8 beam under the kitchen where old insulation had cracked at the staples used to attach wire to the beam. 8x8 wooden beams do not conduct electricity. They burn. And they had extension under the floor and into the basement. Worker.

"Leeeave the light with me. Go baaack to the engine and help with the hydrant. Tell Flanigan to run a 2.5 to Engine 5, then get the Scott on and geeet back here." Gary hustled outside and down the driveway along the side of the house out to the sidewalk where the owners of the house, an elderly woman, and her rotund, bald husband stood perplexed and frightened, and oh shit.

The old man dropped to the sidewalk and smacked his head on the pavement. His wife shrieked and everyone thought at first that he'd just fallen and knocked himself out, but when the driver from Engine 5 brought a light, they could see that he was conscious, gasping, clutching his left arm, and in serious pain. "Lieutenant!" the driver yelled, and when his lieutenant hurried out of the house and out to the front sidewalk, he barked back, "Call the ambulance," and the driver hustled back to the cab of Engine 5 to radio downtown for the ambulance while the lieutenant turned to Gary. "You have a resuscitator on Engine 8." It wasn't a question, it was an order, and

Gary didn't stop to check. He jogged as fast as he could in the heavy boots up the street and yelled at Jack Flanigan, Albe's driver, to get the resuscitator, which meant he forgot all about the need for the hydrant line and the woman suddenly started shrieking nonstop. Her husband had stopped breathing, and she'd gone into shock. Oh shit. He grabbed the resuscitator case and hurried back to the downed old man.

Beck saved his ass when he walked up behind Gary, who'd never trained on the resuscitator, and took over, opening the case, setting up the mask, turning the tank on, knowing the old man on the ground didn't have a chance. Nobody in the department would be an EMT for another two years, although some had advanced first aid, some not. Beck placed the mask on the dead man nose and mouth and told Gary to take care of the women who was rigid, panicked, still shrieking incoherently at the top of her lungs, starring off somewhere into another dimension, neither down at her dead husband nor at the house nor into space. He felt like a complete ass when he said, "Ma'am, it will be all right" when the ambulance driver walked up, took one look, and yelled back to his partner, "Get the bag." She still shrieked while they bagged her husband and a seen-it-all-before cop walked over and said, "Ma'am, can you give me his name?" Shriek.

"Wheeere's the hydrant line?" Albe barked.

Gary and Beck hurried back to Engine 8. Gary dragged the 2.5 down the middle of the street to Engine 5 where the driver grabbed it and connected to an intake port while Beck and Flanigan connected the soft suction to the hydrant at Engine 8 and Beck started turning with the hydrant wrench while Flanigan yelled "Water on the way!" and Gary headed back to the house without a Scott on to back up the 1.5 now down in the basement where the truckies were pulling the ceiling to find hot spots, but it looked like they had most of it. What a mess, Gary thought. What a frickin mess.

"Aaaaat least it didn't get into the walls," said Albe.
After a half hour of overhaul, the Captain released Engine 8, they drained and rolled their hose line, put all their gear away, including the resuscitator, then headed back to the station. So okay, Gary thought, turning back to look at the house and the old woman now collapsed and crying on the sidewalk with a neighbor finally with her to console a helluva lot better than some rookie firefighter or a jaded cop. So okay, we show up, make a mess, and then leave, Gary thought. The house is still standing.

Nobody said anything back at the firehouse other than Beck giving orders to repack the hose, and Gary helped, but then, when the pumper was ready again, he shuffled into the kitchen, never bothering to take his boots off, sat down at the table, and looked at the television without seeing it. Albe finished his log entry and joined them, but couldn't help a sardonic smile when he saw Gary at the table. "Thaaat bother you?" Didn't seem to bother anyone else but him. Guess they'd seen people die before and heard people scream like that. It made that woman at the car fire sound muted. Damn.

If you think Albe or Beck or one of the other firefighters from Engine 8 took Gary aside or took him out for a drink and a man-to-man talk about how tough it is to see your first death, and said either "You'll get used to it" or "You'll never get used to it, but you learn to live with it"--forget it.

The old man was a heart attack waiting to happen, and the stress of the fire, of literally being run out of his own house into the November cold with his equally elderly wife while firefighters tore up the floor in the kitchen and pulled the ceiling in the basement to get to the fire and check for extension was too much. At least it was massive and quick and he died on his own property if not in the house.

The fire department's job, Gary had to learn, was to respond to the emergency, manage the emergency, then leave and be ready for the next one. Other people or agencies had to take care of the property and psychological damage due to fire, smoke, and water. The surviving old woman had relatives, and if she didn't the Red Cross would help.

So relax Gary. People die. You did your job. If you let this stuff or Pasquale get to you, then maybe you should stick to being a bus mechanic.

4 washdown

Tis the season for giving and slipping and crashing and trees indoors that go dry and burn easily. The season of candles that burn homes and cars that slide out of control. In spite of all the annual warnings issued by the NLFD fire marshal's office to keep Christmas trees watered, to not overload circuits with too many lights, to turn off the lights before going to bed, the usual one or two holiday structure fires occurred, and Engine 8 caught one of them.

But they stopped it in the living room because it was early evening and the neighbors spotted the flames in the front window while the owner and his family were at Mass to celebrate early so they didn't have to haul the kids to church at midnight on Christmas Eve. And, using flawless logic, they figured they'd leave the lights on while they went to the service because the lights looked so white, red, blue, and green pretty from the street, and they could also see them from outside in the dark when they pulled in the driveway returning home after Mass. The kids would love it.
They saw the lights from Engine 8 and 5 and Ladder 1 and the Captain's car when they arrived. B-Line had the duty, and he was nice

enough when they pulled up first due to not order the front window broken out to ventilate. Beck and Gary popped the front door with the Halligan, then got down on all fours and crawled in with an 1.5 to attack the fire that had burned the tree and the curtains at the front window and had started to crawl along the ceiling. They knocked it down in five minutes while the crew from Ladder 1 hung the smoke ejector in the front door and turned it on full blast to ventilate. They killed the power, disconnected the tree and one lamp by the curtains that had burned, then turned the power back on after making sure the fire had no extension in the wall or ceiling, which meant they pulled some of each, but not a lot before B-Line, then the Captain told them to take up.

The family arrived when they were draining and rolling the pre-connect, and they weren't happy, of course, although the father at least had enough courtesy to thank them for saving the house. Luckily, no presents were under the tree yet, and the damage was limited to the tree, the curtains, that one pole lamp, wall board, wallpaper, and carpet, although the smoke damage also affected most of the downstairs. Gary felt bad for them, but knew enough now to move on. They'd fix the house up and get another tree and be certain never to leave the tree lights on again when they were not home.

But then between Christmas and New Years, a drunk, in broad daylight, stopped for gas but didn't really stop and skidded on the packed snow into the pump at the gas station on the corner of Broad and Coleman. With gasoline gushing from the broken pump, the station owner ignored or forgot the emergency shut off and yelled at his employees to get the hell out, then went to haul the drunk out of the car before the whole place blew the hell up, and then he dragged the drunk across the street before he finally called the fire department from the car dealership.

"Station A," Captain Vosconi, the duty officer said by radio to dispatch when he arrived, "Call Ladder 2 back and send me all four pumpers." At which point Engine 7, a 1947 Seagrave arrived and the driver, not the sharpest tack in the box, proceeded to drive right into the flood of gasoline in the intersection. Big, burly Vosconi's leadership style was to yell at people, but he outdid himself that day when he reamed the Engine 7 driver and tore him a new one. "What the hell are you doing, you dumbass? What the fuck are you doing? Back the hell up to that hydrant back on the next fucking block and when you get there, open the hydrant, douse the damned cigar, and eat it. What the fucking hell is wrong with you?"

Technically it was a washdown. No hazmat existed. The dictionary didn't have the word. Nobody ever heard of the term. At accidents or the source of any other fuel spill, the fire department just pulled the booster or a pre-connect, charged it, then flushed the fuel, gas or diesel, down the nearest drain, the assumption being that the supposedly diluted fuel no longer posed a hazard--above ground anyway. The Captain positioned each of the four engines at a hydrant on each of the four quadrants of the spill, had them connect with a soft suction, then ordered one 2.5 put into service from each pumper to force the gasoline to stay in the intersection and down into the storm drains while Vosconi and one other firefighter waded back to the gas station and found the emergency cutoff switch.

With every pumper in town, all four of them, committed to the washdown, Waterford was called for mutual aid to send in three engines, one to cover Engine 7, another to cover Engine 5, and another to cover Engine 2 at headquarters in downtown New London.

The job was long and messy with everyone sliding and a couple of firefighters falling on the ice that formed once most of the gasoline had been flushed off the street and the freezing water had turned it into a skating rink. They city eventually sent a dump truck to sand the intersection, and Engine 7 had to stand fire watch until midnight to keep flushing the storm drain while everyone else went back to a warm firehouse to pack hose and pour a hot cup of coffee---until the next run.

You'd think all that camaraderie stuff happened after a run, and some did among the vollys, but the rift had widened between the paid and non-paid firefighters, so the union guys didn't make much of an effort to get friendly with the vollys other than to be polite, with the exception of Pasquale, and a rumor had started among the volunteer company that the IAFF had convinced the city to add a third man (women need not apply) that year to each fire company, which was the equivalent of a full time, fully paid department. For routine fires. The irony, of course, was that for anything other than a single alarm working fire, all off-duty firefighters would have to be called in, some of whom did not live in New London, so larger fires really needed the immediate staffing volunteers could provide, all of whom lived in New London. If anything other than second alarm happened, the all-volunteer Waterford fire companies would be called in for mutual aid. But the paycheck trumped public safety logic.

So even though it was important to get to know people with whom you conducted potentially explosive washdowns, Gary never got to know too many of them beyond their firehouse personalities. Seigel was the only exception when he invited the vollys to the basement of his home once to watch 8 millimeter porn and drink beer while his wife and girlfriend were both home upstairs. Yes, he was headed for a divorce, and yes his wife was a shrew, but, yes, Seigel was no prize himself with his pinched face and hips wider than his shoulders and bigoted attitudes.

The union people stuck with other union people, and that was that. The only other exception was the day Gary happened to be at the firehouse when a car load of boisterous Italian women showed up with a silent Marco riding in the front seat. They brought him by to get his paycheck, and it was easy to see why Marco was a quiet man for the most part. He wasn't used to speaking his mind, and undoubtedly suffered the consequences in stereo for doing so.

No sports, either, other than as an occasional topic of conversation. None of the paid men were athletes, and the vollys sure weren't except for occasional touch football among the younger guys when they had enough people to play, which was maybe once a year. Nope. Men smoked and sat in firehouses on duty after performing a few required chores, such as making sure the engine had enough gasoline and a scheduled equipment check to make certain all the gear was on board and stowed in the right compartment. Putting tools back in the right place was a cardinal rule. From one shift to another, from one fire to another, everyone, paid and volunteer, needed to be able to go to the driver's side rear compartment, for instance, to get a hose strap. At a fire, no one had time to rummage around in the compartment or ask anyone within hearing distance: "Honey, have you seen the hose strap?"

But exercise, no. Men naturally grew a gut when they hit middle age, if not younger. And smoked. And died of a heart attack, preferably at a fire where it could be considered death in the line of duty.

Beck and Gary and Joey were the exception. Maybe because they were younger, maybe because they all had physical jobs and didn't smoke. Beck the red-headed electrician had nonstop energy at work and at the firehouse, and he also seemed to spend a lot of time chasing Lora Dominick, the daughter of a former New London firefighter who had to take an early retirement because of a heart condition. She never would go out with him, not for months after he asked her out the first time, and who would go out with someone who drove around in a red Ford F-150 with a scanner and a large whip antenna. Not exactly romantic. Gary thought about trading in his red Beetle for something sexier, but he hesitated because, as with many firefighters, pragmatism in his mind always dominated romanticism. The VW could be driven to fires in all kinds of weather, and he'd already modified the interior with a bracket to mount his scanner where the radio normally would have gone. And he took out the front passenger seat anyway to make more room for his gear when he carried his bunker gear away from the firehouse. It would not fit in the small front trunk of the VW, but with the seat removed, he had plenty of room, and the VW, like a Seagrave, became a purely utilitarian fire response vehicle, complete with blue light mounted on yet another bracket he had screwed into the dash.

Yeah, well, maybe someday he'd find a woman willing to go right to the back seat, but not so far. Besides, who the hell would date a grease monkey, even slim and not too bad looking, who came home from work each day smelling like oil and gasoline. And no matter how hard he washed his hands, they never seemed to get entirely clean. But the job did keep him in shape and did teach him important skills he'd need if he ever did get a paid job as a firefighter, like how to shift without a clutch. Even with a clutch, it seemed Seagrave drivers had to know how to shift without one because the Seagrave wasn't synchro, and the driver had to catch the gear at just the right RPM. Being a mechanic, he also gained experience with pumps and hydraulics, with gears and transmissions, with driving gas and diesel in all kinds of weather on any road surface. He learned how to do brake jobs, how to get chains off and on, and how to balance a truck tire.

And he learned more than the average paid man or volunteer about fire rigs. He studied Seagrave, of course, and Mac (favored by FDNY at the time), Pierce, Pirsch, American LaFrance, Ward LaFrance, Crown Fire Coach (favored by LAFD at the time), and a bunch of off brands that sold cut rate pumpers mounted on commercial chassis. He studied pumps and settled on two-stage Waterous as being the best for urban spec bid pumpers. Although he understood the need for cities to use the bid system for making purchases to prevent corruption, he also knew the consequences of low bid junk. New London itself succumbed over the years to being penny wise and pound stupid by purchasing a gas powered Ford. Gary was certain using a commercial chassis for a fire engine was almost always a mistake. Even though fire trucks did not accumulate a lot of mileage, they weren't built for delivering beer from one state to another. They were built to run hard on a cold engine and pump all night at maximum capacity if necessary. That was Seagrave. Though a gas engine and 12 cylinder at that, the 1954 Seagrave at Engine 8 started like a diesel, with the push of a button, and never flooded. The V-12 was so well balanced, it generated hardly any vibration, and the pump was solid brass that would never rust. And the Seagrave would give you 150 psi pump pressure all night at 750 GPM without breathing hard.

It had to not too far into the next year when the Pequots returned.

5 Pequot Revenge

When the rich and powerful decided to create a Gilded Age summer resort at the mouth of the Thames (once named the Pequot) River on the south end of New London where private white beaches faced Long Island Sound, they chose to name it the Pequot Colony for some unknown reason. Why name an exclusive resort for rich white people after a slaughtered tribe with only 66 surviving members at the turn of the 20th century and call it a colony? Very odd, but so it was, and the colony bragged of its hotel, casino, bars, cottages, and fine Victorian homes displaying broad porches where the rich could find summer idyll in sea breezes and needed fire protection beyond what the city of New London offered to the hoi palloi, the masses, the many without access to the private beaches along Pequot Avenue.

Formed in 1906 to protect the colony, the Pequot Engine Company was led by an army colonel who served as its foreman until 1923, but the new fire company could do nothing to save the Pequot Hotel in 1908 when it (and several cottages) burned to the ground, the third hotel to do so since the 1850s, followed by a fourth, the Lighthouse Inn, in 1979. Call it the curse of the Pequots, though arson was suspected as the cause of the Pequot Hotel fire.

Throughout the 1630s, conflict waxed and waned between the Pequot, the dominant tribe in southeastern Connecticut, and the English and Dutch and their allies among the Mohegans and Narragansetts who did not like the Pequots. It was the same old story of human conflict. The Pequot were expansionist and competed with the Narragansetts, Mohegans, and other tribes for land and trade with the whites. Conflict ensued at the level of tit-for-tat clan vengeance violence until the whites in Massachusetts Bay, Plymouth, and Connecticut chose total war to end Pequot power once and for all. With their Mohegan allies led by Chief Uncas, in the spring of 1637 the English attacked the Pequots, who had allies only among one branch of the Niantics, a tribe demonstrating a subservient loyalty only because it lived next door to and had to live with Pequot power.

The conduct of the English during their 1637 campaign against the Pequots became the template for treatment of native Americans by Europeans for the next 300 years and beyond—a scorched earth, no mercy warfare. The English decided in the spring of 1637 to first attack the fortified Pequot village at what is now New London, but found it too well fortified and opted instead to attack the fortified village at what is now Mystic, Connecticut. Forts, of course, can easily transform from sanctuary to fire trap, especially if they're made of wood. A high wooden stake fence surrounded the Pequot wooden homes when the English attacked at dawn on 26 May 1637 with most of the Pequot warriors absent on a raid of their own.

Though the Pequots fiercely resisted, women, children, and old men were no match for the English fire power and fire itself---the standing order of the day. The whites burned the village to the ground and killed an estimated 400-700 Pequots, most of whom died trapped by the fire. The Mohegan waited outside the village to kill any Pequots who escaped. Captain John Mason said God made them do it. God "laughed [at] his Enemies and the Enemies of his People to scorn making [the Pequot] as a fiery Oven . . . Thus did the Lord judge among the Heathen, filling [Mystic] with dead Bodies." "We had sufficient light from the word of God for our proceedings," wrote Captain Underhill, another of the raid leaders implementing a deliberate policy of genocide. That's an overused word, but it's the one that fits. The English set out to and nearly succeeded in removing the Pequots from the surface of the planet.

The English returned to their ship burning anything Pequot along the way. The surviving Pequots scattered but were hunted down, and in one case, their severed heads were offered as tribute by other tribes to the barbarian English, who killed with a gusto never seen among native Americans because God told them to do it—the Mohegan were appalled. Those Pequot not beheaded were sold off into slavery to other tribes and to whites or shipped off to slavery in the West Indies, and the name Pequot was outlawed--for a while anyway. The Puritan law was ignored by the Pequot Colony, which had no interest whatsoever in preserving or restoring the tribe. They just liked the name, for some reason, and, due to their profound ignorance, failed to realize they had chosen a name for their fire company associated with arson and massacre.

A July 1893 New York Times article reported on the summer social life among the oblivious Pequot Colony idle rich. "Dullness has largely prevailed among New-London's [sic] Summer [sic] people so far this season, the desire seemingly being for quietness rather than gayety [sic]. Outside of formal dancing in the hotel parlors, an occasional yachting party and a little quiet entertaining of the cottagers nothing has occurred to disturb the serenity of seaside life since the hotels opened." Standard, boring, late Gilded Age society page stuff. No massacres that summer.

In 1922, the firehouse that protected the Pequot Colony was doubled in size when a second bay was added, and in 1926, the Locomobile, the first pumper powered by a combustion engine, was replaced by a real pumper, a mighty Ahrens Fox with that distinctive front mounted piston pump that served well until 1954 when the Seagrave arrived to fight the neverending Pequot revenge. Or maybe it was just white stupidity thinking wooden buildings, even with a brick facade, would not burn when gas was piped to lamps inside to be replaced with electricity that also had its hazards as did coal then oil fired furnaces for central heating that replaced equally flammable inside fireplaces. They even installed a gasoline pump on the carriage floor inside Pequot Engine Company No. 8, which seemed like a good idea at the time for easy refueling of the fire engine. At least the Pequots, the real Pequots, had the sense enough to keep their fires going outside their wooden huts. It took the English to burn them down.

So you could call it either Pequot's revenge or white stupidity that led to big fires rising up in New London once or twice a year, such as during the 1938 hurricane where several downtown businesses burned to the waterline as did the headquarters station of the New London Fire Department.

The revenge appeared again for Gary's first big one that January, a New England January with temperatures he used to look forward to as a kid when the thermometer dropped close to single digits for a hard overnight freeze that made good skating on pond ice the next day, but he learned quickly that good weather for skating meant lousy weather for firefighting.

The call came in around 6:15 pm, early evening, but already dark in the third week in January, and cold. A pedestrian walking past Mahan's Fine Furniture on Bank Street stopped by headquarters to report that he thought he smelled smoke, although he said he couldn't see anything through the large display window facing the street: "It looks like the lights are all out inside." Engines 1 and 7, Truck 2, and the ambulance responded as the usual first alarm assignment with eight people and one duty officer, the shift captain. Sean O'Conner was driving Truck 2, and, on orders from the Captain, tossed an ax through the display window. And the word "toss" is correct. On orders from the Captain, who suspected the worst, they positioned all apparatus in the middle of Bank Street away from the three story brick facade building, and then everyone stayed at their apparatus ready to react to whatever happened after O'Conner threw the ax from ten feet at the glass just like a Pequot warrior swinging a club at the skull of an Englishman.

Backdraft. The window, already weakened by heat, shattered and smoke and flame blew out into the night. No need to ventilate now, at least not from the front of the building. The Captain's experience and judgment had saved the lives of several New London firefighters, and, of course, fighting the fire internally was out of the question, and, of course, now that the building was opened up, given the load factors of a furniture store (meaning a lot of stuff to burn), the fire would move quickly and vertically into the walls and extend to the second and third floors. The good news was that all four walls of the store were brick, which meant NLFD firefighters had a chance to containing the fire to that one building if they acted quickly.

Five minutes after the box for the first alarm rang into every station in the city, the still phone rang in the other stations with that one long shrill ring. John Gary kicked off his shoes, stepped into his boots, and, for first time decided to crawl up into the catwalk between the hose beds during the run to get out of the wind and to get added time to snap his turnout coat closed before buckling the wind flaps into place. His coat collar was up of course, and after fixing the coat, and getting the ear flaps down on his helmet, he pulled his gloves on, but he never seemed to warm up. At one late December car fire, he learned the thermal paradox of winter firefighting. You cooked on one side and froze on the other. At car fires, he'd cook his face and freeze his butt. For a second, he'd wished the fire would not go out to stop the cold and dark from returning again, but the fire had to be put out, so he'd grit his teeth and shiver until they returned to the warm firehouse with the warm bunkroom .

While he was sitting in the day room after one fire with his boots off trying to warm his feet again, Beck told him, "Put water down your boots." Gary looked up as if Beck were crazy. Beck laughed. "The boot doesn't breath. It's like a wet suit. The water in your boot will heat to body temperature and keep your feet warm. Try it." Sure, thought Gary, I'm not falling for that one.

Engine 8 arrived during the usual setup chaos at a multiple alarm working fire, although the term "multiple alarm" was a running joke in New London where the entire fire department barely equaled a first alarm assignment in New York City. Two alarms in New London meant committing all four pumpers and the two ladders and leaving the rest of the city unprotected until Waterford could provide mutual aid. That was the dispatcher's responsibility. The Captain, in charge of the fireground until the Chief and Deputy arrived from home, ordered Engine 8 to stop at the alley entrance on the south side of the building, haul hose to Ladder 2 where it was setting up in the alley near the back of the building to open the roof then flood the building from top down with a ladder pipe through the ventilation hole.

They had no choice. The officers knew they couldn't enter the building, knew the fire would climb the walls and the ceiling and the stairwells and the freight elevator shaft to reach the roof, but they couldn't see the fire in the dark through billows of thick smoke, had no way of finding the seat, and knew the building also had a basement. Sending men inside would be suicide. The strategy was surround and drown to confine the fire to the building and hope it didn't collapse or start throwing embers onto other downtown building. Tactically, it meant one ladder in the alley, one ladder on the front left corner, each with a ladder pipe—one through the roof from the alley and one aimed through the third floor windows where smoke was now showing. Each ladder required one pumper to feed it and that meant one hydrant each per ladder. The third and fourth pumpers fed 2.5 hand lines setup on the sidewalk in front of the building to throw streams of water through the blown out display window into who knew what and into the second floor windows. Faint flickers of flame appeared now and again back in the thick black and gray smoke, but after the backdraft, the fire hid inside. They could do little more than throw water inside and hope it soaked the contents of the building, meaning thousands of dollars worth of furniture, to keep them from feeding the fire.

Gary and Beck dragged both sides of Engine 8's 2.5 hose to the ladder after Gary grabbed the double female in case the ladder needed one. Beck yelled "Go!" at Engine 8 once the hose lines were connected at Ladder 2, and Engine 8 slowly drove 200 feet down Bank Street, dropping both sides until it reached the hydrant. "Go help at the hydrant," Beck ordered Gary, who slipped and slid down the street where ice was already forming to the hydrant to help Pasquale with the soft suction. Pasquale had already connected each 2.5 to a discharge port, and he was connecting to the large intake port on the pump panel and didn't say a thing when Gary grabbed the hydrant wrench from the tailgate where he left it when they hauled hose to the ladder. He unscrewed the hydrant discharge port, then set the wrench in position on the stem to open up as soon as Pasquale smacked the soft suction connection on the hydrant with a rubber mallet to get it as watertight as possible in the cold weather; no leak, no ice. He tried to take the wrench from Gary, who glared at him. "I got it." And opened up, turning the stem 15 times counter clockwise to shove the ball valve down into the main until it would turn no more, daring the little bastard to try to grab the wrench again. Then he followed standard procedure and left the wrench in place on top of the hydrant. "You need anything else?" Gary half yelled.

Pasquale didn't say a thing, so Gary skated back up the street to the fire building with a hose strap stuffed into each pocket and checked the 2.5 ladder feed lines as he went to make sure neither had kinks as they jumped and snapped with the pressure of being charged. Setup was a pain in the ass, but somebody had to do it.

His was already starting to lose feeling in his toes when returned to the building and took up a position on one of the two hand lines shooting a 200 GPM stream through the smoke with hope of hitting the fire. With the hose strap wrapped around the line, he knelt and held on to relieve some of the back pressure on the two paid men in front of him. Off duty men were being called in and other volunteers who usually never showed up at smaller fires or routine runs also showed up so first due crews could start taking breaks from the cold.

Not yet being a 20th century fire department, NLFD had no canteen, but fortunately the drug store on the other side of Bank Street stayed open so the firefighters could gather inside for free coffee and warm air, but that was it. Nothing else was open downtown, because stores usually closed at 6 pm in that era just before suburban malls with longer hours threatened downtown business and forced longer hours. People went home in the evening, and Mahan's Furniture was no different and normally closed at 5:30 pm during week days. It took just that 45 minutes after closing for a cigarette butt to start it all.

Beck found Gary again two hours into the fight with smoke still rolling out of the building and Gary could no longer feel his toes, even after a break for coffee; he didn't want to be a wimp by complaining about it, but he sure as hell wanted to move around and jumped (or more like stumbled) at the chance to help Beck. "They need help in the alley," Beck half shouted above the roar of water and pumps and engines.

Beck led him to Truck 2 where they took the battering ram to the brick alley wall that had no windows and started, with the help of two other firefighters, to make a hole. Curious, Gary asked why they didn't just pop the door in the back of the alley or cut through the overhead door on the loading dock. "They're both hot," said Beck. "The Chief wants us to work back down the alley to the doors, first. Then pop them."

The ram was six foot of solid cast iron with a blunt round head and four handles, and it took four people to hold it and swing it with enough force to punch a hole in the brick--after a dozen or more hits. Ready. Heave. Bam. Ready. Heave. Bam. Ready. Heave. Crack. At least the exercise warmed him up, but he still couldn't feel his feet and took Beck's advice after they had a hole open a foot in diameter and stretched a charged 1.5 line to poke through it. Gary grabbed the nozzle, said "Excuse me a second," and filled each boot up to his ankles before shoving the nozzle into the hole. "Son of a bitch." Beck looked at him. "You okay?" he said with a tone that indicated not concern for Gary but concern for his ability to continue the fight. "Yeah," said Gary, not meaning it but knowing he needed to say it.

And now he had something to do besides stand or kneel out front. As soon as they'd soaked that hole for five minutes, they started the routine again, moving another ten feet down the alley to punch through the brick again. Swing. Bam. Swing. Bam. Swing. Crack. Swing. Crunch. Through brick, a stud, and wall board. To make things move quicker, Beck found Joey, and they rotated off the ram to take turns shoving the nozzle into the building to soak down whatever was on the other side of the hole. A smash and soak strategy.

Near the back of the alley, at the metal door, Beck took his glove off, felt the door with the back of his hand and announced that it was hot but not as hot as before. "Get the Chief and a Halligan. We need permission to pop this door open."

The Chief sent the Deputy, who walked down the alley and surveyed the work along the way and offered a question when he was within shouting distance. "What the fuck do you want?"
"Permission to pop the door open. It's hot."

"Do it," said the Deputy, half perturbed that they had to get him in the first place.
Okay, thought Gary. Just imagine Pasquale's face. He rammed the crowbar end of the Halligan into the crack at the edge of the door just above the knob and yelled, "Ready?" meaning do you have the 1.5 ready because we don't know what's on the other side of this frickin door. "Go," Beck yelled back, and Gary leaned on the bar, pushing it in toward the building, then pulled back to shove the fork in deeper, then leaned again toward the building and it popped open and he ducked as flame and smoke shot out into the alley. Not a huge amount, and it was no backdraft, but enough to clearly indicate the fire in the back of the store hadn't been touched yet. The 1.5 opened up as Gary crawled out of the way with Halligan in hand. Man he was suddenly tired. But he couldn't quit and got himself up and moved to the right of the hose line to pull the door back as far as it would go and held it open while they hit the fire and the Deputy Chief yelled, "Stay the hell out of there. Hit it from outside." Beck yelled back, "Get the smoke ejector and hang it in the door." Five minutes later, Joey and Gary had it off the ladder truck and hung in the door. Five minutes after that, when the Deputy walked back out front, they started to work the line inside the building until Beck put his foot through the floor, then they backed out to the door again and stayed put. It was a long, cold night, and it was getting longer and colder.

The last in first out rule applied six hours into the fire when the Chief declared control had been established at around 1 am the next morning. Smoke coming from the building was minimal, which meant they'd finally poured enough tonnage of water inside to reach the fire or had soaked the interior of the building to an extent that the fire had no place to go and had burned itself out. The fire marshal would make that determination the next day, and, by the way, discover that the seat of the fire was in the basement where the store operated a furniture refinishing and reupholstering business. A cigarette butt in a trash can was most likely the cause, and the fire could have been stopped there with sprinklers, but the old building had none because it was grandfathered into an old fire code. The Pequots must have been smiling.

Take up was easy because they had to leave all the 2.5 on the street frozen in place. They drained it and left it there to get the next day when the sun warmed things enough to pull the hose out of the ice without ripping it apart or they had enough light to chop it free without hitting the hose. But nobody could relax back at the station. Beck, as usual, had everyone working the minute Engine 8 backed in packing the hose beds with the dry spare hose--that is, after they helped each other out of frozen turnout gear. Gary's coat buckles were ice cubes and his hands didn't have enough strength to force the buckles open. Beck smashed each buckle lose with a spanner, and Gary returned the favor for Beck and other firefighters, except for Pasquale, who didn't have ice to worry about. After the hydrant connection was set up and he charged the lines, he didn't have much to do beyond watch the gauges for six hours and dance around next to the pumper to keep warm.

In a half an hour, Engine 8 was ready to go again, and Gary dragged himself up to the bunkroom where he gave serious thought to calling in sick the next day when he realized with a huge sigh of relief that the next day was Saturday. He pulled off his boots, dumped the water down the toilet in the second floor latrine, dried his feet, pulled on dry socks, set his quick hitches next to the bunk, thought about taking a shower, which was the last thing he remembered before his head hit the pillow and he passed out into a dreamless sleep.

6 Dump Fire

That furniture store fire proved to be the last big thing until May. They had a few false alarms, a couple of grass fires, food on the stove, and one bomb scare in a rooming house down near Ocean Beach Park that turned out to be nothing. Everyone, meaning the whole country, had the jitters because of radical action here and there and demonstrations and riots, but none of it really touched New London. And another car fire, but a lot less dramatic than the Mustang; it was actually a grass fire that turned into a car fire because some idiot parked on dry grass with a hot engine, ergo a hot exhaust pipe, ergo ignition.

Boring might be the word. Months of tedium. Moments of terror. Gary thought about looking for a better mechanic's job, but hesitated because his boss, Isaac Levine, still had a tenuous connection to the fire company and had given him the job because of that connection. The classic paradox of staying in a crappy job with hope of getting a better job. He had to work every day with the head mechanic, a short, greasy, chain-smoking Alabama cracker as ignorant and bigoted as they come, but working with the little bastard gave him a chance to drive trucks (okay, buses, but close enough) and to work on them. And that summer he'd take more fire school classes to add to his training, so maybe someday soon he'd get paid to sit around a firehouse. Besides, the transit union got him another nickle an hour raise, one of the school bus drivers had the hots for him, even if she was married, and one of the charters he drove turned out to be to a convention in Manhattan, the home of the legendary Rescue 1.

Rescue 1 at the time responded to any alarm from 125th Street south to The Battery, responded from a nondescript three story building on a one-way side street where the Mac was backed onto a carriage floor that barely left room to walk between the rig and the wall. Rescue 1 was just as cramped inside the rig, loaded with gear, including plenty of Scott Packs and spare tanks. Gary couldn't believe how many Scotts they had on board. New London was definitely operating in the Stone Age.

The FDNY lieutenant called one of the men on duty out of the kitchen to give a guided tour, which he did, telling Gary at one point to smell a Scott mask, stating emphatically when he held the mask up, "The smell never goes away." He was talking about the smell of smoke. No matter what they tried at Rescue 1, they could not get that smell out of the rubber seal on the edge of the mask.

Not ten minutes later, they had a run so Gary had to leave the building. Fire department policy. No visitors, even other firefighters, in the house when they were out on a run. A retiree from the neighborhood was the only one trusted to remain inside at the watch desk after the doors were closed and the Mac took off down the street to the alarm.

Gary also drove a another charter that definitely motivated him to get a fire department job. He began to understand why the Italians and Irish wanted the union jobs and how they fought to keep them, and, hell, he even started to understand why the IAFF policy meant the end of volunteer fire departments if at all possible, although he still disagreed with how they went about doing it.
The bus charter took a group of people from Connecticut to Rhode Island for a Dare to be Greedy conference, a rally held across the state line, because in Connecticut it was considered a pyramid scheme

without a product, and therefore an illegal con. But that worked to the advantage of the handlers in their polyester suits who started hyping the minute people got on the bus. "You will not believe this, but you can make $2000 dollars tonight before you return. We are looking for four people who want to be leaders. We will be focusing on just four leaders, until they also have four new working leaders under themselves. This isn't hard. It is just a fact we can only work with four people at a time, train them and help them on their way to a solid future with a company that is 25 years old and is run by honest and ethical people. There is a lot to be said about longevity whether it is a company or products."

Gary didn't pay much attention and focused on driving the old diesel coach that threw black smoke out the exhaust every time he shifted.

Then the people found themselves trapped in a Rhode Island conference hall with guards at the doors while the main attraction, huckster Ben Terner, started the show. Gary didn't stick around, because he knew a revival meeting when he heard a revival meeting, having grown up in protestant churches. It didn't matter if religion had anything to do with the meeting or not, the approach sounded the same. Build the audience to a fever pitch with outrageous promises and then get them to buy either with money in the collection plate or a "share" in the pyramid ("We will be focusing on just four leaders . . ."), although the pitch presented the scheme as anything other than a pyramid where the only person making money was the man at the top, and maybe a few people a few layers below. Each share bought for $500 gave the owner the right to turn around and sell other shares to $500 each with a cut of each $500 going to each layer above. No product existed. Nothing but a promise. Once the pyramid got tall enough, the man at the top didn't have to sell a thing. He'd just sit back and collect his percentage. Terner would be convicted of mail fraud and abetting a pyramid a couple of years later and served five years in federal prison.

Late into the evening, a bus load of harried, harassed, and fatigued people still holding on to their cash climbed back on the old Levine Bus Lines charter coach for the return trip to Connecticut. Their handlers stood up front the entire return trip trying to get one person, any person, to buy a share. When the bus trip ended in the parking lot of the Waterford Mall right outside of New London where the trip started, the two handlers, who had yet to make a sale and were visibly angry, refused to move from the front of the bus, continued to harangue those on board, and ordered Gary to drive downtown to drop the passengers off at the Pequot Hotel (yes, they built yet another), and then to leave. Nobody spoke up and Gary falsely assumed the handlers could extend the charter to the hotel. Stupid.

Levine let him know Monday morning that the charter always ended where the bus originally met the passengers--especially if that's where they parked their cars. Several people had called and complained about being kidnapped and forced to go downtown when they just wanted to go home and to bed.

And then there were the frickin kids who jumped out of the back emergency exit on the school bus when he had to fill in for one of the drivers who either quit or called in sick. Or the kid he had to haul into the principal's office for starting a fight one morning on the route in. Or the corn binder, the old International school bus with a clutch that failed one afternoon, but, he told himself, at least he learned how to drive a stick that day without a clutch. All a matter of timing engine rpm with transmission rpm and hoping not to break your arm if you missed the gear and the shift lever kicked back at you. Fun stuff.

Hell, he'd take a dump fire any day of the week over that crap. Call it a resume builder that added hours and hours of firefighting experience. The paid men gladly allowed volunteers to help at the dump. Any time. The Bates Woods Landfill now sits as a park in New London, but in 1970, a dump was a dump no matter what the euphemism, and as with dumps at the time, it burned every once in a while when a load of hot trash landed atop the piles of paper and old furniture and tires. Earth Day my ass. Re- What? Recycle?

So, yeah, sometimes Gary learned that he gained a little status in life when he road on the tailgate of a big shiny red Seagrave with its siren screaming down Montauk, and stepped off the back like a hero at the hydrant and made the connection. Sometimes he got to roll up on a nice day in April and pull the booster to spray water on a grass fire and go back to the station satisfied that he performed a vital community service that gave his life a real purpose.

Then he volunteered for dump duty, but what the hell, he wasn't driving a bus load of suckers or snotty middle schoolers. He got to watch while the paid man started up the trailer pump, connected it to the dump hydrant, and charged two 1.5 lines, but they did allow the vollys to connect each six foot dump nozzle, the name given to an extra long bayonet nozzle. They let the vollys spend hour after hour all night long shoving the bayonet vertically into the trash at one spot, then stand there while the water soaked in before moving it again. "Keep doing that," said the Captain, "Until you don't see smoke any more. I'll be back in the morning to check on it."

Once a decade, New London would get a spectacular tire fire at the dump that generated a column of smoke visible for miles, but this fire smoldered below the surface and proved less an emergency than it was a public nuisance that had to be removed because it couldn't be ignored. The city manager wanted it out. So they soaked and soaked and soaked some more and spent the time between pulling the nozzle up and shoving it in somewhere else shooting the shit.

"Do we have a radio?"

"No," said Joey. "Vollys can't use radios."

"What if the portable runs out of gas?"

"It won't."

"You hear they're hiring a third man for each station?"

"That's the plan."

"You taking the exam?"

"Not this time. Some people I don't want to work with. I'll wait for an opening somewhere else."
"You staying in the bunkroom ."

"For now."

"Beck said they want to shut down Engine 8."

"He talked to Judge White. That stopped it."

"Who's Judge White?"

"Some bigwig who lives down near the station. Big supporter of the Pequots."

Joey left at midnight. He had to work the next day and had no plans to be anything more than a volunteer firefighter and welder. Welders made good money, better than firefighters, and after the first Millstone nuke project ended, they planned to build a second power plant. Steady work for a few years to come thanks to the modern miracle of nuclear power.

Gary stuck it out and worked with Joey's replacement, a loud-mouthed, carrot top accountant by the name of Denny Reilly, one of the other handful of younger men in the Pequots, but he hedged his bets and also had a membership in the Oswegatchie (an Algonquin word meaning black water. Not a tribal name) Fire Company in Waterford. Reilly could and did respond in both New London and Waterford and could remain active in the fire service as a volunteer even if New London shut down the vollys. He'd also have the satisfaction that at least a couple times a year and maybe more, New London, being as under equipped as it was and as stupid about running an effective combination department as it was, had to call Waterford for mutual aid. In Waterford, the volunteers ran the department. But for one paid man who drove the first due engine during the day, volunteers drove and operated apparatus, volunteers fought fires, and volunteers formed the officer corps from chief down.

"Hey. How they hangin?" Reilly grinned and slapped Gary on the back.

"Thought you had to work, Denny?"

"Thought you had to work, John?"

They both laughed and Reilly pulled out a cigarette and lit up.

"You could start a fire."

"Fuck you." Reilly laughed again.

"Let's move the nozzles over there about ten feet."

"What the fuck for?" For an accountant, Reilly swore a lot, or so it seemed to Gary. Maybe Reilly had a need to be one of the boys once he got out of the office, or maybe he got so sick of being polite and restrained all day long that he liked the chance to spew an obscenity now and again, and what better place than a fire?

"Why not?"

"Because this place burns all the time anyway. We just come out here every once in a while because someone complains to city hall about the smoke, so we soak it down for a night, then call it good. You'll never put the fire out. It's buried so deep, they'd need to dig up the entire dump to find it."

"Okay. I'll move one just to do something. You can watch this one."

Reilly laughed, flicked the cigarette ashes in no particular direction, then took another drag while Gary pulled the nozzle up and dragged it ten feet out further into the trash to bury it again, but had to stop when his left boot punched into an air hole. "Damn."

Reilly laughed again but didn't make a move to help while Gary struggled to free his foot. He didn't want to lose a good boot. The department provided cheap gear to the volunteers, so he'd bought his own pair of good Servus boots. He shoved the bayonet nozzle in until it hit something solid, then used it to hold onto while he pulled his foot up and out, including the boot. Angry at the damned dump, he pulled the bayonet up, then jammed it down into the garbage again the full length of the shaft. Six feet down. Then opened it up, turned, and carefully stepped back to the place he'd been next to Reilly.

"You're too damned gung ho. Relax." He flipped the cigarette out into the night without a thought about where the butt would land, lit or not.

Gary had to laugh at that one. Yes, he was gung ho. He'd been at damned near every fire with the Pequots his first year, and he had no plans to let up. He shutdown the nozzle next to Reilly, disconnected the bayonet, then open the nozzle and aimed the straight stream in the direction of Reilly's butt. "Right." Then just for the helluva it, to break the tedium, he swing the nozzle back and forth into the darkness to soak down whatever was out there.

Reilly smiled.

Gary swung the nozzle again. "You going to fire school this summer?"
"Been to them all. Some of them twice. We're running a pump operation workshop at Oswegatchie in July. Stop by."

Gary said he would, then shut down the nozzle, reconnected it to the bayonet, shoved it back into the garbage, and opened it again.

The dump still smoldered at sunup, but Sean O'Conner from Truck 2 showed up with the department pickup truck to shut down the trailer pump and return it to headquarters station. Gary and Reilly helped disconnect, drain, and roll hose and load it in the back of the pickup, then helped O'Conner lift the trailer onto the hitch ball. Reilly offered O'Conner a cigarette from the second pack he'd opened overnight and O'Conner accepted with a nod in thanks before he drove off. Reilly had his own way of dealing with paid people. Groveling and bribery. He bribed his way into riding shotgun in the pickup with O'Conner on the way back. Gary drove his VW out of the dump and back to Engine 8 for a shower, breakfast, and a good cup of coffee.

7 Second

That one long ring woke them at 3:33 am, and Beck shot out the door, followed by Gary, Joey and then the new third paid man, and the lieutenant. At least no school buses had to be fueled, so Gary had regular hours during the summer, and his boss, also a volly, would know he would be late if he got stuck at a working fire. By the time Lt. Albe was down the stairs, everyone was on the back, and Flanigan had the Seagrave started and the lights on—headlights, tail, and that one rotating red light on the cab roof.

They rolled down the ramp, turned right and took off down Lower Boulevard, and, to tell you the truth, it was hard to believe the call was anything serious. The August night was warm and still, the kind of night Gary lay out on the beach on a blanket and counted stars with his girlfriend, the one who stayed with him an entire week until she got tired of competing with fire calls. And the streets had no traffic, so the lieutenant had no need for the siren. The south end of New London was primarily residential and the fire department didn't want to wake anyone in the middle of the night if there was no need to do so. A stealth run, as if they were sneaking up on whatever it was they were sneaking up on. Even after they turned right onto Pequot and drove along next to the private beaches at the mouth of the Thames River, they had no reason to buckle up coats or pull on gloves. They left their turnout coats open to the breeze until Engine 8 got closer along Pequot to the corner of Neptune Avenue in the neighborhood where most of the homes were old Pequot Colony summer places or rooming houses for the lower classes who worked for the robber barons where the Thames met Long Island Sound.

As they approached the final right turn from Pequot onto Neptune that led across Ocean Avenue and down a short hill to the Ocean Beach Park entrance, Beck nudged Gary and they all saw it at the same time. No one spoke. They didn't need to. It was that sudden, as if the sun had popped up three hours early. They hung onto the back with one hand and with the other began to buckle their coats, check the straps on their helmets, get their gloves on. Still nobody spoke and everybody listened on that last turn to that unmistakable rumble of a fully involved structure fire, the kind that start in the middle of the night when no one is on the street to see the flicker of flame in the basement when a wire sparks where old insulation that should have been replaced years before finally wears completely through to the bare wire. Or maybe it was a leak in the oil furnace tank in the basement or maybe somebody smoked a joint in the basement and dropped a hot butt and at that moment it didn't really matter. Whatever it was, and the fire marshal would try to make a determination after it was all over, whatever started it waited until everyone was asleep and built up enough heat to blow out basement windows, and boom, the flashover, and up through the floor, up outside the basement to light up the front porch, and then, with plenty of fresh air to breath, it rolled up over the porch roof, heated up the old, single pane glass in the second floor living room, blew out the glass, and entered unannounced and took over inside and outside.

The fire was having a fine time burning tons of the best fuel old New England rooming houses had to offer—wood, wood, and more dried out old wood. Plaster and lath walls with wood, wooden floors varnished again and again and again, clapboard siding, open interior wood stairs, curtains, overstuffed chairs, newspapers, and carpets. The whole block was lit up and the conflagration produced enough heat as it soared over the peaked roof, melted asphalt shingles, and burned overhanging tree branches to ignite the Oldsmobile parked across the front lawn on the curb. Convection at work. The house was cooking that Oldsmobile without touching it with one bit of flame. You could have stood across the street and roasted a marshmallow.

Engine 8 stopped in the middle of the street just above the fire and sat there. Mistake number one. Albe didn't yell any orders because he was busy on the radio calling in the second alarm with a speech impediment while Flanigan waited for orders and Beck thought they were committed, so he yelled, "Make the hydrant," and the game was on. Gary grabbed the female 2.5 and dragged it across the street to the hydrant on the opposite corner, which was mistake number two. Now hose ramps would have to be deployed to allowed second due and second alarm apparatus to cross the hose without cutting off the water supply to Engine 8, and that two and a half would only feed one heavy line from Engine 8, which led to mistake three.

While the hydrant line was being connected to the intake port on Engine 8 and the hydrant opened by Gary, Beck and crew pulled the male 2.5 off the back of Engine 8, having to drop hose by running away from the fire to get enough line off before connecting it to a discharge port and screwing one of the heavy pipe nozzles on the business end.

Once the 2.5 line was charged and air release from the nozzle, Beck doused, or more accurately, blasted the car with water to put the fire out, then led the crew across the side yard and up the metal fire escape that climbed to a door on the second floor. The door opened onto a hallway that crossed the building right behind the front room on the second floor. He was an aggressive bastard, Beck, and thought he was going to fight an interior fire on the second floor of a building with a solid wall of flame from basement to roof peak, if that tired old metaphor applies here. Flame is not solid; it is a gas. You can put your hand into it if you want to have the skin burned off. Flame won't stop you, but the pain will certainly stop you as would any cement wall, and that you'll know if you've ever tried to get close to any serious fire, or even a campfire or cozy fireplace. The heat gets uncomfortable, and you can feel it even though you're not touching anything—but gas, superheated gas. Convection. So it might as well be a wall. You'd never walk through it alive. If you take one breath, it would not sear your lungs but your trachea before the heat ever reached your lungs. Then the trachea swells shut and nothing will save you.
Up they dragged that damned heavy stream line, up the metal stairs to that second floor door, but at least Beck and the paid man hanging onto the nozzle decided it smarter to punch through the glass in the

door rather than open it given the fire rolling along the ceiling toward them. And fire does roll like that along a ceiling, especially if it senses a new source of oxygen, and it's the oxygen it wants, not just the air. No oxygen, no combustion.

Below Beck on the stairs, Joey struggled to keep the big line in place, holding onto it with hose straps, straining against the weight and against the desire of the hose to straighten itself out, and hoping Beck and the paid man did not let go of the nozzle, which would have whipped around and clobbered someone. Part of fire school training was learning how to get control of a heavy line if the nozzle got loose and succumbed to one of the fundamental laws of physics. All that pressure shooting out the end of the nozzle had to have an opposite and equal reaction, which was a nozzle flying around, whipping left to right until it came into contact with someone's head or blasted an eye out with the water pressure. The training advise was don't let go. But, if it got loose, jump on it and hang on until you get help or manage to grab the nozzle handles.

If that weren't enough to worry about, assuming the fire escape was up to code and would hold, the fire did not seem to be affected at all by that one little hose line squirting 200 gallons a minute into the hallway and living room. The water evaporated instantly and the fire seemed to grow stronger and roll faster along the ceiling toward the door as if to welcome the fools and let them in.

No time, though, to find out, because the Deputy Chief had arrived and he yelled even louder than usual, directly at the fire escape. "Get the fuck off," he yelled, and had to yell and swear a second time before they realized he meant them, yes, that group of idiots on the fire escape. Get off, get down, the building is clear, we're using exterior tactics, I don't want anyone on or in or near the building . . . And down they came and set up the line on the side lawn next to the building for a siege just as the front of the house collapsed into the first floor with the boom of thunder.

Now it was just a matter of sheer gallonage, tonnage of water. But first the Deputy Chief had Beck's line shutdown, drained, and disconnected while he yelled at Flanigan to reposition Engine 8 at the hydrant on the same side of the street as the fire and hook up the soft suction so they could feed two heavy hand lines. In the meantime, Engine 1 fed a ladder pipe on Truck 1, and Engine 5 fed a ladder pipe on Truck 2, and Engine 7 had two additional hand lines in operation on the opposite side of the rooming house, and when everyone opened up, the fire never had a chance. 2000 gallons, eight tons a minute pouring onto the flames, and by sunup, the actual sunup, the battle was over, the chemical reaction stopped by water, the heat dissipated, and nothing was left to do but overhaul.

First due, last out was the rule. All other companies were released but Engine 8 once the front half of the building was reduced to a smoldering, steaming ruin that would be condemned by the City that day and demolished the next. But first Albe ordered Gary and Joey into the basement with a booster line and a short pike pole to dig around in piles of burned junk to soak anything left that smoked or smoldered until they were certain it was out, dead out.

But, of course, as in the plot of any B western, the villain makes one last gasp effort before being shot dead, really dead. Gary could never understand why the good guy always shot the bad guy and then turned his back without first putting another bullet into the bad guy's head to make certain, very certain, he was dead, really dead. But the standard action plot allows the villain one last shot. The fire had no flame left, no sudden, dramatic explosion. It simply put a nail through the boot of the Fire Marshal when he stepped down into the basement for a look around for the seat of the fire. He yelped "Damn!" when he stepped onto the upturned plank and drove a nail through his boot and his foot;

he stepped onto the plank again, but with his good foot, yanked the wounded foot off the nail and limped back out of the basement to head off to the hospital for a tetanus shot. Engine 8 rolled up the last link of hose shortly thereafter, retracted the booster, and returned to the firehouse.

After the hose had been packed on the pumper, Beck headed out the door to work followed by Gary, who stopped him to apologize for the hydrant screw up.

"Not your fault. Albe needed to have the pumper positioned on arrival. We sat there while he called in the second, so I made the call."

"Guess so. Who's the new paid man?"

"Don't know."

"Does he have any training?"

"Don't know and don't give a damn any more. I'm bunking in Waterford starting next month. The vollys are dead in New London. Big mistake by the city. We had a full crew tonight with vollys, but without them first due personnel would be half the NFPA standard. Gotta go."

"See you later." And there it was. A fire department of paid incompetents replacing a fire department with a volunteer system that trained personnel. Nobody in NLFD made one ounce of effort to create a combination department. Nobody even introduced the third man to the vollys. They'd fought a second alarm with some no name without knowing what he could and could not do. Great teamwork. Before he left for Waterford himself, Gary got to see the other third man on each shift. One was a cloned Pasquale; the other was this little guy who looked like a grade school kid in turnout gear given the job, with little doubt, due to being the son of a captain in the department. He didn't work out so well. He had the luck to work with Marco and Pasquale. He tried and tried to become one of the guys, but reticent Marco and sarcastic Pasquale made him feel worse than a volly. A paid volly. The poor little bastard got so desperate for inclusion and attention he thought telling how he and his wife had screwed the night before would make a connection. "We tried it doggy style." Wince. He quit not long after that, which offered a sure sign to Gary that he didn't want to belong to that department, paid or volunteer.

Maybe Waterford, or maybe Groton where two paid positions opened up after two full-time firefighters found themselves without a job.

8 poquonnock bridge

John Gary, when he crossed the Thames River from New London to Groton, didn't give a damn about moving from Connecticut College and the Coast Guard Academy and the private beaches once part of the exclusive Pequot Colony to the gritty, working class world of Pfizer Chemical, General Dynamics, and the Submarine Base. For him the move was up from grease monkey at a bus company to paid firefighter, a job any working stiff would leave home to get. It meant a steady paycheck, a uniform, not having to get dirty all of the time (just some of the time), and a little respect at $3.02 an hour.

He placed second on the exam given by the Poquonnock Bridge Fire District to hire two firefighters to replace the two fired for failing to respond to a structure fire call at the small airport in town. A maintenance building burned, and they didn't leave the station until the third phone call. Bad idea. That made Gary acutely aware that being gung ho had benefits once he crossed the river, because even though PBFD had four paid people on duty Monday through Friday during the day, and two on duty at night and on weekends, and a paid chief who also served as fire marshal, the department was predominantly volunteer and nobody would hassle him as a paid man for responding off duty. He could run to fires day and night.

Though Groton had decent apartments not too far from the station, Gary chose a place as close as he could be to the firehouse on Fort Hill Road, better known as U.S. Route 1, the same Route 1 that ran from Maine to Florida. He found half a shabby duplex on Depot Road down the street from the town hall at 45 Fort Hill Road, an easy walk to Fort Hill Road, location of the two story, white, wooden firehouse built in 1946 by the volunteers on the Poquonnock Plain near the Poquonnock River in the heart of Pequot country. Each side of the duplex offered the luxury working class accommodations of a front sitting room next to the kerosene furnace, a front bedroom Gary used for storage, a back bedroom he used for his bed, scanner, and quick hitches, a bathroom with a sink, toilet, and metal stall shower--and the kitchen. A back door from the kitchen opened out onto a ratty yard with half dead grass, all surrounded by a low chain link fence.

The short driveway on Gary's end of the duplex had room for two cars, and he backed his red VW in next to the yellow Dodge Charger owned by the sailor who lived next door with his wife and a small child when he wasn't at sea in one of the boomers. Three months out, three in.
It was old, allegedly temporary industrial housing built during World War II for workers when Groton built the US submarine fleet. After the war, the government sold the houses for about $900 each, and some went to private owners, including a couple of the PBFD paid men and several volunteers, and others went to landlords like the one Gary rented from. The first windy day he found out the caulking around the windows had rotted, which provided really good ventilation on warm days. On cold days the heat did not exactly circulate beyond

the front room, so he moved his mattress out there on the floor to stay warm at night during the winter. But the great location made for a short commute and quick response off duty. The location also sent a signal that he was one of them. PBFD paid men worked a 24/48 schedule that averaged a 56 hour work week at pay that forced most of them to find a second job. One ran snow plows in the winter. Another drove an oil truck. Another worked at a gas station. The volunteers worked blue collar jobs at General Dynamics, called The Boat, as electricians, welders, and the others worked construction, worked for Groton utilities, collected trash, or collected a retirement check. One old guy who stopped by the station to visit every once in awhile liked to joke that "he got even with the bastards," meaning the railroad, because he'd been collecting a pension for 28 years since he retired at 65. Yes, he was that old.

Gary fit right in and learned right away that no two fire departments are the same. Yes sir, PBFD had newer rigs than New London. Not an old Seagrave in sight. Out of that one station on Fort Hill Road, they ran three pumpers. The 1964 Ferrara cab forward ran first on all fires with a 1000 GPM single stage Barton-American pump and a 500 gallon booster tank and no power steering. For structure fires, the Ward LaFrance cab forward with a 1000 GPM two stage Waterous ran second due also with a 500 gallon tank and no power steering or power brakes. Just hydraulics. Second due on car and brush fires meant the 4x4 1960 International with a 500 GPM pump and and 500 gallon tank, but it did have power steering and decent brakes. The same two second due firefighters took either the Ward or the corn binder, depending on the type of run.

And they did run. Four times the number Engine 8 ran in New London, because they covered 20 square miles, including I-95, an airport, shopping centers, schools, churches, trailer parks, housing subdivisions, apartment buildings, commercial buildings, a state park, an asphalt plant, and mutual aid for every other fire district in Groton.

Being centrally located, PBFD ran on second alarm calls to the City of Groton, Center Groton, Noank, Mystic, and Old Mystic. The sub base, the Boat, and Pfizer each had their own fire station, but if they had anything big, the city and PBFD would be called in. So the load hazard mix ran from rural to suburban to urban right there in the middle of the military industrial complex.

But John Gary, firefighter, did not give a damn about that complex. The Pequots killed their neighbors, the Calvinists killed the Pequots, millions killed each other during World War II, the war that created Poquonnock Bridge with its Midway Loop housing project for war workers. The Vietnam War still fumbled along, and the sub base certainly had a big target painted on it if nuclear war with the Soviet Union broke out, which meant Groton would be vaporized. None of it mattered. At least, John told himself, I'm where I can do something before being vaporized. I am one of those who responds to emergencies rather than sitting around waiting for someone else to do something. Nothing noble. No working class hero stuff, no Walter Mitty dreams of glory. Just a sense that he had some control over chaos and wasn't alone when he faced it. When Benedict Arnold led the British attacks in September 1781 that burned 143 building in New London and attacked Fort Griswold on the Groton side of the river, the massacred American militia, commanded by Colonel Ledyard and outnumbered 800 to 150, did not die alone or in vain.

Gary's first day of duty arrived 190 years after Benedict Arnold's attack. And that had a nice ring to it, the word "duty." He no longer had a job, no longer went to work. He was on duty and had an obligation to protect thousands of lives and millions in property for $3.04 an hour Monday through Friday from 7:45 am to 5:15 pm with no time off for lunch, no breaks. Firefighters eat at lunch time unless an alarm rings in. They get a cup of coffee, unless an alarm rings in. They complete daily chores, unless an alarm rings in. They visit the

head, unless an alarm rings in. Always on duty, in or out of the
station. Always committed to helping others.

Wearing his navy blue work uniform, Gary reported for duty his first
day, nervously, of course, because he had to meet a lot of new people
and get to know the rigs and the equipment they carried, but that's the
next chapter.

9 Second due

Gary left his little red VW parked at the back of the lot on the right
side of the station and walked to the front entrance just to the left of
the two overhead doors behind which Engines 31 and 32 sat facing US
Route 1. He walked straight through the door past Engine 31 and down
the stairs marked Members Only to the day room where John Dill and
Ernie Taylor sat at the round table with a cup of morning coffee. He
introduced himself, and they shook his hand and asked if he'd like a
coffee. Yes. Then the size up. Where'd he work before, and so on,
but the conversation didn't go too far because the next shift arrived.
Each man had to officially arrive by finding the man he had to relieve,
but the shift change always happened in the basement day room first
thing in the morning, making it easy for one shift to find the other.

Joe Murray walked in, all gray hair with a key chain dangling from his
belt, to relieve the senior man, Taylor, then the other new man
followed, Jack Shawnessy, to relieve Dill. Couldn't get much more
American than that for two new firefighters, John and Jack, but
nobody said much other than hello and goodbye. John Dill lit a
cigarette, his second of the morning, when Shawnessy arrived, and
headed out the back door of the kitchen through the back bay to his
truck and home to the wife and kids, all four of them.

After shift change, they hiked up from the day room to the carriage floor and then up another flight at the back of the carriage floor to the second floor to be sworn in officially by the Chief and given their badges. Gary and Shawnessy trooped back down to the carriage floor where the Lieutenant, who had no need to meet anyone in the day room, gave them the tour with much more information than they'd ever remember the first day. The Lieutenant never took time to shake hands, and spoke with a no nonsense, flat, matter-of-fact tone. Joe Murray sat the morning watch at the desk on the other side of the carriage floor--the nerve center with all the phones, the radio, the tape machine, the alarm panel, the maps, the intercom, and the weather station.

"Keep your gear," meaning the helmet, boots, and turnout coat they'd been issued, "next to Engine 31. Shawnessy, you're driving and Gary, you ride. Engine 31 is second due, so Shawnessy takes care of dispatch first, then drives 31 unless there's a brush or car fire, then you both take Engine 34 from the back bay. We'll go down there in a minute." They both knew their assignments, but that made it official. Top score on the exam had the higher paying 24/48 shift job and drove second due, and second on the exam had the Monday through Friday day job as fourth man on duty who also filled in for one of the other drivers when he took a day off, or road shotgun on first due when the Lieutenant took a day. NFPA minimum personnel standards and all that to guarantee a response with four men during the day, five including the Chief. No crew shortage worries on nights and weekends, though, when plenty of volunteers were home from work.

And, yes, that's right. No 9-1-1 way back then just before centralized dispatch. It was in the planning stage in Groton with its seven fire districts, each independently taxing, each with a board of commissioners, each with its own fire equipment but for one, Groton Long Point, which contracted with PBFD for coverage. The hodgepodge system persisted because Groton really did not exist. The City of Groton did, chartered in 1705 as a borough independent from New London across the Thames, and it sat on the river shore and had a downtown, but from the Thames to the Mystic seaport of whaling fame, no downtown Town of Groton could be found. Shopping strips existed just north and south of I-95. Neighborhoods like Poquonnock Bridge, Center Groton, Groton Long Point, Noank, part of Mystic, and Old Mystic filled the rest of Groton with clusters of population. The Mystic fire district straddled both Groton on the west shore of the Mystic River and Stonington on the east shore. Each district had its own emergency number, a seven digit number that a resident had damned well have written down on the inside of the phone book. Trying to find the right number to call without having it written down could prove fatal.

They circled Engine 31, the Ward, and the Lieutenant didn't say much other than to tell them to take the time before lunch to go through all the compartments to learn where the gear was stowed. "Just one thing, Shawnessy," said the Lieutenant, opening the driver's side door of the Ward's cab. "When you start the engine, pull the choke all the way out, and then push it back down half way when the engine catches. If it floods, push the choke all the way in and crank with the gas pedal to the floor until it clears. Not exactly a Seagrave, Gary thought, but not aloud, of course.

The phone rang at the watch desk and the Lieutenant stopped talking and stood rock still. They could hear Murray say, "Poquonnock Bridge Fire Department." Then a pause. The Lieutenant turned to walk around the front of Engine 32, but stopped as Murray said, "2311 Indian Field, correct?" Pause. The buzzer sounded. "Car fire, 32, 34." No, John Gary, you are not in New London any longer. Firefighters knew where they were going and more or less what they had before leaving the station. The Lieutenant pushed the button to raise the overhead door in front of Engine 32, then the button that changed the flashing yellow light in front of the station on Route 1 to red, before he climbed into the cab. Having dispatched in Noank, Shawnessy knew the drill. While Murray climbed into the cab of 32 and cranked the engine, Shawnessy quickly keyed the mike at the watch desk and announced, "Station PG to all stations, signal 50. 2311 Indian Field." Now all of New London County knew PBFD had a run--just in case.

"32, 53." Engine 32 was on the air and in route.

Gary had already pulled his boots, coat, and helmet on and had found his way through the meeting hall behind the front carriage floor, down the half flight of stairs through the alarm shop, past the district pickup in the small bay, past more racks of hose than he'd ever seen in his life, to the back double bay where the 1937 parade Mac sat parked next to the 4 x 4 International he'd ride. Shawnessy showed up just after Gary pushed the overhead door button and climbed into the cab. Shawnessy grinned, "Good thing I stopped by yesterday to see what I saw driving."

The corn binder cranked right up, and they left the back bay through the parking lot with the electronic siren at full howl to be damned sure stopped traffic could hear them coming and didn't think of moving again until 34 reached the street. Gary keyed the mike: "34, 53."

They could see 32 in the distance about a hundred yards ahead when they straightened out on Fort Hill Road and followed eastbound. Murray drove cautiously, slowly almost as if he wanted to be certain 34 saw him turn left onto Newtown Road. They did, and they saw him turn right onto Indian Field a quarter mile later and followed, smelling the smoke immediately.
The Chief stayed in his office upstairs. He left only for structure fires and let the Lieutenant run the show and take the report at the small stuff.

"32, 72." Working fire, but quick work. Murray positioned 32 in the middle of the street in front of 2311 just past an old Ford F-150 smoking in the driveway. A lot of heavy black smoke billowed out from under the hood, but no visible flame, which meant caution. The Lieutenant ordered Shawnessy to park 34 back fifty feet short of the driveway and "Both of you head up here." Murray had the pump operating, the lieutenant barked at Gary to get the Halligan mounted outside just behind the cab and told Shawnessy to pull the rider's side booster. The LT stood next to the cab, opened the driver's side door, and, with the hose and Halligan in position, just said, "Okay," and popped the hood latch. Gary didn't have to think. He shoved the crowbar end of the Halligan under the front of the hood and leaned down on it just as Shawnessy opened up. He had to duck and turn his head as flame shot out, but managed to hold onto the Halligan as Shawnessy worked the booster close enough to shove the nozzle right up next to the slightly open hood.

"Let's open it all the way." The Lieutenant found the lock latch, released it, then lifted the hood up as far as it would go while Shawnessy swept back and forth with a fog pattern until black smoke turned into white steam in a minute. He kept the water on it until most of the steam had disappeared as the engine cooled and the lieutenant propped the hood open and talked to the truck owner for the report.

"I came out to go to work and started it, and it wouldn't start, then started to smoke."
"Gas line broke?" asked the Lieutenant, though not knowing for certain what caused the fire before taking a second look to see that the air filter had been removed. "Was that off when you started it?"

"Yes."

"Did you spray some of that starter juice into the carburetor?"

"Yes. It wouldn't start at first."

"When was the last time you had it tuned?"

"Don't know. I sprayed the stuff, set the air filter back on, but didn't latch the top in case I had to spray again, then tried to start it. Never did this before."

"It backfired," the Lieutenant said, "and lit off the paint under the hood, the oil built up on the engine, then the wiring insulation. I need your full name and the name of your insurance company for my report."

When they picked up, Gary almost laughed out loud at the ease of pulling the booster back on the reel by pushing a button. Each of the two booster reels mounted behind the jump seats on 32 retracted with an electric motor. Yes sir, modern firefighting.

Before lunch, they had 32 and 34 returned to the station, washed down, backed in, and topped off 32's water with the overhead fill hose. After lunch, Shawnessy and Gary took the clipboard for the Engine 31 inventory, a routine weekly task and went compartment by compartment to make certain all the equipment sat in the right places-- all lights, hose clamps, hose ramps, hose straps, double males, double females, Scott packs, hard suction, soft suction, ground ladders, roof ladder, bolt cutters, smoke ejector, wheel chocks, shovel, rope, Halligan, pike pole, bayonet nozzle, pre-connects, 2.5 inch male and female hydrant line, 2.5 nozzles, deck gun, reciprocating saw, ax, dry powder extinguishers, first aid kit, hazmat book, and Herman Melville could fill a whole chapter on the technology used to subdue a primal force of nature. Facing whales or fire, humans stood helpless without technology. Gray found himself impressed again by PBFD when they reached the back of 31. It had the usual split hose bed with 2.5 male packed on one side and female on the other, but no catwalk to a jump seat. Ward positioned the hose bed higher to allow for more compartment space, and they built the jumpseat right behind the cab, so nobody had to ride the tailgate anyway. The most impressive gear, though, is often the simplest. At PBFD the hydrant ring took the prize for innovation. Just a three foot diameter metal ring attached with a rope to the hydrant line, the female side. Even if the driver worked alone before volunteers arrived, he could stop the engine, pull the hydrant line, drop the ring over the hydrant, then drive off without worry about the hydrant line being dragged down the street if a coupling snagged in the hose bed. If a firefighter working with the driver pulled the line, he could drop the ring over the hydrant and be certain of a connection.

It's the little things.

Jack Shawnessy relieved Murray on the watch desk after they completed the inventory, and Gary joined him and studied the shades mounted on a wall rack. Again, innovation. No computers then, but somebody had the inspiration to have subdivision and trailer park maps printed on window shades they could pull down for fast address location. Nice. And then he and Jack reviewed the communication and alarm equipment, knowing that they could be interrupted at any moment by another run; besides policy forbid discussion of religion or politics on duty. They all had to get along based on what they had in common. After the watch desk equipment review, Gary chatted about firefighting in New London, and Shawnessy chatted about his eight years in the Navy on boomers. After basic at Great Lakes, the Navy had moved him to sub school at Groton and stationed him there once he finished, a good location close to his home in New Jersey. He stuck around after discharge, married, had no kids, a good sense of humor, black hair a little too long, a slight beer paunch, and a part-time job off duty working at a gas station to save for a down payment on a house in Noank on the water.

"Poquonnock Bridge Fire Department. Yes ma'am. What's your location. We'll be right there."

Loud buzzer. "Engine 32, 31," said Jack with his best Navy efficiency, "Station PG to all station, signal 50, 215 Buddington Road. Possible structure fire."

The overhead doors rolled up, and the Chief beat them out because it was potentially a structure fire, and because he'd left his car on the ramp when he returned from a building inspection after lunch. 32 rolled down the ramp and the air horn on top of the station blasted out the box location without concern for disturbing the neighbors. Gary sat in the rider's seat in the open cab ready to go when Shawnessy started the Ward with a rumble and a cloud of blue exhaust that filled the carriage floor. They both glanced at each other, eyes a little wide, glad it hadn't flooded. Out the door they went, lights flashing, the mechanical siren cranked up loud, and again right onto Route 1, then the first left up Buddington Road where 31 roared up to 50 miles per hour in fourth gear, running close behind 32, but both engines slowed when the Chief radioed that they had an overheated dryer. "Engine 31, return. 32 proceed in to standby on the street."

Second and last run of the day. Gary went home at 5:15 pm with an odor on his work clothes that smelled a little like burning car and a little like exhaust from a 600ci monster Waukesha starting in a confined space. First day over as long as the scanner didn't wake him that night, and it didn't.

10 scanner

Home sweet home. But not for long. Gary ate his blue collar bachelor dinner, a frozen pot pie heated in the oven on a cookie sheet covered in foil, and had settled into Friday evening in front to the TV at the end of his first week as a paid firefighter when the PBFD tone squealed from the scanner sitting on the night table next to the bed his parents had donated for his Depot Road palace. At least he hadn't spotted a cockroach. Yet.

"Station PG to all stations, signal 23, Rt 12 at Tollgate. 34 only for washdown." Borwin's voice--big Don Borwin who worked the shift with Hannigan after Shawnessy and Murray. Big Don because he personified burly truck driver and did just that off duty, jockeying an oil delivery truck for a local fuel company. He looked like an aging, barrel chested, middle linebacker. Borwin's shift partner, Rob Hannigan, a young man of ordinary dimensions, after high school before civilian fire service, spent his four years in the military on Air Force P2 foam crash trucks, which kept him out of Vietnam and stationed most of the time up in Massachusetts. In fact, Hannigan arranged the donation by the Air Force of a silver proximity suit to PBFD should the remotely possible become the immediate horror of a plane crash at the Groton airport.

Gary had his red VW cranked up just in time to hear "34, 53" on his other scanner in the car. A long run, five or six minutes or more up Long Hill and under I-95, especially in the underpowered International, and Gary decided then that it was time for a bigger car, one with a real engine. He'd taken a lot of grief during the week about the little red VW. "Do you mow the lawn with that?" "Give that clown car to a kid." "Does it really float?" "Buy American." That sort of thing. Besides, Groton encompassed more than eight times the territory found in New London, with PBFD protecting half of that first due and all of it second due, so having a ride off duty with a real engine seemed like a good idea anyway for long runs like this one.

The accident involved an overturned jeep. The driver had tried to make a sudden lane change and flipped the jeep on its side, an easy trick for a vehicle with a short wheelbase and high center of gravity. The roll bar protected the driver's head from concussion and his face from developing a serious case of road rash, but he had smacked his arm and seem to be in mild shock, common to accident victims, so the cops called for Groton Ambulance to give the kid a ride to the hospital, and called PBFD to wash away the gallon of gasoline that dribbled from the tank fill, and to standby in case more gas leaked while the wrecker righted the vehicle and towed it away.

Hello, thought Gary, as he pulled up behind 34, who is that brunette wearing the red Groton Ambulance jacket with the big white cross on the back? She and two other women unloaded the gurney expertly from the back of the Ford one ton and wheeled it over to the victim, applied an air splint to the banged up arm, checked for concussion, then strapped him in, and off they went to the hospital, lights and siren but at a cautious speed used for non-life-threatening transport. Gary heard Groton Ambulance held first aid classes in their quarters, and he decided the time was now to take the advanced first aid class after work and maybe join the ambulance company. More runs, more action, more skills, community involvement, and women. So he definitely needed a new car.

Her name was Violet, and he called her Violent once in awhile, because she had a temper, but then, who didn't? Violet and her mother, Trudy, ran Groton Ambulance, and spent all of their spare time at the ambulance building down near the airport. Gary sauntered over to Hannigan to find out if Violet were single, and he smiled and said she was about 24 and worked in the school system office with her mother. He asked Hannigan to sign up for the first aid class with him, but Hannigan laughed and said no, he had other ways to get laid. With a dead serious, deadpan tone, Gary glared at Hannigan when he answered: "You impugn my motives, sir."

Hannigan laughed louder. "I do what?"

"Heard that line in a movie," said Gary. "I'll let you know if I get lucky, and I'd like to get more medic experience. Paramedics are the future."

Gary also signed himself up for his first fire technology class as part of the two-year fire tech degree program run by Norwich State Tech, and luckily the class met upstairs in the nice new brick City of Groton headquarters station on Wednesday nights, so he didn't have to drive all the way up to the main campus in Norwich. The district reimbursed the cost of the class.

Time, in other words, to start building a career, and do anything but sit around the rest of his life in that dump he rented only because it was a short drive from there to the station, and because the cheap rent meant he could save a few bucks just in case the job didn't work out, and if it did, he'd want to move into a better place eventually. Maybe buy one of the old houses and fix it up like Taylor, Borwin, Murray and a few of the volunteers had, including the guy across the street who no longer ran to fires because of a heart condition, but lived there in the Bridge in his working class home pulling down his working class wages from a job at the Boat building America's submerged nuclear arsenal.

After the run, he hung out at the station for a few minutes to meet some of the other volunteers, the welders, the machinists, the carpenters, the tile men, and one accountant who worked inside at the Boat. They usually coagulated in the day room after a run at night or on the weekends, drank a beer from the pop machine, watched TV, maybe even started a card game, until one by one they'd drift off toward home.

But not before hazing the rookie, a necessary initiation right for any bubba men's club. Brian Winneger led the pack. A short, wiry Boat steel fabricator with a hawk nose, Winneger spoke in one tone--loud. "I hear New London runs junk."

"Seagraves, a Mac, a Ward, American LaFrance," said Gary, bracing himself.
"Like I said, junk," said Winneger, "and Christ, you drive a German piece of junk."
Then Gary made the mistake of turning his back on Winneger and saying, "Well, guess I better get home in my German junk."

"What for? You're not married." That got a laugh, then Winneger threw his left arm around Gary's shoulders and announced loudly to the room, "I like this guy" and pinned Gary from behind using both arms with the strength of a steel worker. Gary felt a little embarrassed, laughed along with the joke, "What, are you gay?" and made a token effort to break the hold, thinking that would be enough for Winneger to let go. He didn't.

Okay, thought Gary, enough's enough, and he buckled his knees to gain leverage to lift Winneger, then turned and backed him into the nearest wall. Winneger bent his legs also and perfectly countered Gary's move by pulling him backward off balance, so Gary just backpedaled, then threw an elbow and Winneger let go and laughed. "I like this guy," yelling above the din of other men yelling, "Watch it. What the fuck? Take it outside." And it was over. He'd passed the Winneger likeability test.

Home again, flip on the tube, drink a Coke, eat a small bag of chips, wash up, go to bed, and sleep until about 3:15 am when the tone woke him.

"Station PG to all stations, signal 23, Long Hill Road at Stop and Shop." Hitches on, out to the VW, drive past the station along Fort Hill to Long Hill, all Route 1, following the tail lights of Engine 34, then turn into the supermarket parking lot to get off the street with a few other volunteers who showed up to help out when the Deputy Chief ordered the ground ladder deployed on the driver's side of a Chevy Impala that had climbed the guy wire of a utility pole and sat perfectly propped against it, still running with all four wheels off the ground. The rear bumper sat squarely on the sidewalk so no danger existed that the car would roll in either direction. But the driver did not appear in the window and no voice answered from inside the car: "Yo! You okay?" So they immediately had to assume he or she had been knocked out. They also had to get at the ignition. Gary helped foot the ladder while Winneger climbed to driver's side door and leaned in through the open window to get a good whiff of beer and whiskey stench.

"He's dead drunk," Winneger yelled down to everyone. "Out cold across the front seat. No visible injuries and smells like a six pack." He turned the ignition off and took the keys.
The Deputy decided to let the drunken son-of-a-bitch sleep it off while they waited for the City of Groton tower ladder to arrive to remove the bum with the bucket. As a precaution, legal more than medical, the Deputy also requested Groton Ambulance to stand by to check the guy out one more time for injuries before the police hauled him off to the drunk tank and the wrecker hoisted the Chevy off the pole.

"One lucky bastard," said Winneger to Gary, but Gary had his attention on Violet again when she and her mother pulled up in the medic van. Winneger turned when Gary didn't answer and laughed and elbowed Gary. "You want that?"

"As long as I don't have to get married."

Winnegar laughed louder. He was married. "Why the hell not?"

"Feminismo."

"What?"

"Women use men to get what they want."

"Can't live with them. Can't live without them."

"Like firefighters."

Gary decided to end it there. The conversation threatened to disintegrate further, and it was 4:15 am and he suddenly had a need to get home, such as it was, and get back to sleep for a couple of more hours before he got up to shop for a new used car. "See you later, man."

"See you later," said Winneger.

He bought a new used one that Saturday, a gray 1968 Pontiac LeMans powered by a 350 four barrel with a three speed Hurst on the floor. Who needed four speeds with a 350 four barrel? He could get it up to 50 in first anyway, and even skipped to third from first entering the Interstate right after he bought it. With the blue light flashing on the dash when he ran to alarms off duty, people moved over, which didn't happen often when he ran to fires in the clown car, even a red clown car.

11 medic

By November, the certainty of uncertainty of any permanent relationship stayed with Gary. He felt a bit more secure in the job. He'd handled everything during those two months or so it seemed. They had a tractor trailer crash on I-95 that involved no fire but extrication of the driver from the cab. They had a middle-of-the-night single car crash on I-95 with a flipped vehicle with a gas tank lit off like a giant Bunsen burner. He responded from home on that one and learned for the first time that Joe Murray loved 100 pound nozzle pressures on pre-connects. Firefighters had to lean hard into any line Joe charged. And they had the usual fall brush fires, including one along the railroad tracks caused by a passing train, a booster line and shovel job. Another one involved a backyard grass fire next to a storage shed with gasoline cans, but again they stopped it cold before extension to the structure. Not to mention false alarms and standbys and the annual October fire safety display at the Long Hill shopping center, and the school visit. Hannigan and Gary took Engine 31 to a grammar school and charged the booster line. The kids loved it and the next week, the Chief called Gary up to his office. The secretary smiled and the Chief smiled when he handed him the drawings the kids had done on large sheets of paper for "Mr. Fireman." He had to spend the rest of the day getting razzed about those drawings, but he kept them and even taped them to his living room wall for a while.

Nothing big. No structure fires anywhere in Groton, but he knew that with winter approaching workers would occur in the not too distant future, including his own place maybe with that old kerosene furnace that seemed to burn constantly to keep just the living room warm. The place had no way to circulate the heat that blew out into the living room and stayed there. He'd heard stories on duty about the regulating valve on the burners failing, and they did have a call like that one day when the furnace kicked on full flame in one of the Midway Oval homes and could not be adjusted. By the time they arrived, the inside of the duplex felt like a sauna, but the fire still remained in the furnace. Their only actions involved shutting off the fuel valve on the tank behind the house and using a dry powder extinguisher on the furnace to knock down the flame. From there the problem belonged to the furnace repair people. And light fixtures. One in a business that started smoking. Another that shorted in a home kitchen ceiling. They cut the power and pulled the ceiling, but no real extension.

Routine stuff.

But getting married? A fiancee, a girlfriend? Not yet. If ever. But getting some, getting laid, having a little fun. Sure. Booty, snatch, pootang, bush, beaver, getting bred, and every other sex euphemism in the Navy town lexicon that floated around the firehouse in daily babble. Taylor, the expert on women, offered this one day when the conversation turned to Groton Ambulance. "You know what she needs," he said about Violet. It wasn't a question. Taylor, who believed he should always find fault with his wife's cooking to keep her in her place, offered the wisdom that every woman just needed the big one, the prick, the hard on, the wally. Okay. Gary used that last term, a nickname for Mr. Penis he invented in 10th grade to refer to a pubescent part of his anatomy that seemed to have a mind of its own. Just one look at a girl's thigh in class, and he had to spend the rest of the period figuring out how to hide the bulge in his pants. And if it didn't subside by the end of the period, he had to walk to the next class with his notebook in front of his crotch. Being a grown up mechanic kept his mind focused on work rather than women, or more accurately, sex with women, but for that married school bus driver who hit on him because her husband neglected her, or the occasional down home remark from the cracker supervisor who said one fine day, "When you're old, you put it over the fence. When you're young you have to put it under the fence." As in fence rail. The cracker had eight kids. When you're young you can never keep it down, and that seemed to be a problem--if biological determinism is a human failing as the Victorians would have us think. Taking the night course helped keep his mind busy, but joining Groton Ambulance sure didn't. Running to medical emergencies was not, as mentioned, the only reason he joined. Boys just want to have fun with girls who just want to drive ambulances.

Besides Taylor, other role models included Shawnessy, who seemed headed for divorce. He wanted children but said one day with disappointment that he "blew her tubes" without any other detail on his wife, who couldn't have children. Children, preferably a lot, demonstrated virility among the Navy and ex-Navy guys. Dill seemed headed for divorce, kids or no kids, and liked to tell the joke about the barmaid who lost a bet to some drunk who told her she couldn't piss on his face if he blew on her asshole. Har. Har. Murray had a political marriage to the sister of one of the district commissioners. With a scowl and hawk nose like the wicked witch of the west, she showed up on payday to stand over Murray until he handed over his endorsed check. The Lieutenant never talked about his wife other than once a month when he announced that he "got a piece" the night before. "Just rolled over and put it to her." Rumor had it that the Chief and his wife slept in separate bedrooms. Only burly man, Don Borwin, seemed happily married. His wife drove by the station each day he had the duty and dropped off his lunch as an excuse to visit with him for a few minutes. They talked quietly to each other with a sly smile like they were sharing the same joke for years and still finding the humor. Hannigan, the bachelor, lived in a trailer park just up Route 1 from the station and didn't seem to have any steady woman.

Violet remained all business until the advanced first aid class ended, because she had the good sense to keep her distance from everyone enrolled to avoid any appearance of favoritism when she had to make judgments to award or deny the advanced first aid certificate. He passed and began to hang around the ambulance building on weekends and a couple of evenings a week when he didn't have to study for the insurance course, a requirement for the fire tech degree.

One Saturday afternoon, PBFD, which dispatched Groton Ambulance, took the call, got the address, and relayed the information with a call to the ambulance house.

Violet picked up the phone and wrote down the address. "Elks Club. Possible coronary. Got it."

"G-301, 53." Trudy drove and Violet road shotgun. Gary sat in the back with the stretcher. "Just follow our lead," they told him. Women in charge.

"Roger 301." Gary recognized Hannigan's voice.

They arrived at the Shennecossett Road location in under three minutes, pulled up in front of the main entrance to the one story brick building, went right in, and Violet made an immediate assessment. "Get the spine board and the stretcher." A gray haired man wearing a blue plaid sport coat and bright blue slacks lay on the floor in the entrance lobby half conscious but still breathing and barely acknowledging the half dozen worried people who stood around him in their JCPenney evening wear for some sort of event at the start of the holidays. Just behind the lobby, the double doors opened onto a crowded banquet hall packed with people chatting and drinking, the two favorite sports among the Elks.

They needed the full length spine board to keep a solid surface under the man just in case they needed to start CPR there or on the way to the hospital, and the stretcher, more of a gurney, had a thin mattress that would give and negate some of the force of the compressions. So they rolled the man on his left side, slipped the board under him, rolled him back flat, strapped him in, then lifted the board onto the stretcher with it lowered. Up they lifted the stretcher and rolled it out to the van, shoved it inside, and, without a word, Trudy went up front to drive while Violet climbed into the back with Gary and the heart attack victim. But before they went anywhere, Violet pulled out a sphygmomanometer and a stethoscope, then collected a reading on BP and pulse for Trudy to relay to the ER. "230 over 110. Pulse 120 and weak."

"G-301 to PG," Trudy said, calmly, "We're in route with one male, aged 57 with a history of coronary disease. Conscious, but with unstable vitals." Then she drove off slowly without the siren, which was not recommended for heart attack victims. Maybe in New London where the meat wagon never had more than a five minute drive from Lawrence Memorial, they could risk full arrest with lights and siren all the way, but not from Groton where they had to get to the bridge, cross, then drive south through New London to the hospital, the only hospital for New London and Groton. Groton Ambulance policy required stabilizing the victim and keeping him or her stable on the run. In the back, on the small shelf just above the right side where they locked the stretcher securely for the run, a red, yellow, or green button could be pushed as needed to signal the driver to stop, use caution and drive slowly, or go like hell. Violet had already pushed yellow.

"G-301, hospital notified," said Hannigan.

"Roger. Thank you."

He went in and out of full arrest all the way over. Violet had Gary work the ambu bag while she did the chest compressions until the man lifted an arm, then they'd stop and allow heart and lungs to function on their own. When his eyes rolled back they started again and made it to the ER without losing him. New London, Gary thought, would have just body bagged the guy. He felt good that he'd help save a life, but nobody said anything. Violet and Trudy got in the cab and he road in the back for the trip back across the Thames. Maybe he'd see if he could get Violet alone away from her mother for a moment when they returned, but the siren interrupted that thought. Half way across the bridge another call came in.

"PG to 301." Borwin's voice this time.

"301," Violet answered.

"Respond to Long Hill Road at Kings. Two car accident. Engine 34 in route for stand by. Groton police on scene and report two injured."

"Roger. Thank you."

One victim, a young woman, sat in the police car bleeding from the head. The police had her hold a compression bandage against the wound, but she still bled profusely as is the case when the skin splits over the skull. The driver of the other car, a middle-aged woman, showed no visible injuries, but did not move and seemed in shock at first glance.

"Get the kit," Violet told Gary, and he grabbed the large box with all the first aid bandages and tools. "Help Trudy with the bleeder while I check the other driver. And get a cervical on her." Meaning cervical collar. A wound like that usually meant the victim's head had been snapped in one or more directions, so even if she escaped with nothing more than a bad headache and a few stitches, the chance always existed for a ping pong cranial fracture or spinal injury, so always always stabilize the neck. Gary waved at Hannigan as he hustled from Engine 34 over to the police car. Hannigan nodded and smiled. Helluva a way to get a date.

Just as Gary opened the kit and pulled out a bandage, Violet yelled over, "Leave the collar and bandages with the police and have them transport the head wound. Get another collar, the back board, and get over here." Semi-conscious, irregular, rapid pulse, pupils uneven with one dilated. Luckily, when the bleeder's car ran the intersection and T-boned the victim with a concussion and internal bleeding, the driver's side door had popped off on impact rather than jamming shut as often happened.

Hannigan ran over to help by climbing into the backseat to hold the woman's head steady while they placed the collar on her and strapped her to the backboard. Gary held the stretcher in place while Trudy and Violet eased her out and onto the stretcher. "Lift her up. We want her in a seated position." Avoid aspiration, thought Gary. Concussions can lead to convulsions.

The police car got into position to lead them back across the bridge, and off they went, fast this time, screaming sirens the whole way.

"Just hold her steady," Violet told Gary, meaning hold the stretcher steady while she kept a close eye on respiration and heart rate, kept the stethoscope on the woman the whole ride. She never said a thing on the way to the hospital, and it must have been that thick wool winter hat she had on that prevented any skull laceration like the other driver suffered. And she died, they learned later after they'd returned to the ambulance house. The ER called to let them know she arrived still living but bled out rapidly due to a ruptured spleen and really never had been conscious after the accident; the blow had knocked her cold, slammed her brain inside her skull. The lights were on, but nobody was home.

One for two. Gary decided not to ask Violet that evening if she'd like coffee sometime and left the ambulance house shortly after a couple of other volunteers showed up for duty. "See you tomorrow." He walked out past the understanding if slightly bemused smiles of Trudy and Violet. They'd seen it all before. He'd get used to it. "See you tomorrow."

Sometimes you're better off alone, he thought as he drove home, nearly stopping on the way for a quart of beer, but decided against it.

The surviving driver took a few stitches in her head after they shaved it clean, stayed overnight for observation, and went home the next day with a headache and the need to find an attorney to help her with the charge of vehicular manslaughter in addition to DUII.

12 workers

Yes, he did get some. Not Violet, not at first, but the school bus driver who wasn't getting enough attention from her husband. Nothing like a guy with a badge and a steady job to attract a working class woman.

"He just goes out after work with his buddies and never comes home," she said after he opened the door and let her in. She'd called ahead and then showed up at the door. "He thinks I'm at a movie, but I didn't stop by to talk about him."

"Which movie?" John Gary asked, stupidly.

She smiled. "Does it matter?" Then sat on the couch.

"Do you want something to drink?"

"Maybe later," and she put her hand on his thigh.

"Okay," he said and ran his hand through her black hair, and from there on hormones took over. They pulled the mattress from his bedroom to the floor of the living room where it would be warmer and the neighbors wouldn't hear as much. She liked it from behind and hissed when he slipped it in, and he started pounding away thigh to ass when she implored him to push harder and harder.

After the second round, right after, the scanner tone made the most noise. To her amusement and slight annoyance, he said, "I have to go."

"So do I," she said.

"Bye," and a quick kiss as he pulled on his hitches, a T-shirt, grabbed his jacket, and hurried out the door. "Can you close it behind you?"

She did, and Gary drove the Le Mans up Depot Road to Route 1 with his blue light flashing on the dash, then waited as Engine 32 rumbled by, siren howling, heading east. Rather than wait for 31 to leave the station, he gunned the Pontiac and followed 32 up to Newtown Road to the Indian Field subdivision, then pulled off to the right curb when 32 stopped at the hydrant on the left 30 yards before the house on Ring Drive deep in the subdivision, an ordinary one story suburban cement slab home that had fire rolling out of what was once the big bay window in front.

"Engine 32, 72."

Gary jumped out, ran across the street to pull the hydrant line off 32, and dropped the ring over the plug just as 31 pulled up behind him close enough for him to hear Dill say, "Go Ernie," and Taylor drove down to set up in front of the house. He had the 4.5 port cap off and helped Dill connect the soft suction, then ran down to 32 and hauled a second hydrant line back to 31. They had everything connected just as Dill yelled down the street, "Water!"

"I got it," Dill said, then turned the hydrant wrench while Gary grabbed the Halligan and hurried back to his car, opened the trunk, pulled his coat and helmet out, and put them on running back toward the end of the house where the bedrooms were located. The heavy fire roared out of the front of the house and the first arriving volunteers had a 2.5 line pulled and connected and charged and opened up by the time he and another volunteer reached the first bedroom. Nobody knew for certain if the family had gotten out or not.

The window smashed out easily, and with a ten finger boost from the other volunteer, a husky off duty cop, Gary half dove, half fell through the window into what seemed to be a kid's bedroom. The cop got half way in and Gary grabbed the back of his turnout coat and pulled him through the rest of the way. "Anybody in here?" Gary yelled, and they crawled along the walls in the smoke-filled darkness, coughing, bumping into bureaus, then the beds, and sweeping their arms underneath checking for kids hiding, then, coughing and wishing they'd taken the time to get Scots on, they found the closet and searched it and found no one. They kids had gotten out.

But that was it. They couldn't go out into the hallway to try for another bedroom. The fire pushed in toward them along the ceiling and walls through the open door, pulled along by the window they'd opened and pushed in as the hose crew tried to work from the front lawn into the living room. Another crew had a second line working on the garage where the car, paint, oil, gasoline cans, sundry other chemicals, and stored domestic detritus like newspaper stacks made for nasty work, but there they wore Scott Packs. So Gary and the cop turned around and dove back out the window to clean, cool air, and took a moment to breath again. Without a word they got up and headed for the second bedroom, but other firefighters had already taken out the glass and conducted primary search.

"John Gary!" He turned and saw the Deputy Chief waving from the backyard. "Get a ground ladder and a roof ladder and the saw. We need to open up more. Check the attic."

The living room crew could not get in any farther nor could they check the attic for extension until they'd ventilated. Well, now, nothing like a little truckie work. Search and ventilation. He and the cop pulled the ground ladder off 32 and carried it back behind the house while Winneger, after he yelled, "Hey rookie," grabbed the folding roof ladder and the saw and followed them across the lawn. Winneger went up the ground ladder and stretched to extend the open roof ladder far enough to hook across the peak, then he stepped off onto the smoking shingles. "Come on up, Rookie."

Gary climbed with the saw and handed it to Winneger, then held the back of his coat while he cranked it up and went to work cutting a three by three hole through the shingles and sheeting. "Hang on," Winneger yelled and set the saw down on the roof ladder. "We need an ax." The cop had climbed the ground ladder to the gutters with the Halligan and handed it up to Gary, who passed it along to Winneger. "Not an ax, but it'll do." Gary held the saw with one hand and Winneger with the other while he swung down hard onto the roof and smashed the square cut down into the attic. That did the trick. Smoke, then fire shot up out of the hole and they ducked down and carefully backed down with the saw. "Not bad for a rookie," Winneger said.

Inside, the living room the ceiling had started to sag, but that was a good thing and made it easy to punch out with a pike pole. After the ceiling dropped down onto the couch and dining table and carpet and years of memories, the fire moved up rather than laterally now, and the firefighters pushed inside all the way to knock it down completely, then started pulling the rest of ceiling, then the walls, especially the wall between the living room the the garage until only the studs remained. Gary volunteered for the overhaul, sticking to his role as a truckie. With pike pole in hand, he worked next to the hose crew, smashing the tip and hook into burned plywood, then yanking down and ducking to avoid getting water in the face when they opened up again.

An hour after Gary pulled the hydrant line, they started to pickup. Shutdown the hydrant, disconnect and roll the hose. Stack the rolls in the department pickup truck Hannigan had driven from the station. Put all the tools back on 32 and 31, including the saw, the pike pole, the Halligan. Put the air packs in the pickup. The Scotts and hose would have priority when they returned to the station. Get ready for another one as fast as possible, then relax, have a beer, shoot the shit in the middle of the night. Psychobabble experts called it debriefing. "Thanks," said, the cop, who introduced himself as Mike Donatelli, "The only thing I could think of were my kids, the kids that might have been in that room. Gary smiled, shrugged, and didn't know what else to say but "Sure thing."

He started to leave the firehouse when Ernie Taylor stopped him with a half smile and half smirk when he asked loud enough so the whole carriage floor could hear. "How did you get there so fast?"

Gary had served a few 24 hours shifts with Taylor, including one with a middle-of-the-night false alarm. He'd been amazed to see Taylor head straight for the bunkroom bathroom when the box started to blast in. The air horn mounted on the roof of the station was aimed right at the bathroom window, but Taylor stood there and pissed without hesitation before he left for the run. Gary had already run down the stairs, opened both overhead doors, and made the radio announcement by the time Taylor climbed into 32 and started out the door. He stood at the watch desk waiting for 32 to clear the carriage floor; otherwise, he could have had 31 started before Taylor left the building. The answer was easy. "What the hell took you so long to get there?"

Taylor laughed as did the half dozen other volunteers getting ready to head out the door. Still being on probation and not wanting to push it too far, Gary added, "And I keep my hitches at home and the car backed into the driveway."

Back home, nobody waited. She'd gone and left nothing, not a note, nothing. One night stand, he guessed, correctly, because he never heard from her again. And he didn't really want to talk to anyone and sat on the couch still in his hitches waiting for the adrenalin high to subside. Sometimes it took an hour, sometimes longer, before he could stop reliving the fire and get his mind onto other things. This time he kept thinking about what Donatelli said about the kids. So maybe one night stands were a good thing. No commitment, no kids to worry about dying in a fire or worse, living without a father who died in a fire. But hell, he thought, he still had three months to go before he had a permanent job anyway, so who the fuck wanted to think about getting married. He just wanted to keep saving as much from his paycheck as he could--just in case.

In the meantime, get a little sleep, then get your ass up, shower, get breakfast, then study that goddamned fire insurance textbook. He had a test coming up on Wednesday night at the City of Groton firehouse. Three hours later he drove over to the firehouse where it was warmer than his drafty bachelor cheap rent, said good morning to the Sunday crew, Shawnessy and Murray, then walked out to the back bay to sit in the old Mac parade pumper to read the deadly insurance prose. Most of it had to do with risk determination by building type and protection, as in sprinklered or not sprinklered. Also a lot of information on probability of fire by time of day and time of year and on type of fire by time of year. Yawn. Any firefighter could tell you that most structure fires happened at night, brush fires burned on schedule in spring and late summer. And just when he thought he couldn't take it anymore, the phone rang at the watch desk and echoed throughout the station on the PA speakers.

"Location ma'am. Try to stay calm so I can understand you."

Gary set the book down on the seat of the Mac and ran to the front of the firehouse. No other volunteers hung around on a Sunday morning, so he had a chance to ride shotgun in 32 for the first time, getting his boots on and throwing his coat and helmet into the cab just as Murray cranked it up.

"Station PG to all stations, signal 50, C Street, High Rock Trailer Park."
"Get the mike," Murray said. He liked to focus on his driving.

"G-32, 53." Just over a mile and a half, a five minute run along Fort Hill and Poquonnock Road, then eventually left on High Rock.

"G-31, 53."

They could see the smoke the minute they took the left bend in Poquonnock to turn south.

"Tell Jack," Murray said with a dead calm voice, "to take the hydrant at the corner of High Rock and A Street. We're going straight in. We have a trailer fire. Pull the pre-connect. While it's charging, take out the door with the Halligan."

Gary relayed the information and heard Shawnessy answer, "Roger."

"One more thing," said Murray as they turned onto High Rock, "Duck after you open that door." The metal skin of a mobile home created an oven inside, one that didn't vent as easily as a stick built home like the one that had burned the night before when the furnace failed.

"32, 72." Murray positioned 32 fifty feet from the burning home with the pump panel away from the fire. If the propane tanks blew, the pump operator would be protected by 32 and could keep a water supply running. That meant, of course, that Gary got out on the fire side, but it didn't look too bad in spite of the volume of smoke forcing itself out around the door and the windows. No visible flame. He got his coat, helmet, and gloves on, then grabbed the Halligan with one hand and the 1.5 nozzle with the other and pulled one length away before turning toward the fire, confident Murray would pull the rest of the 150 feet clear of the hose bed, and he did. He set the nozzle down at the door, checked the door. Locked. He used both hands to jam the crowbar end of the Halligan between the door and the frame and pulled away from the door to make an opening, then he rammed the Halligan in deeper and got a good grip and pulled. The roar and being thrown back and the shouting seemed to happen all at once. "Get him back. Get water on those propane tanks. Shut off the gas. Get water inside. Jacob! Jacob! Oh my God! He's in there! He's in there."

They found Jacob's body with the clothes burned away from red and charcoal skin or what was once skin in the back bedroom of the trailer, the end away from the only door. Poor bastard never stood a chance when the propane blew inside, probably due to a pilot light that went out while he took a nap. No automatic shutoff or one that didn't work, but he died fighting, his legacy the marks on the wall where he tried to claw his way out away from the searing heat, at least for a breath or two until his throat was closed by toxic superheated gases. Somehow Gary managed to get back on his feet and follow the nozzle man into the trailer to knock down the fire, and he didn't react at all to the sight of what was once a human being, an old man who had just retired from the Boat and only wanted to live quietly in a trailer near the golf course. But things, noises, people, still seemed to be at a distance. The Chief's voice was the last he remembered. "Call Groton Ambulance."

In the back of the ambulance, in the middle of Gold Star bridge crossing to New London, the siren woke him. He had the oxygen mask strapped to his head and Violet, seeing that he moved, told him to lie still in a no nonsense voice but with a hand on his shoulder.

"How bad?"

"You'll live. Slight concussion and first degree burns on your face."

"How about a coffee later?"

She smiled and he passed out again until the RN in the Lawrence emergency room woke him with smelling salts.

They kept him overnight for the standard observation, and the Chief told Jack Shawnessy to pick him up the next morning.

"You look like hell. You stayed out in the sun too long."

"I feel great."

"The Chief told me to tell you to take a day."

"I can work."

"Sure. What'd they give you for a pain killer?"

"Some sort of shot."

"I can tell. You can hardly walk straight. Go home and sleep it off."

"Roger that."

And he did.

13 mutual aid

Now he knew he'd crossed the boundary. After John Gary survived the back draft at the trailer park fire, everyone from the Chief down started using his first name instead just Gary do this or Gary do that. He'd been awarded the unspoken, unofficial red badge of courage. Or more accurately, red face of courage. The burn healed liked a sunburn, and he had to endure a few days of jokes about trying to get a tan in winter, but nothing else. The concussion went away, too, and life returned to the routine of car fires, electrical fires, MVAs on snow days, and all the other events due to routine human stupidity or bad luck or an act of God as the insurance textbook called them.

But the real initiation arrived with the annual meeting in January. Not the district meeting with all the commissioners present to answer any questions from the press or public about the new budget, a pro forma gathering with one or two voters seated among the hundred empty folding chairs set up in the meeting hall behind the carriage floor. The fire district commissioners, all volunteers firefighters in Poquonnock Bridge, let the Chief answer the one or two questions from the one voter, a polo shirt wearing middle aged middle manager from the Boat who showed up, Gary found out, each year to grouse about money. That January he wanted to know why the district needed a Hurst tool. "Don't you have tools already to get people out of cars?"

"Nothing like the Hurst," the Chief said. "It can tear a car apart faster than any tool we've got, and, I think you'll agree, extrication speed is critical in accidents with injury."

But the sonofabitch would not back off. One of those Republicans who forgot that the entire economy of Groton depended on the federal defense budget. On tax dollars. "Can you name two instances when you could have used that Hurst thing this past year, or is it excess like those extra air packs you bought last year?"

The Chief stayed as calm, as unflustered, as he did at a fire. He knew the one reporter in the room wrote down each of his answers, so the moron actually provided him with an opportunity to make a public statement of support for the district budget that would reach everyone who read the Groton News. "We have used the extra air packs on several occasion in the last year at structure fires, and the more of our men who have them to wear, the fewer cases of lung cancer the taxpayers will have to support financially down the road. And two weeks ago, we had a car wrap around the pole just down the street from the station, and we finally had to use the winch on Engine 34 to move the car away from the pole to get the driver out. We could have cut the roof off the car with the Hurst and gotten the driver out in half the time. We had a semi driver on I-95 pinned in a crushed cab, and it took us an hour to get him out. In both cases, we couldn't risk use of the circular saw because of the fire danger and risk of further injury to the victim."

The good citizen backed off, not because he thought the Chief had presented a convincing argument, but because nobody else showed up for the meeting. He sat there, a constituency of one who, for some perverted reason, decided that keeping a couple of extra bucks in his pocket seemed like a fair tradeoff for reduced fire protection. Every town or city had them. Cheapskates who figured their neighbor's house would burn before theirs ever did. A community of one, he probably wouldn't carry car insurance if the law didn't require it.

No. Not that meeting. The other annual meeting two weeks later when all the white males gathered in the hall and filled the seats to elect new officers for the volunteer company, then cheered and yelled while the stripper gyrated, but only after she shot a look of disgust at her manager when three guys sitting in front pulled out spiked dildos and wiggled them around. Sitting three rows back from the dildo kings, on the aisle, Gary became the sudden center of attention when one of the volunteer captains, Harry Peterson, an accountant at the Boat, waved the stripper over and pointed. "Do the rookie!"

She strutted up the aisle and gave him a ten second lap dance with her perfumed, unnaturally round breasts shoved into his face. The place roared and howled with testosterone laughter. The rookie had been bred. Only if you're liked by the tribe do you suffer the honor of public humiliation from a stripper. That's how he knew he'd been accepted both as a paid man and as a PBFD volunteer. Even though the probation didn't end officially for two months, he knew he'd moved from New London and found a home among the heathens.

After the stripper ended her routine, the Chief declared the meeting at an end and recommended all members adjourn to the day room or the back of the station for refreshment, which meant beer and card games.

"You should have seen the look at your face," Peterson said, sucking on a cigarette and still laughing at Gary. Gary smiled back.

"Hey rookie," yelled Winneger from across the hall, "Did you get her number?" More guffaws.
Hannigan, who had duty that night and stayed near the back of the hall in case a call came in, added his two cents. "I think she liked you."

Christ, thought Gary, everybody's here. Shawnessy, Murray, Dill, Taylor all had to either slap him on the back or offer a grinning insult. "Did you propose?" Har har. "You know you have to marry her now." Har. "Does Violet know about her?" Har. "What's that bulge in your pants?" Har.

They thought he and Violet still had something going on besides running together on Groton Ambulance. And they did, for about two weeks. After one grisly automobile accident that left one DOA in the street and another victim rushed to the ER bleeding profusely from multiple cranial lacerations, both due to bouncing their heads off I-95, she accepted the offer for coffee while they swabbed down the stretcher to clear the blood off and stretched a new sheet over the pad. Coffee led to dinner led to a movie led to bed. The usual progression, but in her place, a nice one bedroom apartment on South Road not far from the ambulance house. And the sex? Excellent. She went right for his belt the moment they closed the door, and loved to suck on Mr. Wally, loved oral sex and taught him a thing or two about how much she liked him to slurp between her labia until she started to shake, shiver, and utter something between "Whoa" and "Wow." The first time he thought she meant whoa and he stopped until she shoved his head back down. "Not yet. Not yet."

And fun in the shower, soaped up, fucking her from behind, feeling her butt shiver when she hit orgasm, then turning on him for a second go when her beeper went off. They both said, "Shit" at the same time. "Gotta go," meaning they both had to dress as fast as they could and head to the ambulance house trying to look like they had not just been playing with soap together.

They knew the old woman who called, because they'd taken her to Lawrence for the same nose bleed several times before. She told them to drive slowly, because the doctor told her he could do nothing to stop the bleeding that came and went. "One of these days," she told them each time, "the bleeding won't stop." One of these days a massive cerebral hemorrhage would be her last nosebleed. Violet held her hand in the back while he drove with lights on and no siren. Trudy had to work at a high school PTA banquet that night, and because Violet lived so close to the ambulance house, they arrived first. Usually they waited for a crew of three, but they knew they'd only need two for the old woman who calmly awaited her fate and went to the hospital only because her neurologist told her to go. The ER would help stop the bleeding, if they could, and keep her overnight before sending her home again. Violet would just pack her nose with 4x4 gauze pads in route and hold her hand.

"That stuff ever bother you?" he asked on the way back.

"Interrupted sex?"

"Very funny. Death."

"Death and sex?"

"Right. That's it."

"You want to go back to my place again?"

"Not tonight. That killed the mood."

"People die, John. Don't let it ruin your sex life, and I don't plan to propose."

"Why not?"

"Why spoil the fun? And I don't have time for marriage. Tried it once. Married a sailor and found out he'd used me to keep the Navy from knowing he was gay. I found him in bed with his boyfriend one night after work. They beat me up to keep me quiet."

"Did you?"

"Called the cops, divorced him, and called the Navy. He's still in jail for assault."

"Sorry."

"For what? It's not your fault."

"Sorry for having to leave. I started another class this week and need to get home to study."

"See you next time stud."

They both smiled.

The next time he had to leave when he heard the firehouse horn blasting out a box alarm. He and Violet were locked together again, humping like rabbits, and he did the worst thing possible. He finished, pulled out, and left her with her motor running and no orgasm. Not cool. Even the chauvinist pigs at the firehouse knew that women liked orgasms and razzed anyone who bragged about getting off and leaving the woman humping air. "You mean you don't finish her?" Not cool.

But still being a probie, in spite of his esteem boost at the trailer fire, Gary had to go. Okay, he wanted to go, fire being the only element on earth that would pull him away from sex. He did not want to miss the other action, even a false alarm. He had to keep the reputation he'd built and had to help. Helping in an emergency proved time and again the only rush in life equal in satisfaction to sex. "Won't be gone long."

He dressed and drove to the firehouse as quickly as he could on the packed snow and arrived after both 32 and 34 had left for a car fire at the shopping center. Since no one had the watch desk, he set his turnout coat and helmet down on the desk and took over there until one of the older guys showed up.

"32. 72 in front of ShopRite. One vehicle," said Murray.

"Roger 32." He got up to close the overhead doors to keep the heat in and the flurries outside.
The City of Groton tone interrupted the winter quiet.

"Station G to all stations. Signal 50. Nautilus Theater."

G-1, G-10, G-11, G12 all seemed to sign on at the same time. And G-1 reported the 72 two minutes later. Nothing in the three square miles of the city was far from anything else.
"G-1 to Station G."

"G on."

"Heavy fire. Call General Dynamics and ask for their ladder. Call Poquonnock Bridge. We need another pumper."

The call rang in, not from the City dispatcher but from Gary's boss. "You go ahead and take 31 on mutual aid," the Chief said, "34 is returning to cover the station."

"Yes sir." During the holidays, when the shift people started taking days off, Gary had duty driving both 32 and 31, including a couple of runs that involved pumping. His rep improved even more so at one car fire over on Midway when he positioned 32 perfectly and had the pump engaged and the booster charged by the time the first arriving volunteer grabbed the right side booster. "He put the nozzle right in my hand."

Gary made the announcement. "Station PG to all stations. Signal 50, mutual aid, Nautilus Theater, City of Groton." And then he hit the door switch, pulled on his coat, helmet, and climbed into Engine 31, drove out onto the ramp and stopped long enough to wait a second for Winneger to climb in the rider's side. "Let's go, Rookie."

The canvas winter cab cover flapped as he drove west on Route 1, then turned left onto Poquonnock Road, slowly. No chains on, and even with just a bit of snow on the road, he did not want to skid. Then an easy run down Poquonnock into the city at Mitchell Street where the plan had been to renovate the old Nautilus for summer stock to rival Waterford's O'Neill Theater. The proverbial welder's spark had lodged between two floor boards too close to a painter's tarp, and nobody noticed anything because they'd closed up at 6 pm and gone home. Flames tore through the roof by the time G-1 arrived, and the Chief immediately ordered an exterior attack. No one in the building. Surround and drown with ladder pipes and deck guns.

The City chief waved for 31 to stop in front of the theater next to the General Dynamics ladder. The City ladder had already been raised and operated with a 500 GPM deluge nozzle. "Drive down the block to that open hydrant and connect there to feed the ladder." City firefighters pulled both sides of the 2.5 from the 31 hose bed, and he drove slowly down to the hydrant where he and Winneger connected the soft suction to the 4.5 port, then open the hydrant, connected both 2.5 lines to discharge ports on the pump panel side, and radioed G-3. "31 to G-1. Water ready."

"Charge it."

Gary pulled the valve handles out from the pump panel and the 2.5 lines jumped with the pressure and danced down the street with Winneger following the flow to check for and remove any kinks on the way back to the ladder. Then he cranked the panel throttle, enjoying a bit the rumble of the Waukesha as it rose up from idle to meet the demand, and the pump pressure climbed to 100 psi. He could calculate the friction loss from the distance and the 50 foot height of the partially extended ladder, but chose instead to keep his eye on the deluge stream, waiting until it cleared all the air from the line, then jacked the pressure to 120 psi and settled in for the siege.
John Gary loved machines, loved having the knowledge to setup a portable water system and pump station in five minutes or under, but he knew the trade off was being stuck at the pump panel and missing the action at the fire just as Pasquale had been that night at the

furniture store worker. Tedious work, but somebody had to do it, and he needed the experience on the pump. He set the wheel chocks in place front and back of the left rear tires, double checked the lock on the stick shift, which was critical to keeping the engine in gear and the pump engaged, then stood there to watch the show.

That's when both he and Violet decided that anything other than, as they called it, a professional relationship, was not going to work. The emergency services equivalent of "Let's be friends."

On their last date, they just went for coffee again and talked for a while until her beeper did what beepers do.

14 hero

One month rolled into the next and gave John Gary's life the security of routine, or as secure as it could get when the job was dealing with uncertainty day after day so others could pretend life could be predicted, and, if not, then protected with one phone call. He moved from probation to full appointment as a paid PBFD firefighter without any ceremony, but still wore the rookie name patch on his work uniform and still served as a volunteer off duty seven nights a week and weekends. So nothing really changed from probie to regular. The runs remained the usual mix. They had car fires like the one at the shopping center where Hannigan severed the battery cable with bolt cutters and a spark popped the battery. It didn't explode; it just threw a quarter-sized piece of plastic and a little acid against John Gary's turnout coat, but he didn't notice the holes until he returned to the station and silently thanked God or somebody for not letting the acid hit his face or eyes. And the VW bus fire down in Poquonnock Bridge. And the 3 am rollover on I-95 caused when the driver fell asleep. Or the car fire after the 20-year-old kid in his Camaro had a fight with his fiancee and roared off along Drozdyk Road until he missed a curve, went airborne and landed nose first against a six-foot diameter oak tree that refused to budge--just like New London. The Camaro crumple zone went from the front bumper to the rear seat where the undertaker removed the body parts from behind the engine block after the PBFD had the fire out.

Or runs like the two vertical propane cylinders that lit off behind a restaurant, and they had to stand there keeping them cool with water from two nozzles while the propane burned off. And the guy who decided to clean car parts in his kitchen sink with gasoline, a sink next to the open flame of a propane water heater in the Bridge. People suffer the delusion that they can duck fire and explosion, but that only happens in the movies in slow motion. In reality, no human has time to react, and that idiot had only time to yell "Shit" and do the same in his pant when the gasoline fumes found the flame and flared with a foomp right into the sink before he had time to even flinch. He was burned on his hands, but lucky compared to the moron who dug a pit in the ground in his yard deep enough for him to lie in without having to jack up the car while he worked on the leaky gas line from tank to engine without the slightest thought given to gasoline fumes being heavier than air. Apparently crawling out from the pit to take break to smoke proved too bothersome, so he lit up right in the pit, from head to toe, from tires to roof, burned to a crisp. He could have been simply asphyxiated if he had not decided to smoke, which was, yes, hazardous to his health.

But one structure fire John Gary decided to be the most ironic, a word he learned--even though he'd lived it constantly--from the writing course he had to take as part of the fire technology program. No, not the basement restaurant fire or a fire that cooked the store room, because that type of worker repeated itself from time to time when a restaurant owner attempted insurance fraud by torching his or her business. Restaurants cooked frequently. But the irony of that house fire in the Bridge that burned out a family while they attended the circus that paid a visit for a day or two each summer and required, by Connecticut law, one fire engine present to standby during performances. All because of the 1944 Hartford circus fire. The Titanic syndrome, Gary called it. You put enough lifeboats on the ship after it sinks. You reform the fire code after enough people get killed.

The idea of the modern in public attitude toward fire and fire suppression translated again and stupidly again into never again. People forget or want to forget conflagrations because life would be impossible lived with heightened fear, so denial was and is necessary to get up each morning to drive on roads where thousand are killed each year in cars or being hit by cars. Denial is needed to live in houses with gas lines running into them, or oil lines, and electrical lines. Denial is needed to walk into and stay seated in places firefighters dread, such a churches, theaters, bowling alleys and circus tents--large open spaces with no fire stops, meaning no way to compartmentalize a fire like they do on board ships to confine it to one area of a structure.

The canvas used in the circus tent on July 6, 1944, in Hartford, Connecticut, stood saturated with paraffin diluted with gasoline as waterproofing. But the burning tent did not kill the estimated 170 who died, nor did it cause the injury of 700 others among the 7000 in attendance that day. As happens in sudden fires in large, crowded spaces, people panicked. Orderly exit disintegrated almost immediately into chaos as people ran from the stands, running over others, or jumped from the stands, or ran in circles in a panic. Those trapped under the tent that rained fire like napalm were burned beyond recognition, incinerated into body parts leaving any accurate body count impossible and forever an estimate.

So there sat John Gary on special fire watch duty in the cab of Engine 31 on a bright July day at the circus where the performance went on safely while one family inside enjoying the elephants, the tigers, the clowns had no idea their home burned due to another example of human stupidity equal to waterproofing canvas with gasoline-- bypassing a fuse. The owner, the father, had bypassed the fuse box to run a refrigerator in the basement rather than install a new box with enough circuits.

"Station PG to all stations," Gary heard on the 31 radio knowing he had to stay put on fire watch, "Signal 50, 531 Depot Road," which was down toward the end of Depot, well away from his place. "32, 53."

And a minute later, "34, 53."

And three minutes later, "32, 72. 34 take a hydrant."

After the circus, after he returned 31 to the station and signed off fire watch duty, which paid time and a half on a Saturday, Gary drove down to the home that burned because he was gung ho, yes, and hated to miss any run, and because he wanted to learn. The Chief had stayed on the scene in his fire marshal role and found the illegal shunt, but Gary found the most interesting sight to be the phone that melted to the wall in the kitchen. "A hot one," he said, knowing he'd made a statement of the obvious, a statement the Chief ignored with a brief smile.

Job security. Those runs over the months reinforced the importance of the job of protecting humanity from the unexpected, both natural and from the bottomless well of human stupidity. The fire service protected them from themselves and the consequences of alleged modern technology that promised again and again falsely that nothing like it would or could ever happen again. But firefighters knew it would, even on days when nothing happened, days that would stretch into a week, even at the busiest firehouses. John Gary hated those days and wondered aloud once, but just once, if they were needed, because is was, yes, quiet, too quiet.

"What are we being paid for?" he said by mistake one day, feeling a stupid, preacher's kid Calvinist guilt for collecting a check for what he thought was sitting around.

Hannigan, the former Air Force firefighter, happened to be on the receiving end of that stupid comment as they both stood in the balmy air of late September in the open back bay door a year after he started the job, and Hannigan reamed Gary out for five minutes without a talking a breath, then said, "I'm getting something from my locker. Stay here."

Gary, thinking Hannigan would most likely not ask him again to go fishing on Long Island Sound from the tone of his voice, still looked out past the parking lot toward the Poquonnock River when Hannigan returned. "Here, read this." He gave Gary a copy of Report from Engine Co. 82.

"You read?"

"Funny," said Hannigan, who had a good working knowledge of fire service history. "Peshtigo, Chicago, Boston, New York, Washington, D.C. and even little old New London, fucking burned, and it can and will happen again."

"What's this about?"

"The Bronx is burning. Stuff burns all the time. And we're it. We're the only fucking protection people have unless they install sprinklers in each home and business. We're fucking it. We're paid to be it, to be here to guarantee a fucking five minute response time, because shit happens, and shit will always fucking happen. People are stupid. Fact of fucking life. Fire takes full advantage of that stupidity every single damned fucking day. If not here, then somewhere. And even Engine 37 in Boston, one of the busiest in that city, has gone two weeks without a run, and they have days when they get sixteen runs on a shift. Nobody yet has invented a way to predict when emergencies will occur. The genius that does can put us out of a job and have all fire departments run on call with the call people told when to be at the station before the fire."

"But, I didn't . . ."

"You didn't what, college boy," Hannigan shot back, a statement, not a question.

"This job won't make you rich, but you can sure as hell know that it's the best damned job on the planet and that you're needed. You're paid to be here, to be ready, to get the hell out of the station as fast as you can, to know what to do even when you don't, and to get killed if it happens. If you're bored when it's slow, get a hobby, study on duty, work out on duty, but never fucking never ask anyone what it's about. You sound like one dumbass shithead when you say things like that. They all need us from the garbage collector to the doctor. Lesson learned college boy?"

Gary nodded, "Acknowledged and understood, sir."

"Good."

He became a true convert to the religion of public service, especially given that five minutes after Reverend Hannigan finished his fire service sermon a sign from God rang in at the watch desk followed a

20 seconds later by the buzzer as they sprinted from the back bay to the front of the station.

"Station PG to all stations. Signal 50, 44 Pamela Avenue."

"Engine 32, 53."

"Engine 31, 53."

Five long minutes later, the Lieutenant reported, "72. 31 take a hydrant."

The job, in the basement of a single family detached home, proved to be a nasty, dirty little fire. They didn't know if the motorcycle they found in the basement started the fire or why the hell anyone would store a motorcycle in a basement, but they did know it wouldn't run again and did know that they stopped the fire from moving out of the basement. A good stop, and they saved the house.

31 connected to the hydrant and dropped a line to 32, then backtracked with a second lay to the hydrant, and setup with soft suction to feed both 2.5 lines to 32. They weren't needed, but the water supply would be ready if they did need it if the fire had climbed out of the basement. John Gary helped with the initial hydrant connection, road the 31 tailgate down to 32, dropped off, broke the line and gave it to Big Don to screw onto a pump intake port. Hannigan, he knew, would handle the reverse lay, so he pulled on a Scott pack, pulled a pre-connect from 32 and lined into the basement behind the LT, who also had a Scott on, through the storm door. The two volunteers who showed up charged a second line and checked the first floor of the house for extension.

They couldn't see a damned thing in the thick black smoke in the basement, including any flame. No visible seat of the fire, no nozzle opened. Rules of the game. To stop damage by fire, water damage had to happen, but no need to cause more destruction than necessary, and crawling blind through a smoke-filled basement did not fit the definition of good tactics, especially since they knew everyone had escaped the house, so Gary asked the LT if they needed to ventilate, which was a statement of the obvious, so they backed out, set the nozzle down, retrieved the smoke ejector, hung it in the basement door, and let if suck smoke out while Gary circled the house with a Halligan and smashed out every basement window he could find. By the time he returned to the storm door, a hose team of volunteers lead by the LT had pushed back into the basement and had the fire under control.

Another day at the office.

Hannigan looked across the cab on the ride back to the station. "Any questions?"
"None," said John Gary, firefighter.

"Well, maybe," said the good citizens of Chelsea, Massachusetts that October of 1973 while PBFD ran around town dousing the usual grass and leaf fires during fall brush season, including one stubborn job down on Bluff Point. Maybe, after the Great Chelsea Fire on Palm Sunday, April 12, 1908, the good citizens of Chelsea, Massachusetts decided that major urban conflagration was a thing of the past with modern fire apparatus powered by high torque gas or diesel engines and 1000 GPM pumps that could respond quickly and connect easily to good water mains through hydrants on every block. In 1908, the Chelsea fire burned 3000 buildings, left 18,000 homeless, and killed 18. On April 12, 1908, the Chelsea Fire Department responded with 77 people, 21 full timers who worked 24 hours a day for eight days solid without a day off (the labor assumption being that firefighters only worked at working fires), and the rest responded as call men paid $200 each a year. Oh, and Chelsea had 24 horses to haul three steamers, 2 hose wagons, one chemical wagon, one ladder truck, and a buggy for the chief. But, what the hell--irony intended--fires didn't happen that often, even with the rag shops, and with a little more fire prevention, well, no need to expand the department for such a small city of two square miles. Half the city burned to the ground in 1908, but maybe it wouldn't happen again. It couldn't.

On October 14, 1973, Chelsea still had a rag district, but the general salvage business that boomed during World War II had dropped off and left much of the district with abandoned buildings filled with or surrounded by scrap, already the scene of several serious fires. And as in April 1908, the dry October 14, 1973, weather turned breezy, creating the right conditions for a rag district fire to spread quickly, and it did, starting 200 feet from the origin of the 1908 fire. But this time the modern, motorized Chelsea Fire Department, with the help of 66 other fire departments from Massachusetts and one from New Hampshire, limited damage to a swath of territory one mile long and a half mile wide, and did so without resorting to that tried and true 19th Century method of creating a fire break with dynamite, the method used in New York City, for instance to stop a lower Manhattan conflagration, the method used as well as to make a stop in the great San Francisco conflagration that followed the 1906 earthquake. Chelsea firefighters made a stand at a natural fire break, the 60-foot-wide Everett Street. Firestorms can't be stopped with water alone because the water evaporates before it does any good, assuming firefighters can get close enough to put enough water on the fire. During the desperate hours from first alarm at 3:56 pm until after 11 pm, the Chelsea strategy evolved from attempts to extinguish to containment to making a calculated stand at the fire break and letting everything up to the break burn, including one pumper from Medford.

In Poquonnock Bridge a month later, a routine grass fire not long after dark raised no suspicions, nor did the second fire in a trash can set on the curb for pickup the next morning. But the third call did. Engine 32 pulled up near a burning utility pole lit up like a giant candle due to the creosote used to waterproof the wood. The investigation after suppression pointed to a grass fire started at the base of the pole that climbed up the pole. At midnight, the fourth run led to a fully involved car parked on the street in the Bridge where Don Borwin stopped Engine 32 a hundred feet short of the car, set the parking brake, dropped the transmission into fourth, flipped the PTO, then slowly let out the clutch to be certain the pump engaged. When it did, he climbed down from the cab, opened the valve on both booster lines. Gary had one, a second volunteer pulled the other, and they quickly knocked it down. Engine 31 stood by down the street next to the closest hydrant--just in case.

After that run, the Deputy Chief, the department's top volunteer, assigned men to stay the night in the firehouse, three each to ride 32 and 31, one to drive 34 if needed, and one to handle the radio. Gary, assigned to Engine 32, could not sleep because of the noise of all those snoring people in the bunkroom , and because he wanted to be on the carriage floor if and when the next call rang in, which it did at 1:03 am, a box alarm in the Bridge. Already in his bunker gear, Gary had the overhead doors up and sat in the cab waiting for Borwin to climb in. The arsonists had graduated to a duplex, a vacant one, but the fire had not gotten a good start, and the crew on 32 knocked it down quickly in the one room where they'd used old newspapers to start it. Nobody slept for a while after they returned to the firehouse. For an hour they hung out in the basement day room expecting a sixth run at any moment, but when nothing happened, everyone assumed that stepped up police patrols in the Bridge kept the arsonist or arsonists at bay--nobody knew until days later after the state fire marshal investigation solved the case, that four teens drove around with matches that night.

At 4:07 am the sixth call that night woke the station, including John Gary, who had dozed off at the watch desk. The police used the intercom line. "You've got fire at the Board of Education building, a lot of fire. Send everything you've got." The arsonists had broken in and lit off a windowless supply closet that offered the fire a good chance to build before detection, which it did, being spotted by a passing patrol car just after it blew out into a hallway and ventilated itself through the nearest window.

Gary acknowledged the report, hit the buzzer, but the boots had already started thumping down from the bunkroom as he pushed the switches for both overhead doors. The old timer had been dozing down in the day room and reached the watch desk just as Gary climbed in the rider's seat of 32 a step ahead of Borwin and the two volunteers riding the jump seats.

"Station PG to all stations, signal 50. Board of Education building."

No street address necessary, because PBFD members knew the location in the heart of the Bridge. The BOE building, a sprawling one-story wooden structure with two main wings at right angles to each other, served as an unofficial town hall and community center during the war, and then after the war the federal government deeded the property to the Town of Groton. No sprinklers. No internal fire stops. And never room in the budget for fire safety updating, but they had extinguishers in the hallways that met minimum state fire code, and, besides, they had plans to build a modern fire proof building, and what with modern fire suppression . . . . Two long, open corridors with no fire stops connected one wing to the other, each lined with offices, storerooms, and the all-important student records room filled by a large mainframe computer and a row of backup tapes along one wall. They did have money for that.

The Deputy Chief responded in his pickup truck from home in the Bridge a block from the building, and reached the scene first to offer a quick sizeup. "72. Heavy fire in the south wing. Smoke showing under the eve of the north wing." The south wing actually pointed to the southwest, and the north wing to the northwest, joining at the main entrance. The parking lot formed an asphalt wedge between each wing, and at least someone, when they ran water mains into the bridge, had sense enough to put a hydrant in the parking lot. The other three hydrants surrounded the building on the streets. If they'd only spent a little more for sprinklers. Titanic syndrome.

"32, 53."

"31, 53."

"34, 53."

With the old timer at the radio, all three pumpers could get out one right after the other.

"32, this is G3." The Chief had arrived. "Setup in the parking lot. Get ready for an interior attack through the main entrance. Two and a half only. Deluge gun outside."

"32, roger."

"G3 to 31, take the hydrant on the street at the end of the north wing and set up to run one two and a half inside, a second outside. And ventilate the roof. We may have fire running the attic."

"31, roger."

"G3 to 34. Stand off in the neighbor to stop spot fires. We've got embers flying everywhere."

"34, roger."

"G3 to PG."

"PG on."

"Mutual aid. Second alarm. " That meant another ladder and pumper each from the City of Groton and Mystic.

And the game was on. One large wooden building with a severe load hazard of wood and paper. The Chief planned a pincer movement to trap the fire in the south wing. Borwin positioned 32 next to the hydrant where he and Gary connected the soft suction while the volunteers led by Winneger pulled a 2.5 line across the parking lot to the main entrance and connected a large bore pipe nozzle while they waited for water. They also carried a battery lamp and a Halligan and an ax to take out the doors when the line charged, but nobody wore a mask. The south wing fire had ventilated itself through the roof, which meant inside smoke posed no serious problem, and in the dark they wanted to see as well as possible.

"Need help with the gun?" Gary yelled above the roar of the fire and the rumble of the Waukesha.
"No," Borwin yelled back, "Go. I'll get it setup."

Gary lashed a hose strap on the line to position himself just behind the nozzle man as the line jumped with water and Winneger took the Halligan and smashed the glass panels in the entrance door on the left, then the one on the right. The polite tactic would have been to pry the lock open with the Halligan and prop the door open to minimize damage. The smash tactic allowed them to move quickly through the busted out panels without worry about a clear route back out or worry about the automatic door closer operating and trapping the hose.

They cleared the glass away so it would not cut them or the line, stepped through, then moved in and wrestled the charged line around the right turn into the south wing corridor, into a furnace, getting down on their knees and inching forward, sweeping the ceiling, then the walls, then moving another inch forward, but the heat stopped them just twenty feet later where the fire simply evaporated the 250 gallons a minute they shot right at it.

Outside, firefighters smashed out windows on the the south wing that had not already blown out from the heat, then started doing the same on the north wing, and when the City of Groton ladder arrived, they put a crew on the roof with a saw to help 31 open up with the hope that another 2.5 could be advanced into the building after ventilation, but they had to back off immediately after the first cut about half way along the wing when the fire blew up from the attic through the vent hole, and the roof felt spongy. "Get the hell off the roof!"

And get the hell out of the building. The Deputy Chief stepped inside and made a quick assessment. The 32 hose crew could not advance down the south wing, but the fire sure as hell moved toward them, and they sure as hell had fire in the attic. "Get out. That's an order."

Fire spreads exponentially, so the south wing interior hose crew had already backed off to the entrance by the time the Deputy told them to back out. And just as he gave the order to pull out completely, the roof of the south wing collapsed, sending even more embers flying off toward the houses in the Bridge and the 32 deluge gun had to open up. With the fire running the attic, the chief could not let anybody back inside. Time to surround and drown and hope no serious fires started in adjacent homes--until the superintendent of schools showed up and pleaded for an attempt to get to the mainframe to save the six backup tapes with all the student data. The Chief said no, but she insisted, pleaded again, almost in tears for removing the line item from the budget that would have paid for an off site backup system. "Please, please try."

The Chief stepped inside the entrance just as the hose crew reached it. "I need two people to go down the north wing hallway about half the distance to the computer room on the left. Take a Halligan, bust in, and get the six backup tapes from the back wall, then get the hell out of there."

"Back this way?" said John Gary.

"Negative. We'll keep the two and a half here to block as long as we can. We can't risk putting the 31 hose crew inside, but they'll be at the north wing exit at the end of the hall. Get out that way. The computer room has no windows. Go."

And they did, Gary and Winneger, hustling down the hallway with the light and the Halligan and ignoring the sagging ceiling. Five minutes later, of course, the ceiling caved in just as they had the tapes off the spools ready to bring outside. Instinctively, both firefighters ducked. But the beam directly above the room caught them both in the head.

15 -- epilogue

No John Gary did not die, nor did Winneger. They both ducked instinctively when the ceiling fell, which softened the blow, and the massive mainframe computer stopped the beam from crushing them and protected them when they fell to the floor, clutching the precious tapes. Winneger took the hit across the right side of his helmet and blacked out briefly, then started calling to Gary, who still lay unconscious. "Rookie? You okay?" Winneger couldn't crawl over to him through the flotsam that crashed down from the storage shelf built over the false ceiling of the computer room. They had to keep all those blank punch cards somewhere.

And the firefighters outside went right to work getting water on the north wing, dousing the fire fully exposed in the attic after the collapse. One deluge gun from Engine 31 and two handlines kept a steady shower of water on the pile as other firefighters brought saws whining to life and began to ripping through the wood to free Winneger and Gary, yelling as they did. "You okay in there?"

Winneger yelled back, "Just fine. The Rookie's not talking. Call an ambulance."

"It's on the way. Hang tight. We'll be through soon."

"Not going anywhere."

Winneger and Gary road in the same ambulance, Winneger seated, Gary moving in and out of consciousness because of his second fire service concussion. Pulse and respiration seemed fine to Violet, and they put a horse collar on both him and Winneger just in case of a cracked vertebra, but other than that, the blow on the back of his helmet did not cause any damage other than knocking him cold. He'd have a goose egg larger than Winneger's, and it'd be a while before either of them could put a helmet on again.

But no epiphany, as you might expect if this were some sort of academic existential narrative. Firefighters would have an epiphany each day given what they see and live. Nope, no consciousness transformed. They already knew how good life could be without near-death reminders, which was, as far as Gary was concerned, so much college bullshit. What did those idiots know sitting on campus, as he'd tell himself more than once after being forced to resign due to permanent disability and then deciding go to college full time to maybe find something better in life than returning to being a bus and truck mechanic with an ignorant and bigoted cracker. No sir. Not that again.

The decision did not arrive easily, and he thought at first he'd return to duty. The doctor kept them overnight in the hospital to be certain they did recover from the blow and to be certain no sign emerged of brain or cervical swelling. John Gary felt not too shabby when he left the hospital, which may have been from the painkillers, but the pain had started to subside the moment he woke up after the first night to see the Chief and Hannigan standing there. Good to have friends. They'd driven over to New London together in the Chief's car. Winneger sat on the edge of the other bed in the room, getting ready to go home.

"About time you woke up," said Winneger. "And you snore."

"Did I miss anything?"

"Yeah. We had to do all the overhaul and cleanup," said Hannigan.

"Sorry. Did we save the tapes?"

"The superintendent is very happy," said the Chief, "Yes, you did."

"We came to give Brian a ride home. His wife wants to know where the hell he's been all night. She had to take care of the kids by herself."

"I better get out of here," said Winneger

"We'll pick you up tomorrow," said the Chief. "The doctor said they want to keep an eye on you another day, and you can keep an eye on the nurses."

"That an order, sir?"

"Do you need an order?"

"No sir."

Fact is, Gary continued his penchant for brunettes and had a date with a petite second shift nurse, Jeanine, lined up by the time he left the hospital the next day. Fact is, while they laughed shoulder to shoulder through "Sleeper" (she liked Woody Allen), he noticed the trouble focusing for the first time, but dismissed it as an after effect of the concussion, which Jeanine confirmed when he asked her after the movie. That first date ended with a kiss at the entrance to her apartment in New London, because her roommate was home, but on the second date the next weekend, at a drive-in movie, they never watched the screen and humped like rabbits the whole time in the backseat with her on top bouncing and rocking so hard he thought she'd wear his dick down to a numb. She brought the blanket to cover them, but they steamed up the windows so fast, the blanket quickly dropped away to the floor, and besides, she came prepared wearing a skirt with easy-off panties underneath. The skirt stayed on as did her blouse with no bra under it.

No third date, though, because she ended the second, after three orgasms, with mention of how much she liked kids, and Gary lost interest fast. Feminismo. He felt like she set a trap and that he couldn't trust her to take her birth control pills, and he hated condoms because he couldn't entirely trust them either, and he knew she'd keep, as a good Catholic girl, any child she produced in or out of marriage, but she would pressure him into marriage. None of them good reasons to marry or even get serious with a woman. Besides, Winneger nearly lost his life and would have left two small kids without a father and left a wife as a single mother.

And Gary's vision after the second date still didn't clear up, so he might not be able to support a family anyway if he lost his job as a firefighter. Back to the doctor's office, to get a referral to see an ophthalmologist who told him that his vision might never clear up, and might get worse as a result of the blow to his head. He prescribed glasses. But the worst news had to be knowing that if he hit his head again, John Gary, firefighter, stood a fifty times normal change of detaching both retinas and going stone blind.

But first, denial. He returned to duty after two weeks with blurred vision and tried to pretend nothing had changed, and he managed to fake it for a while as long as he did not have to drive and could just pull hose and squirt water. But then three weeks later, he worked a 24 hour shift with Hannigan while Don Borwin took a day off, and a mutual aid call rang in that night for Noank. Nothing big. Small electrical fire in the wall of a restaurant, but Noank had one pumper and wanted backup just in case. Just a drive over and back on a pleasant evening, but he kept squinting the whole time and the street signs looked blurry and that was it. Time to do the right thing.

He thought it would be a matter of turning in his notice and leaving, but parting from a fire department is never that easy, because the rumors are true. It is a family, and even if John Gary had been a member for only three years, he had to say goodbye, and they had to say goodbye even though he would travel only thirty miles to the north with his three years of Norwich fire tech credits to Eastern Connecticut State College, the one place he could afford to attend, and attend for one year only. He had to cram two years of college into two semesters and a summer.

"We're sorry to see you go," said the Chief, "But I understand. We'll keep you on days until you leave so you won't have to drive and hope you don't get clunked on the head again."

"Hope not, sir," said John, and quickly left the Chief's office to avoid the embarrassment of tears in his eyes. He had to sit out back in the old Mac for a while to get control again.

He could smile when they gave him, at the next volunteer fundraiser, a model steam pumper, a beer mug with a small gold engraved plate that read "Rookie" on it, and a gag gift. Apparently word had gotten around or Violet had made sure word got around, so she had a big laugh as did everyone else at the table when he opened the eight inch long black box in a plain brown wrapper that held a much-too-large dildo. "You can put it on your mantle," said Hannigan. "Or you could keep it as a spare," said Shawnessy. Har har. And a commendation letter from the Chief for outstanding service as well as a thank you letter from the superintendent of schools for the heroic effort to save the student records. Firefighters don't always save babies.

So, believing the hype about making more money with a college education, up the road John Gary drove to Willimantic and Eastern to improve his mind and learn all about critical thinking with the hope that he'd actually pick up a marketable skill along the way. But Jesus H. Christ, he hated the place from day one. The campus, surfeit with institutional brick, looked like a cross between a prison and a cheap hotel stuck out in the middle of nowhere, the reason the state located the Eastern Connecticut State Fire School in the same town. Even with a map for the small campus, he had to keep asking where this or that building could be found while he muddled through the insanity of registration, and the dorm he forced himself into to save a buck stood as a brick monolith, an alleged high rise easy to spot because it towered nine stories over the other brick bunkers.

Eight years in age, but light years in life experience beyond the five twenty-one-year-old punks he had to live with, John Gary adapted by giving them his black and white television for the living room to stay on their good side while he studied nonstop as a means of escape, and because he paid every cent of tuition himself. No loans. No mommy and daddy. He wanted full return on his state supported higher education dollar. Still he had to put up with the punks calling him "gramps," and quickly gave up telling them about life outside the kindergarten they lived in, especially after one of them said, "You sound like my father." They'd find out, and they did. The kid with the stringy blond hair who burned incense, meditated, and smoked dope in his room got a job pumping gas after graduation. The smart-ass pretty boy who never went without a girlfriend in his bed, coached girls' high school basketball after graduation. The quiet jock, the math major and number one man on the cross country team, crunched numbers in the dehumanizing glass towers in downtown Hartford, the insurance capital of the world, after graduation.

And Gary managed to avoid getting sucked into juvenile, pointless, infinitely stupid dorm bullshit sessions by taking study breaks in the gym to workout, although he failed once by wasting time with this fat Catholic gay guy and the guy who first called him "gramps," a tall, goofy looking geek, about how strict God intended the "Do not kill" commandment to be. "You'd allow your own mother to be shot even if you could defend her by killing the guy attacking her?" The gay Catholic refused to budge from his absolute, do not kill under any circumstances position. Most sophomoric arguments rest on speculation and analogy only. Real evidence was a waste of time.

Gary's mantra became eat, sleep, go to class, write papers and papers and papers and ignore the distant sounds of any siren. Nobody did anything in college but write papers, which seemed the only means of gaining status other than sports and, especially for males, getting into fights--except males who had to avoid getting hit in the head. So he desperately gripped the hope that all the reading and writing would generate tangible value like connecting a hose to hydrant. He couldn't run home to mommy and daddy in the suburbs. He and his holy roller parents had parted on bad terms right after he finished high school. A decent living, he thought, could be found in an honest day's work of sitting through classes on Thoreau, US history to 1877, finite math, international relations, cultural anthropology, social problems, politics and literature, law and the life cycle, European history, American foreign policy, American government, macroeconomics, urban analysis, economic issues and policies, Spanish, and on and on and on.

Taught by one or two good professors, and the rest had to be tolerated like the one who kept saying, "Read my book," the only book he ever wrote and published. Or the one who went off on one tangent after another, making notetaking impossible. Or the grad student who apparently had no training as a teacher and didn't believe in preparing before class and always got this desperate look on his face when he ran out of bullshit fifteen minutes into the class.

But there's no need to linger on this one year. Though no genius, Gary, because of his work ethic, racked up a 3.97 GPA that landed him in the honors seminar where he muddled through by studying the work of four political journalists, feeling out of place among the really smart people. But at least, in that one Eastern year, he learned he had a brain that functioned fairly well, then got the hell out of there in hopes that he'd return to adult world in the MPA program at the University of Connecticut where nobody meditated, smoked dope, got stupid drunk on cheap beer, and streaked across campus naked. Just one affair with a townie during the year for a social life, a working class girl, but for the both of them, as with most of his relationships, the bond beyond sex did not and would not exist. No sense of place, of belonging existed, as it had in Groton, even with all the ignorance and working class attitudes. Life became and remained tentative and transitory. Maybe he could get a new career, and maybe he could associate with a better class of people with this liberal education he'd paid for with his hard-earned working class dollars.

Engine 10

Preface

What follows is my journal for the 18-19 November 2016 shift requested by your firm to aid in the defense of Captain and Acting Chief of the Fire Department, Joseph Ollokut Pierce. I had assistance in producing the document from firefighter Richard Spalding, Jr, who is also an Oregon State University senior in journalism. Dialog has been reconstructed from my journal, Rich's notes, interviews with those involved, and from fire department tape archives.

And, again, yes, I am more than willing to testify under oath at the trial on behalf of Chief Pierce. Without reservation, I can say he is the finest fire officer I have ever worked with, and I would not and have not second guessed his decisions on 18-19 November 2016.

--John Lewis Jones, firefighter and captain (ret.)

Log: 0817, Friday, 18 November 2016: Dumpster behind Kappa sorority house just off north side of campus. Used booster line and one pike pole. No damage, no extension of fire to structure or parked vehicles. Returned 0838.

Journal: Captain Pierce posted the memo from the chief today, but the only thing I read was something about moving the bunks out of the firehouse before dispatch announced the dumpster fire on the PA. Odd time of day. Usually we'd get them behind the Greek houses from midnight on during the usual weekend drunken orgy.

Being the old guy, I drove and let the Cap, Kim, and Dicky boy handle the fire when we pulled up in front of a white, two-story mansion with baby blue trim, as in a lot of air-headed blondes live here. They bounced up and down on the small front lawn as we stopped by the hydrant across the street. Sometimes I think they just lit off a dumpster to see Dicky boy step down off the rig. He loved it.

"Hi," said the pretty boy hunk with black hair and white teeth and a slight paunch.

"Hellooooo," several of them lilted in unison, and laughed and grinned, "Save us Mr. Firefighter. Please save us."

"Use the hydrant so we can keep the tank full," Cap told me just before he stepped down and yelled back at Dicky to get to work and haul the booster line up the driveway to the dumpster that sat smoking across the small parking lot away from the back of the sorority house. At one sorority dumpster fire last week, the girls (they didn't act like adults) pelted Dicky with condoms from a second floor window and yelled down to ask if he needed any help with his hose. Jesus, I thought his face turned the color of the flames shooting up from the dumpster, and we never let up on him the rest of the shift. "Save me, Mr. Firefighter."

I made the hydrant connection with the small port intake two and a half, then charged the booster as Kim and Dick hauled it up the driveway past cat calls and boob flashes. Kim propped the lid open with the pike pole while the Cap kept wonder boy focused on the job. Fact is, the kid had no training. The department dropped the exam, the physical, and the state fire academy requirement on direction from the City Council. Saved money, they said. So we get this kid two weeks ago who got the job in the first place because his daddy was on the Council, and we had to train him, when he paid attention, from day one so he didn't get killed and we didn't get killed. Besides, we had our suspicions. Engine 10 had turned into the token house, as Kim, the Cap, and I called it, before Dicky showed up. The three of us received written offers to keep our jobs at half pay and demotion or resign two years back in 2014 when the Council decided to eliminate all paid firefighter positions in four of the five stations in town. We'd all been officers of one rank or another, but at least we still had jobs. For the time being.

The Chief acted like he was doing us all a favor by adding a fourth to our shift after the cut down to three paid personnel per shift and returning us all to a 24/48 schedule. We figured they would have eliminated our jobs also in the name of efficiency, if we weren't all officially classified as minorities who had education and rank: Me, your narrator, John Lewis Jones, or Jay, as most called me--25 years on the department and formerly a truck company captain. The Captain, formerly battalion chief, Joseph Ollokut Pierce, 15 years on the department, 20 years as a firefighter, starting as a Nez Perce wildland firefighter. And Kim Son Nyugen Douglass, former lieutenant and paramedic, 9 years on the department, and the one who had to put up with Dicky's bullshit most of the time at fires, because she had the nozzle or backed him up or took over when he screwed up, which was pretty much every damned shift.

"Hey, Dick, shut the nozzle down until I get the lid up," Kim said.

"Hey, Dick, point the nozzle down into the dumpster, then open it," said Cap.

Problem was that Dicky did whatever the hell he wanted because his daddy guaranteed the job just like he guaranteed the loan for the three quarter ton 4x4 Chevy he drove to and from work, the shiny white Chevy with the roll bar, balloon tires, gun rack, and sundry intelligent bumper stickers, such as "I'll keep my guns and my money, you keep the change." Or, once Cruz got the votes, "America for the Americans." Plus, of course, the American flag decal.

So Dicky ignored Kim and Cap and opened the nozzle before Kim had the lid up, then sprayed everything in sight before he managed, with Cap's help, to get the water aimed in the right direction--down. At large dumpster fires, it made sense to crack the nozzle before popping the lid, but for campfires like this one, only a squirt or two were needed before Kim stirred up the contents a bit with a six foot pike pole for another short wetdown. It turned out to be the usual ashtray emptied into a trash can just as the housekeeper took the trash out in the morning. Maybe a prank. Maybe just stupid. Most likely the latter. So we thought.

"Take up," said Cap as soon as the smoke disappeared in five minutes.

Dicky boy handed the nozzle to Kim and sauntered across the parking lot to chat with a few of the bottle blonds. No brown skins in sororities these days but for the summer tans worn by blonds, but those faded by November but for one weirdo standing out front staring at me; she looked like she slept on the tanning bed. "You people still in town," she said to no one, but the remark had my name on it. "I was born here," I said, then shutdown the pump and disconnected and drained the hydrant line while Kim and Cap rolled the booster line back on the reel at the back step.

Cap yelled up the sidewalk: "Time to go, lover boy."

Dicky sauntered down the driveway, jogging the gauntlet of blonds, grinning the entire way back to the street. We all glanced at each other and Cap had time to comment to me and Kim on the dumpster graffiti before dumbass returned to the engine.

"You see F-U-E-G-O sprayed painted under the lid?"

"I did," said Kim, but said no more because we all had to climb back in and return to the firehouse.

Log: 0855, Friday, 18 November 2016: Call to medical assistance for a civilian injured resisting arrest by local police. Returned 0947.

Journal: We never made it back to the firehouse after the sorority house dumpster fire. Back-to-back runs used to be rare, but became more common once the city confined paid personnel to one central station, which meant we caught almost all medical calls when the private ambulance service had their one vehicle tied up somewhere most of the time-- when it was running. The City Council, in its infinite wisdom, stopped medical calls handled exclusively by fire/ems as yet another efficiency move, and contracted with a newly formed private ambulance company owned by the brother-in-law of a Council member--a no bid contract for an ambulance service. No matter, people in the city had figured out after the first month of incompetence that they'd rather ride to the hospital in their own car or take a cab than be strapped to a stretcher in the back of a converted delivery van even if it did smell like fresh bakery goods. The brother-in-law also owned a bakery with another sweetheart contract with the City to provide all the donuts for students at the charter schools. Soft drink machines also returned to the schools in a move to end the nanny state interference with local education.

Did I mentioned that the public education system had been shut down slowly but surely. The City Council brought AML (Achieve More for Less) a private education management consulting company in 2014 to run the school system. The consultants, of course, told the City Council what it wanted to hear and presented a plan to run all schools as charter schools competing with each other for students based on "measurable results," meaning student test scores and teacher evaluation. The teacher's union protested, of course, but the union was ignored and union teachers, of course, received low evaluation scores and pink slips by the summer of 2015. In two years, the City Council purged the local school system of any opposition to their privatization master plan, and being so pleased with the result-- meaning teachers earning minimum wage with no benefits and students scores improving with the dumbed down tests--they went after the university faculty.

That brings us to the second run of the day. Dispatch called us back downtown from sorority row to Center Park where the cops had a white guy down on the ground. We had to slow to a crawl to reach the park because of all the protesters crowding the sidewalks along Monroe Avenue and spilling into the streets. They marched in silence with tape over their mouths and carried signs that read: "Free Our Speech" or "Protect Tenure" or "Save Academic Freedom." Not just younger part-time faculty this time, but older gray heads among them, presumably the tenured people who finally felt threatened by local control of the university.

We stopped next to the sidewalk and Kim climbed out of the cab to get the medic kit from a side compartment. I set the parking brake and stood in front of the engine where I could keep an eye on things and offer assistance if needed by Kim and Cap, and to keep the kid out of the way. "Damned hippies," he said to me as he watched the protesters march closer. "Frickin communists." I ignored him and made a mental note to talk with Cap and Kim back at the firehouse when we had a chance to chat away from Dicky boy, and also watched both sides of the street to protect the rig should things turn ugly when the protesters reached the line of rent-a-cops waiting to meet them. You guessed it. The City Council replaced the taxpayer funded police department with a security force under contract after the City tore up the union contract and ignored complaints filed by the union with the useless Oregon Employment Relations Board, then under the control of the Republican led state government. But that's another story.

The bloodied man on the sidewalk looking dazed and frightened had been in the vanguard of the marchers with a can of black spray paint he used to cover the new sign at the park entrance that read: "By ordinance, to enhance public safety, no gatherings of three or more people in this park or any other city park without permit. All violators subject to immediate arrest." The cops had confiscated the spray paint can, but only after clubbing the painter over the head when he tried to paint their face shields. One of them yelled, "Stay down!" when the guy tried to sit up as Kim approached. "Stay the fuck down!" Then he pinned the man's left arm with a boot with the expected result--the man, who looked like he'd just stepped out his university office wearing his crew neck sweater under a tan corduroy jacket with elbow patches, screamed in both pain and protest. Private security, yes, but well equipped. Each officer had a helmet, a plastic face shield, another plastic riot shield, mace, a Glock side arm, an AR-15 assault rifle, and a two-foot riot baton with which to protect and serve.

"Just patch him up," said the goon in charge. I knew every cop in town and this wasn't one of them. Fact is, I hadn't seen any of the regular police officers for weeks.

"After I evaluate him," Kim answered, not even bothering to look at the brute. She'd gotten her training in the Navy, circuit trained, loved karate, and did not rattle, having served one combat tour in Afghanistan as a field medic, or, as she said, a "corpswoman with the

Marines." Kim didn't flinch when the goon stepped closer, but Cap stepped in between. His service history included Gulf War II by Bush the Younger in a tank crew, his ticket off the rez to the middle class life. Though he stood just shy of six foot tall, his Nez Perce glare could stop a charging stallion, and he had the shoulders and arms to back it up from all those years spent in eastern Oregon wrangling on his own little piece of property near Enterprise. He and his wife planned to retire there in the valley of the Lostine River within site of the Wallowa Mountains, but she'd left the city in 2015 with the remaining four of the six children still at home. Cap worked two jobs but drove over as often as he could to be with her. The goon stopped.

"Just patch him up and we'll transport."

"We'll see," said Captain Joseph Ollokut Pierce. "What have you got Kim?" He asked without losing eye contact with the goon.

"Skull laceration that may take 6-8 sutures, bruises on the face, possible broken left arm, shock." She cut the clothing away from the man's left arm to get a closer look to be certain the fracture was not compound, then applied an air splint just as the victim started to pass out. She spoke to him firmly and right at his face. "What's your name? Tell me your name?" The professor didn't answer, but that brought him around long enough for Kim to flash his pupils with her penlight. Uneven. "Cap, we have a concussion. Help me with the collar, then let's get him into the cab for transport."

Hold it," said the goon. "He's in our custody. He's under arrest for assaulting an officer. If you transport him you're an accessory."

Cap took a step to get up close and personal with the rent-a-cop knowing he'd back off because the marchers were nearly at his back. "We're taking him. You can follow to the ER."

"We'll take him in a squad car," said the cop. "We need you here."

"For what?" asked Cap. He didn't see any squad car in sight. Just a lot of Army surplus Humvees still sporting camo paint schemes.

"In case someone gets hurt or we have to hose down the commies."

Cap helped Kim put the barely conscious academic in the back of cab, then turned to Dicky boy. "You stay here to help with riot control." Cap gave him a dry powder extinguisher. "We'll be back for you."

Dicky couldn't argue because we had no room left in the cab with Kim and the victim in the jump seat. I got the rig the hell out of there just as the protesters arrived at the park, but they didn't attempt to enter to avoid more violence and nobody pulled out any more spray paint. They sat down on the sidewalk and surrounded the small block-wide park, sitting in silence while the cops stood by, hesitating for the moment to act further while out-of-town media taped the story. At least Portland had a television station not yet bought out or sued into silence by the Mudrock Corporation. The local newspaper lost count of how many times it had been sued for defamation since the new City Council took office, and when the legal bills piled up to high enough to destroy any hope of financial survival, they had to accept the buyout offer from Mudrock, after which, of course, the defamation suits were withdrawn.

The poor bastard bled all over the jumpseat in spite of Kim's best effort with pressure, and I had to wonder why Cap didn't just let the cops take him to the ER and let him bleed all over the backseat of a Humvee. Cap looked at me as if he knew I was about to say something and moved his head just enough for me to know silence ruled until after the hospital run. Time to focus on driving north up the hill with lights and siren and airhorn.

"We're losing him," Kim snapped from the back. "Move it."

They must have really smashed his head.

"Stay awake!" Kim yelled at her patient and waved smelling salts under his nose that didn't do much more than make his head bob to the side without him regaining consciousness.

"Do you want us to pull over?" I yelled back over the diesel noise. She didn't have her headset on. None of us did.

"Negative. Keep moving."

His pulse dropped to nothing by the time the ER team had him on the stretcher, and Kim was muttering, "What the fuck?" trying to figure out why a whack to the head nearly killed the guy or why they had to whack him in the first place rather than tazz and restrain. For Chissake, the man looked middle-aged and could not have been a threat to anyone other than a sophomore desperate for a passing grade.

Cap saw Kim's face, leaned in, and said almost in a whisper. "Forgot it. Outside."

We huddled in front of the cab before climbing back into the rig. Cap turned off his handset. "I can't leave this off for long before we have to report back in service, but I needed to tell you about the memo I posted at the firehouse."

"The one about moving the bunks out?" I asked.

"Yes. But that's the good news. They seem to have gone crazy since Cruz was elected, but it almost seemed they had this planned and just waited for the election to move."

"Move what?" Kim said.

"Move against all unions. Us, the university. They're already busted the teachers' union and the cops' union and the city workers' union. They've been working on us, in case you didn't notice."

"I noticed."

"No more bunks to make us miserable enough to quit if the longer hours and low pay won't do it like it did for the others. Now they're cutting health and retirement."

"Shit," said Kim, and then, "Jesus Christ. That guy we just brought in works with my husband. I didn't recognize him at first with all the blood on his face. What the hell are we going to do?"

Cap motioned for us to get back in the cab, then paused. "This is going to be a long day and night, but we have to keep doing our jobs until 8:00 a.m. tomorrow. That's all I know for now."

"What about Dicky boy?"

"I'll take care of him," Cap said without an expression. Deadest of deadpan. "Kim is your husband at home?"

"Yes, with the kids."

"Call him and tell him to stay put until things calm down, then, if you both want, he can leave town with the kids for my place. But don't call him from the firehouse. It's bugged. The memo also said the PA system is now a two-way open mike with dispatch and all activity in the firehouse will be monitored. Cameras will be installed on Monday."

Kim used her cell to make the call while I swabbed the blood out of the cab and thanked God or somebody that I was divorced with two grown kids who'd moved away. Cap turned his handset back on and reported we were available for another run and requested that the rent-a-cops give Dicky a lift back to the firehouse as soon as they released him from riot duty, and since the cops had no use for him and got tired of hearing his endless chatter and didn't want him spying on them for his father on the City Council, they drove him back to the firehouse. Not that they cared what Dicky would tell his daddy, but the the police chain of command had unwritten orders to assure the Council had deniability when things went south after the Portland and Eugene media left town.

The tear gas started flying and billowing around ten once the cops knew the last news truck had reached I-5 and they'd temporarily closed the bridges in and out of downtown. Tear gas, pepper spray, mace. Lots of yelling and screaming and running and people down on the pavement, but the chief stopped by our station to tell us in person to remain in quarters "Until the situation has stabilized. For your safety and to prevent damage to the apparatus."

But the real opposition had sense enough to avoid direct confrontations like the battle at the downtown park, if you could call it a battle. More like the massacre at the downtown park. Cops hauled the injured directly to jail for medical attention, if any, which is probably why they wanted Kim and her friends to stay put in the firehouse until the automatic alarm sounded at the university library. The real opposition had already moved to guerrilla tactics.

Log: 1022, Friday, 18 November 2016: Automatic alarm university library. Smoke in the building on third floor. Building evacuated. Fire in third floor men's room across from elevators. Apparent arson. Top of trash can removed. Accelerant odor. Maybe gasoline. Coleman lamp fuel. Extension to the wall and ceiling. Did not return.

Journal: Okay, I exaggerated a bit about Cap and the stallions, although I did see him once slide out of the saddle at a full gallop, drop a lariat loop under the left front hoof of a stallion that refused to listen when he said "Whoa." He wrapped the rope around his back and up over his shoulder like we did in fire school with a safety line for a rookie learning how to rappel off the roof of a building, dug his heels in, yelled "Whoa!" The horse went ass over tea kettle when Cap yanked the lariat taut. You can guess that the horse stopped in the future when told to do so, although Cap complained that it did stop a bit too quickly.

So I had no doubt he'd take care of Dicky boy.

"What's that?" Cap asked when we climbed down after I backed Engine 10 onto the ramp.

"Protection," said a grinning Dicky.

"Get rid of it. We don't carry weapons."

"The cops--"

"The cops," said Cap, getting up close and personal with Dicky like he had with the goon at the park, "don't run this firehouse. I do, and firefighters do not carry Glocks or anything that shoot anything but water, dry powder, or foam."

"My dad--"

"Your dad isn't here, and I really don't give a damn what you tell him when you're off duty tomorrow morning. The Chief told me to make sure you didn't get yourself killed, which means your dad told me to make sure you didn't get killed. You have no training. You've been here two weeks, so you keep doing what I tell you."

"Captain, I--"?

Cap disarmed him before Dicky could get the rest of the sentence out, and dropped the clip out of the Glock. "I'll return this piece to the cops tomorrow morning, and if you ever bring any weapon with you again on duty, I'll send you home for an extended leave. Now get a can of chrome polish and start working on that front bumper. I want it to shine like the front bumper on that thing you drive you call a truck. Understood." A rhetorical question.

The kid eyed Cap, started to say something, then stopped himself, and stomped back into the firehouse to get the polish. He was no threat; though a pretty boy, the kid had already started on a paunch from off duty workouts hoisting a mug at some honky tonk. That dirt smear under his nose may have been a mustache.

"You stop when I tell you to stop," barked Cap as he walked through the carriage floor out the backdoor of the station with me following without having to be asked. We needed to find out what Kim learned.

"Do you trust him?" I asked

"No farther than I can spit," said Cap. "What did your husband say?"

Kim had just tucked her cell phone back in a uniform pocket. She looked worried. "Mike said the tenured faculty organized the march after they received an email from the City Council announcing local control of the university and a policy modeled on the 2013 Kansas Board of Regents policy."

"Sorry," I said, "Kansas?"

"The Kansas policy allowed any state university or college to fire a faculty person, tenured or not, for public statements that did not support the university. Tenure protects speech concerning a given field only, meaning sanctioned professional publication."

"Purge."

"Yes," she said, "Just like the public schools. Mike's not worried, though. He teaches tech writing and never had any job security. Term to term part-time work. No threat to the new world order. There's something else . . ."

The PA system interrupted: "Engine 10 respond to the university library, to Valley Library, for an automatic alarm." We drove up past the downtown park where the demonstration had ended apparently. We saw no one on the sidewalks. They either got too cold to stick around or they'd been convinced to leave.

Theoretically, Engine 10 responded to the west side of the library first and stayed on the street while the second due engine would stop at the hydrant down the block. But now the second due could not be counted on. Many fire departments around the country had well organized, well trained volunteers, as we did once, but no more. Fact is, we used to have qualified students bunk in at the firehouse where we provided desks in a quiet corner for study, but the City ended that practice also to save money--on liability insurance. My Plan B, after I dropped Cap and Kim and Dicky boy on the west side of the library would have been to stay put, then, if they needed a hose line or I needed to feed a standpipe or both, I'd drive down to the next hydrant and drop back to the front of the building. Some days now the volunteers would show up. Some days they wouldn't, especially in the middle of the day or on a Friday at the start of elk hunting season, even though a building of that size should have had a guaranteed minimum response of three pumpers and two ladders.

The Chief radioed before we arrived to say we had smoke in the building and ordered us to the front, so I turned the Seagrave onto the city block sized grass quad thankful that not enough fall rain had soaked the ground yet. We didn't sink in but did leave a nice set of tire marks on the lawn and mud all over the plaza at the front entrance where students poured out and the building alarm rattled on incessantly.

You had to give the Chief credit for being a political survivor, but not much else. Hand picked from among the three battalion chiefs because he stood near six foot four and voted Republican and had a big American flag pin on his lapel and thought Ronald Reagan had walked on water. "Not sure yet where the smoke is coming from. Library people say it's thickest on the third floor. Start there."

Cap ordered me to get the rest of my turnout gear on (I drove in work uniform only) to bring the Halligan and Kim to bring the can, meaning the pump extinguisher full of water. He figured small fire in a trash can in a restroom. "You stay here to help the Chief," he said in a loud voice aimed at Dicky boy.

To which I added quietly when I walked past Dicky, "Touch anything, and I'll kill you." But I'd locked down the pumper air brakes, engaged the pump, and chocked the rear wheels. Turd blossom didn't know squat and wouldn't be able to move it anyway. I was worried more about some stupid ass student or worse playing with the valves.

On the third floor we traced the smoke, sure enough, to the men's room right across from the elevators. Cap took his glove off and felt the door with the back of his hand. "Hot."

Kim pumped up the extinguisher and crouched but we all had to back away after I cracked the door by pushing on it with the Halligan. Thick, really hot smoke blew out.

"Any other units arrived?" Cap radioed down to the Chief.

"One on the way" came the answer.

"Let's get back downstairs, pull the 250 inch and a half and pump from the tank."

"No standpipe?" I asked.

"Negative. All we have is the tank until the second due arrives. No time to move to connect the standpipe."

"Drag the line all the way up from the entrance?"

"Yup. It will reach. Let's go. Leave the can here."

"You smell that?" said Kim.

"Either gasoline or lighter fluid," said Cap once he and Kim had the hose line back up to the men's room while I stood by the pumper. "Charge it," Cap ordered on the radio, and I opened the preconnect valve and cranked the pressure up to 120 psi. "You see this?" I told Dicky, but didn't wait for an answer. "This knob is the throttle. Leave it alone." Then I went up to check the line for kinks and to backup Kim on the nozzle.

She kneeled as low as she could get as Cap opened the door with the Halligan. "Not yet," he said, then: "Push in."

Mind you, we did this without masks, because, you guessed it, no more air masks to save a buck. "They did it that way in the old days, and it was good enough for them," reasoned our esteemed and fearless leader who stayed below wearing his white helmet outside in the fresh air.

We all shoved in through the door and Kim opened up on flames shooting up like a giant Bunsen burner from the trash can right next to the sink, the can with no top on it. Whoever set the fire removed the top to allow extension, and it had jumped up the wall and looked ready run the ceiling when Kim knocked it down with one blast, then stood and drowned the trash can while Cap stirred the wet black mass of smoldering paper towels with the Halligan. We all noticed the wooden wedge jammed into the ceiling sprinkler head to keep it from operating.

"Send Dick up here with a pike pole," Cap radioed the Chief. "Small fire in the third floor men's room trash can with extension up the wall." The wall spray painted with the one word: F-U-E-G-O. "And call the state police arson squad," Cap added. The city had eliminated the fire marshal's office.

We had fun watching Dicky boy finally get a little dirty pulling the burned wallboard and tile with the pike while Kim soaked it and we checked for any fire in the wall, but it was clean. Clean for us. The university would not be happy and would have to shutdown the library for a day or so to get the smoke odor out of the ventilation system.

The single volunteer from Engine 12 on 53rd Street showed up to help us haul hose line back out of the building, drain and repack it in the cross lay bed. "Now you look like a real firefighter," I said to Dicky, who had a soot smudged face until he washed it off at the hydrant just off the quad where we stopped to fill the tank before making ourselves available. But we never had a chance to do more than connect. We never opened the hydrant.

"Engine 10, Engine 12 respond to reported apartment fire in at Bald Hill Village."

Cap keyed his portable. "Which building?"

"Not known. Be advised we have a report of people trapped."

"Acknowledged. Responding. Start the West Hills ladder."

"They've been notified."

Nobody spoke until I had the hydrant disconnected and the fill line back on the engine. The delay could prove deadly, but we had no choice and theoretically Engine 12 would be arrive before we did and conduct primary search. Assuming other volunteers showed up.

Now we had to thread our way along the narrow campus streets, trying to blast our way through the crowds just off campus with the air horn to reach Arnold Way for the connection to Harrison Boulevard to 53rd and a left there to the apartment complex built without codes since the fire codes had been suspended as an impediment to free enterprise and economic development. Not even a smoke alarm in the entire complex. At least a ten minute run. Kim, always prepared, pulled a handful of energy bars out of a pocket on her bunker pants. "Anyone else want one?"

Lunch on the run. Siren at full howl. Air horn blasting. Granola bar.

Log: 1135, Friday, 18 November 2016: Apartment fire in Bald Hills Apartment complex. Report of persons trapped false; one fatality DOA. End of row, two story apt with fire showing in one bedroom window. Stop with single inch and a half line. Checked for extension. None found. Returned 12:51.

Journal: Kim was like that. Well, like most firefighters who think of others first, self last. It's instinct that becomes reflex with training. She carried emergency food just in case, because we don't work regular hours with a lunch break. When you have a call, you go. Doesn't matter what you're doing, you stop it and respond. That's why it's called going "on duty" rather than going to work. We have a duty, a responsibility for the entire community. Just in case something happens, we're there, but we have to be able to take care of ourselves at the same time. If we don't take care of ourselves, we can't take care of anybody else.

I shoved the granola bar into my shirt pocket, nodded thanks, and made a mental note to get an even bigger Christmas present for Kim and Mike this year. They'd saved my ass after my divorce when depression sent me to drink and finally to AA; reciprocation they told me for the times I'd helped with their kids. Mike or Kim would drag me up to the Cascades for long, sweaty hikes, and by the end of the day I was too damned tired to care about any divorce or anything but a shower and a long sleep.

"We're on our own," Cap said, as I passed a car, air horn still blasting. We could see the smoke column and knew we had a worker, but still no response sign on from the ladder. And Engine 12 had to be there, but the driver said nothing on arrival. No sizeup. The Chief stayed behind he said to wait at the library for the state police and to console the head librarian until the university president arrived, and then he'd console him.

Cap keyed the mike. "Dispatch, Engine 10."

"Engine 10."

"Did the ladder truck sign on?"

"Negative."

"Plan B," said Cap. He turned and looked Dicky boy straight in the eye. "You stay with me." He didn't wait for acknowledgement. We knew what to do. Plan B applied at a working fire without a ladder truck or any other back up.

I turned the pumper left onto 53rd, drove the block to the parking lot entrance into a maze of new wooden buildings, each 40 x 100, each with six two story apartments. No sprinklers, no smoke detectors, no external pull station alarms, but at least, for some reasons, the contractor did install hydrants. Two of them anyway. One at the parking lot entrance, and the other at the far end of the complex. So we had a potential total flow of 1000 GPM for the entire complex that among ourselves, we called the Bonfire Apartments. Whenever we had a call there over the last two years since they were thrown up to house workers at the old HP plant, we hit the fire hard, especially after the first worker when we learned the attic ran the length of each building without a fire stop. By the time we had an interior attack started, the roof lit off end to end. During planning, the fire marshal was ignored, the building inspector ignored, and both jobs were eliminated in the first "efficiency" budget the City Council passed. No oversight. No honesty.

"Dispatch. Engine 10 on scene. Single 40x100 building involved. Fire showing in bedroom window D side of end apartment near 53rd Street entrance. Working fire. Engine 10, Engine 12 committed."

That last comment proved to be fiction. The volunteer who'd driven Engine 12 managed to get it into position at the hydrant and connect the five inch supply line, but that's all he'd done.

"Jay. Get water from Engine 12 and charge the monitor. Put it through the bedroom window when I give the signal."

The volunteer shook his head "No" when I asked him if he'd had training on the pump and planned to tell him later how grateful I was that at least he'd figured out how to connect the five inch hydrant line. "You know how to open a hydrant?"

He nodded "Yes" this time, but didn't move.

"Well, get the wrench, man, and get to it."

He didn't move.

Maybe he didn't know where to find the hydrant wrench or maybe he didn't like taking orders from a black man, or a firefighter he classified as a black man (half black really), so I grabbed the hydrant wrench, put it in his hand, and pointed. "Move."

He decided to cooperate when I said "Move" about an inch from his face.

I checked on Cap and Kim while the volly opened the hydrant. Kim had the ground ladder up to the roof line, and headed back across the parking lot for the saw. Cap with Dicky in tow holding the ax had positioned himself with the Halligan at the door to the apartment and waited for me.

The five inch line popped full of water, and the intake pressure looked good. "Bring the wrench back," I yelled at the volly. Standard procedure meant the wrench stayed on the hydrant for emergency shutdown if needed, but I didn't trust the bastard, especially after I noticed the Confederate flag decal on the pump panel. Intake valve open. Check. Pressure relief valve set. Discharge valve open to monitor. Check. I wave okay to Cap, then climbed up to the monitor and aimed it high. I'd open up throwing water over the building, then lower the stream right into the fire window.

"Go," said Cap.

I opened up and dropped the stream right on target, blew through the window and soaked the room.

Cap tried the door. Locked. He mule kicked the door open, got low below the smoke, pulled Dicky boy down next to him, and entered for primary search and to check for extension. "Fire confined to that one bedroom room."

"Water off?"

"Not yet. Primary search and checking for extension."

Cap told me later that the smoke wasn't too bad, and he was able to breath as long as he stayed down for the primary search, although Dicky wasn't much of a help. A minute after he entered the smoke, he started coughing even down on the floor, and then, without permission from Cap, Dicky got up and went for the door, which is when I saw him stumble out on the landing and puke all over the place, and he hadn't even eaten a granola bar. Some can handle smoke and some can't. Maybe he'd ask his daddy to restore funding for the SCBA so we could fill the tanks again.

Cap keyed his mike two minutes later. "The other rooms are clear. No sign of anyone. Kim open the roof."

I knew what that meant. She'd do what we're trained not to do unless we're using Plan B. Plan A meant a response of three engines and a ladder with enough personnel to enter the apartment with no fewer than three firefighters, going on the roof with no fewer than two firefighters, and the other firefighters would help with securing the water supply, laying a charged inch and a half line to the door of the apartment for back up, laddering one window for emergency escape by firefighters inside the apartment, and ventilation, which meant on a two-story residential building poking the glass out of the windows with a long pike pole or using a short pike pole from the ladder bucket. That's right. Sixteen firefighters for minimum response on a structure fire. We had three reliable, and two unreliable. Dicky puked and dumbass stood next to me at the pump panel watching the show.

"You know how to foot a ladder?" I asked him.

He did nod "Yes" and I told him to foot the ladder for Kim while she climbed to the roof with the saw. At least he did that.

Kim brought the saw to life and cut a five by five opening in the sheeting, then backed off. "No sign of extension" she radioed Cap.

"Soak it anyway," said Cap, and when Kim backed away from the hole, I eased the monitor stream up and over to the opening in the roof and gave it a shower. Kim grinned and flashed a thumbs up. Maybe now, I thought, we can get some lunch and took the snack bar out of my pocket for a two-bite knosh to hold me.

Kim climbed down off the roof to bring the saw back to the engine, and damned if the volunteer didn't help with the ladder. And damned if the ladder truck didn't show up just in time for us to grab the smoke ejector to suck all the smoke out of the apartment at the door and pull fresh air in through the windows, air we could breath while we pulled the walls and the ceiling of the fire room, which turned out to be unoccupied. Lucky for us. Only the building to burn. No contents to intensify the fire. Just a body.

"Dispatch," Cap said, "We need the police on scene. One fatality located. Possible homicide." Cap chose his words carefully. He used "possible" because the body looked to be wrapped in a blanket and tied up with a gag in its mouth. It was burned so badly that we couldn't tell if it were male or female, but we could smell that same odor again, the odor of an accelerant like the one used at the university library. He also used the word "possible" because although the body had a bullet hole through the head, Cap was no detective, and he said "possible" to cover his ass and ours from any suggestion that our search for victims had not been completed. Any excuse to terminate any of us and they would.

I couldn't resist. "Dick, come over here and take a look at this."

He did and puked again when he saw the corpse.

"Cap," I said, "Dick doesn't look so good. He might have to take the rest of the day off."

Cap looked over and told Dicky to go out to the engine and wait for us there. We couldn't talk because the two vollies who showed up with the truck helped with overhaul and both wore Confederate flag patches next to the US flag patch on their turnout coats and gave all three of us an odd look when they entered the apartment.

The Chief showed up about then and released us to return to the firehouse while the volunteers finished overhaul and cleanup.

"Chief," Cap said on the way out, "Richard is ill and may need to leave for the rest of the shift."

We thought for sure the Chief would let the kid go home. His dad would not be pleased, we figured, if Dicky had to stay on duty in his condition, but the Chief said, "No. He stays."

Dicky road back to the firehouse with his head between his knees the whole way.

"Take deep breaths," Kim told him. We sat in the kitchen eating our lunch finally after we returned, but Dicky went to the bunkroom and lay on the floor using his turnout coat as a mattress. City workers had removed the beds while we were out and about that morning.

Cap got up to drop his lunch trash in the can by the back door of the kitchen, which was also the backdoor to the firehouse. He turned to glance at Kim and me, then stepped outside. Kim followed a minute later, then I did.

Kim spoke first after Cap shut off his portable. We'd be able to hear the alarm tone from just outside the door. "I wanted to tell you this morning that Mike heard a rumor that one of the tenured faculty disappeared."

Cap's eyebrows arched. "Disappeared how?"

Kim could be counted on for fact. She had a mind that worked from fact only because paramedics have to live that way. They can't let emotions and associated irrational urges distract them when they're focused on quick assessment of a medical problem, initial treatment, then prep for transport. She would unload after a run like she did once we had the beaten man to the hospital, but never during a run. Cool as ice. Smart. And tough. She knew Cap just wanted fact.

"Mike said one of the full professors in the English Department who organized the march this morning didn't show up for the march. He never contacted anyone to tell them he would not be there. People tried to reach him by phone with no luck, both at home and at his office. We can't jump to conclusions."

"Not yet," I said, having already jumped to conclusions.

Cap looked at me. "Bullshit. What are you thinking? We don't have much time."

He was absolutely correct. The alarm tone sounded followed by the mechanical voice of dispatch. "Engine 10 respond to City Hall. Reported car fire."

"Get Dick," Cap told Kim, but Dicky boy had already managed to rouse himself.

Log: 1321 Friday, 18 November 2016: Car fire at City Hall. Turns out to be the mayor's car. Very suspicious in broad daylight. F-U-E-G-O painted on the parking lot payment. Returned 1358.

Journal: Car fires can usually be tricky in any case, Mr. Lawyer, when we have to worry about tires popping, gasoline exploding, and tons of toxic smoke generated by rubber and plastic. And now we had to put them out the old way without any Scott packs, meaning breathing equipment, also known as self-contained breathing apparatus, or SCBA. Scuba. Just like divers, except that we were smoke divers.

Now to add to the fun, an arson war seemed to have broken out in our fair city. How else could we explain why the mayor's Lexus lit off in the middle of the afternoon on a Friday with no witnesses to see who struck the match. And whoever did the job knew how to do it with a little gas splashed under the engine, then a match. None of this rag in the gas fill nonsense. Took too long and easy to spot by anyone walking down the sidewalk, strolling through the parking lot, or just glancing out the window at City Hall. Nope. Bring along a liter and a half plastic water bottle, pull it out of a backpack as if to take a drink, screw the top off, and oops, drop it by the mayor's nice shiny blue car to let the gasoline spill out, then light a match, but not just one match. Detach two matches from a matchbook, insert one in the closed matchbook so only the head pokes out, light the other match, use it to light the one sticking out of the book, then drop it just as the entire book flares. Whoomp. Fire under the car as the arsonist walks away to the bus station and mingles with the crowd. Fire that's spred by all the oil and paint under the car until the engine compartment turns into a furnace. At least that was our theory based on the matchbook find, the odor of gas under the Lexus, and the melted water bottle we found.

The front tires had popped by the time we arrived. Cap didn't have to tell me to stay on the street next to the parking lot. We needed the hydrant because the mayor's car sat next to one of those Humvees that appeared all over town since the demonstration at the park, and the Humvee had to started to cook along with the Lexus.

Kim took off down the street hauling the five inch hydrant line and the wrench while I got the pump in gear and set the wheel chocks. Cap told Dicky boy to stick with him again. "You're going to learn something," he said with a slight grin. "Grab the 150 and follow me." Meaning pull the 150 foot cross lay inch and a half hose. Okay, the small hose, Mr. Lawyer. Or maybe I should say the medium-sized hose, between the small hard-rubber booster line on the reel that looks like big garden hose and the hose that's the size of a man's leg when it's charged. We call that the two and a half, meaning the inside diameter when the hose expands with water.

Anyway, Cap knew we couldn't reach the mayor's car with the short pre-connect on the front bumper we use when the car is on the street, so he had Dicky pull the 150 and haul it across the parking lot to position the nozzle to open up between the Humvee and the Lexus. Save the Humvee to stop the spread, then work back at the Lexus. I charged the 150 as soon as Cap gave the word on the radio and watch it inflate and jump as the water shot toward Dicky. "Keep the nozzle shut," yelled Cap, "Until we're sure we have no kinks in the line. Open it when I tell you to open it." Dicky kept his head down as the wind shifted and blew all that black and brown boiling crud into his face. He tucked that face down into his turnout coat to find good air and held on. I had to give him credit for not backing off, or maybe he was just paralyzed with fear or still too sick to move from the snoot full he got at the apartment fire.

Kim yelled at me. "Connected."

"Open it," I yelled back, and she cranked the hydrant stem until she wouldn't turn any more to let the water up and out from the underground main to the pump on Engine 10. As soon as the supply line filled, I slowly opened the tank fill valve and cranked up the pressure on the 150 when Cap yelled at Dicky, "Open the line. Hit the Humvee first. I'm right behind you." And he was, talking to the kid nonstop to keep him focused and lessen his fear, because two of the worst ways to die are drowning and burning to death. It's instinctive.

Kim grabbed the Halligan and hustled over to help. I stayed with the pumper in case Cap needed a second line pulled, but so far, so good. Dicky opened up with a fog pattern so he and Cap could inch forward close enough to switch to full stream at the base of the fire, such as it was. "Work it back and forth, up and down," Cap instructed, meaning spray both the Humvee and the Lexus left and right, then drop the stream down to the base of the fire rolling out from under the front of the Lexus.

While they worked the water, Kim had the pleasure of opening the driver's side with the Halligan after finding the door locked. She actually smiled when she smashed the window into little pieces onto the front leather reclining driver's seat with optional heating for winter. The public has the wrong impression about firefighters being a bit destructive, but to save the car, sometimes, you have to damage the car, especially if you want to knock the fire down before the entire parking lot goes up in smoke. Or at least one Humvee on the passenger side. She reached in to release the hood lock, but of course the hood being too hot to touch to open the release, she shoved the crowbar end of the Halligen under the front of the hood and put all of her weight on the other end, turning her face away to avoid smoke and flame.

Cap tapped Dicky on the right shoulder. "Go right. Under the hood." He did and that really knocked the fire down to size. "Good. Good," said Cap, which is about as close as he ever came to praise.

Kim actually smiled at Dicky, who couldn't help himself. He smiled back and seemed somewhat pleased with himself. He'd screwed up at the sorority house, so we held him back at the library, and then he'd screwed up again at the apartment fire, but now he finally seemed to get the hang of it. And actually seemed to want to do the job. Not that we trusted him entirely. He had a long way to go. But now Cap had an excuse to keep him with as for leverage the rest of the day and forget about trying to get rid of him.

You'd think the mayor would have run screaming out of City Hall to see what was left of his luxury sedan, but he waited until the smoke cleared, literally, and we began to pick up. He sauntered across the parking lot with his paunch and bald head, flanked left and right by two of the black uniformed goons, the new police, and asked Cap what happened, a very odd question. How would Cap be able to offer anything other than a theory, so he did.

"Arson, sir," said Cap.

"How do you know?" asked Mayor Acklee, who'd made his money as a booze and beer wholesaler, who'd led the right-wing revolt in town with a promise to cut all property taxes in half, if elected, and to return the city for its former red, white, and blue greatness. The newspaper exposed Acklee as the president of the local John Birch chapter as well as a founder of the Oregon Tea Party for America before the newspaper was bought out and turned into a propaganda rag for the Acklee administration.

Cap pointed to the matches, the melted water bottle, and asked the mayor to breath in the wonderful odor of unleaded emanating from the front of his no longer drivable car.

"That so," said the mayor, who had been joined by a group of six other bald, middle aged white men in black waist jackets below which each had a holstered Glock like the one Dicky brought back to the station. The City Council. Dicky waved to his father. Must have been a meeting in progress. When two more goons appeared from City Hall and edged toward Engine 10 as if a pumper at a car fire looked threatening.

"And you might take a look at the passenger side of the Humvee," added Cap, meaning look at F-U-E-G-O spray painted in yellow. The mayor didn't move, but nodded to a black shirt to take a look, but he took his sweet time about it and didn't seem surprised, so then, any doubt about the situation disappeared, or you could say the reality came into sharp focus for us.

"How are you, Richard," the mayor said to Dicky boy.

"Fine, Mr. Acklee."

"And he's doing a terrific job for a rookie," said Cap as he put his big hand on Dicky's right shoulder and nudged him back toward the engine. "Drain the line and repack it."

Kim didn't need direction. She stowed the Halligan and helped me with the hydrant line. I'd already shut down the hydrant and the pump and we both climbed up on the pumper to drain and pull the five inch hose back aboard. Cap stuck right by Dicky and helped repack the 150, then shoved him up into the cab for the ride back, never giving him a chance to chat with the mayor again. The black shirts eyed us as we drove away. "Head for the city yard," Cap told me, meaning the city storage yard off 9th Street where vehicles and supplies were kept for city property and street maintenance as well as diesel fuel. "We need to fill the tank. It's going to be a long night."

Fortunately, for safety reasons, the diesel pump stood out in the asphalt yard away from any building and I made a U-turn to face Engine 10 out before stopping with the pump on the driver's side. Cap knew that meant no one could see us at the pump, at least nobody in any of the buildings. He took a quick look around, then stepped down and told Dicky to follow him around to the pump. "You need to learn how to do this," he said, but the moment Dicky moved behind the cab on the pump side, Cap pulled the Glock he'd taken from the kid and jammed it right into his rib cage and whispered in his ear. "You move, you're dead white man." Cap liked to play Hollywood Indian on occasion to scare the shit out of someone.

"What the hell?" said Dicky, either falling for the stereotype or genuinely surprised, I'd guess, that we were smart enough to add two and two, even though all three of us had college degrees. Cap had his in fire science from the University of Maryland. Kim had hers in biomedical sciences from Cal. Me? A humble degree in sociology with a heavy dose of political science from Oregon. And before the time of troubles, I loved to read fire history on duty on a slow night and an occasional novel.

"Where are the wires?" Cap whispered.

"The wires?

Cap nodded to Kim. "Get the Halligan and help him get the point."

One end of the Halligan, the firefighter's best tool, has a sharp pike at a right angle to a small adze blade. The pike has dozens of uses such as yanking padding locks off doors or for convincing lying SOBs to tell the truth . Kim turned the pike up under Dicky boy's crotch. When he started to block her, she simply said, "Don't move" and lifted higher before he could get his hands on it. Even his turnout trousers would not protect him if she yanked the bar up further.

"Look, I . . ." Dicky sputtered.

Kim pulled up on the Halligan, Cap shoved the Glock into his ribs a bit harder. "You're either with us or against us," Cap whispered. "We know what's going on." The bluff worked.

Dicky opened his coat and his shirt and pulled the wire out. Cap ripped the mike off, dropped it to the pavement, and crushed it with a heel. "Where's the other one?"

"I don't know what . . . ouch!" Dicky buckled to protect his balls from another hit by Kim. "The flag decals on the dash and pump panel. Cap used his pocket knife to pry them loose and cut the wires. "When we get back to the firehouse, you find and remove all of the others."

"If my father--" Dicky started to say as I finished fueling and

Cap shoved him back into the cab.

"Your father may find you dead and scalped in the morning," said Cap without further explanation but the message stuck. Dicky cooperated. Maybe out of fear, maybe because of a slight hint of respect, though I doubted the latter at the time.

As we left the yard, a Humvee showed up to provide escort back to the fire station where the Chief waited for us as I backed up the ramp after Cap, Kim, and Dicky climbed down. Dicky and Kim nodded at the Chief. "Good afternoon, sir." Then walked back into the firehouse while Cap stopped for a chat. The Humvee pulled to the curb and parked.

Cap spoke first, eye to eye. "Did you get an ID on the corpse yet?"

"No," said the Chief, thrown off balance a second by the question, but before he could say anything else, Cap added: "Check the dental records against those of the chair of the university journalism department."

The Chief didn't look surprised, which didn't surprise Cap.

"And tell Councilor Spalding that Richard is doing a terrific job. He'll be able to complete his shift without any problems."

"Captain Pierce, you're fired if anything . . ." the Chief started, then stopped.

"Chief Buttridge, it's very simple. We're all you've got. Our job is to protect this town no matter who is in City Hall, and we're going to do that until 8 a.m. tomorrow morning. If you fire us, you have nobody to stop the arson, no matter who is lighting the fires."

"What do you mean by that?" said the Chief.

Cap didn't explain, but finished with this before walking back into the firehouse and closing the overhead door. "Those volunteers have no training. If we don't respond, the next one could get out of control and then you'll have more than you can handle, which means a big black column of smoke rising up into clear autumn skies, smoke visible for miles around."

The Chief left for City Hall, but the Humvee remained parked in front of the firehouse.

Log: 1421 Friday, 18 November 2016: Fire in basement dorm room. Legitimate call (no arson suspected) with fire caused by illegal grow lamp igniting curtains. Knocked down with inch and a half. Ended 1435. Went directly to next run.

Journal: In a B war movie, this would be the before-the-big-battle scene where the soldiers sit around sharing bits of information about themselves, hopes and dreams, a maudlin moment to let the audience know that human beings (except for the faceless enemy) are about to be killed. But we didn't have time for that and we all knew each well enough already; we wanted to use the moment to pump Dicky for information to try to connect the dots, to see if a pattern to the arson fires existed other than the word F-U-E-G-O appearing several times already. Kim suggested Free University Employees or Get Out. I suggested a literal translation as reason for the City Council wanting to point the finger at the Hispanics on the south side of town. Dicky said nothing. Cap said a radical is a radical, and we had to put the fires out no matter who started them--and stay alive.

We knew Dicky had been planted by his dad and therefore the City Council to keep an eye on the last three union firefighters working, and we suspected they'd try to use information generated by Dicky and eavesdropping from the spyware bugs to build a case to get rid of us with trumped up charges. Getting rid of white male union firefighters had been easy; their only option was filing an unfair labor practice complaint with useless Employment Relations Board, a board dominated by right-to-work Republican appointees. Getting rid of Kim, Cap, and me meant an ERB complaint followed by a big fat civil rights complaint.

So no, Mr. Lawyer, we didn't kidnap the kid. We had to protect ourselves. We had to know where the bugs were hidden. We had to know what he'd been reporting, and, by the time we pulled a loaded pistol on him shortly after a murder-arson fire, we felt a need to protect ourselves. As long as we had Dicky with us, we had leverage. Not sure why the Council didn't just find some other white guy off the street they could sacrifice. Maybe they didn't feel they could trust anyone other than a relative, which made sense given their pattern of awarding no-bid contracts for city services they thought best handled by free enterprise, which meant all city services. The tea partiers promised to cut property taxes in half; but they never mentioned the big shift in revenue that went to the private contractors who then charged a fee and paid kickbacks to Council members. A tax by any other name. A fee for garbage disposal, the law enforcement fee, a law enforcement service fee (if you called a cop, you paid added charges), and the same for fire and emergency medical services. A base fee and a use fee on top of that if you used the service. But no competition, so no real free enterprise. The city still had only one fire and one police department, and it's hard to comparison shop when your house is burning down. A monopoly by any other name, and a public service run by a private company is a formula for corruption that makes government anything other than efficient. But I digress.

Cap acted on instinct and told us after lunch to the stuff our turnout pockets with food and put a liter bottle of water each in the engine just before the building alarm rang in from the Cheney Dorm, one of the old three story brick dorms just off campus the university had recently renamed after famous far right politicians. "Engine 10 responding."

The Chief didn't bother to respond because he thought the box to be a false pulled on a Friday afternoon by some drunk sophomore getting an early start on inebriation or because he knew where the arson fires would be ahead of time and this wasn't one of them, although we had no direct evidence of the latter at the time. Besides, they had the black shirts in a Humvee and Dicky to keep an eye on us, or so they thought until we squashed all the bugs. The ones we knew about. We still needed to sweep the firehouse.

Smoke odor and a light haze filled the street in front of Cheney Dorm and students had emptied the building when the alarm sounded. They coagulated on the sidewalk to watch the show. First due, Cap gave the size up for dispatch and any other responding companies to hear. "Odor of smoke. No visible fire. Building alarm sounding. Residents evacuating. Investigating." That last word meant we needed to find the origin of the smoke, because, yes, where there's smoke, there's fire, and we don't spray water on smoke.

"Hydrant?" I asked.

Cap nodded and looked Dicky in the eye. "Pull the 150 and have it ready at the entrance. Kim, you're with me. I got the light. Grab the irons." The irons were the Halligan and the fire ax.

As Cap and Kim hiked down the walkway and disappeared into the building, I grabbed Dicky. "Pull that 150 as soon as you pull the hydrant line down the block with me. See that hydrant?" I grabbed the connection of the five inch hydrant line, put it over my shoulder and walked away from the engine toward the hydrant for ten feet, stopped, turned, put the connection over Dicky's shoulder, and said, "See how that's done? I'll be right behind you with the wrench to smack you upside the head if you do anything funny or try to run home to daddy."

I got no argument from him, and he did help me connect the hydrant, and did seem to listen to my instructions when I told him how to open the hydrant--when and if we needed to. "Now get the 150 and haul the nozzle to the door like Cap said," I told him, and he pulled the cross lay pre-connected hose to the door and waited.

But only for a second. Kim shoved the door open, jammed it open with the ax before turning to her left, and smashed out the second window from the door with the Halligan. The usual comments floated over from the sidewalk superintendents. "Why didn't they just open it? Why do they have to smash everything? They let gooks join the fire department?" Answer: Standard procedure for ventilation of a fire room. Cap had found the fire right at the window where the curtains had lit up around the window. And yes they do. Sarinya Srissakut serves with FDNY. "Charge the line," Kim yelled over to me, and I opened the valve for the 150. "Water on the way. Dicky hold on." As the line snapped full of water under pressure, Kim followed the kid through the door into the building, or more accurately, she shoved him through the door and stayed right on his back. "Stay low. Take your first right," I heard her bark, and a minute later, water shot out through the window just as the next alarm toned in on the radio.

Log: 1435 Friday 18 November 2016: Fire in stairwell trash can in admin building. F-U-E-G-O spray painted on the wall, but fire confined to a trash can as in library and put out quickly, but building sprinklers fail to operate. Chief inspected sprinkler problem. Ended 1503. Went directly to next run.

Journal: "Engine 10, respond to the university admin building. Reported fire in the basement."

Basements seemed to be the popular location for fires at the moment.

Cap keyed his mike. "Send Engine 14."

"Engine 14 is out of service."

"Engine 12?"

"Standby duty at the apartment fire until investigation is complete."

"Be advised our response will have a slight delay."

"Noted Engine 10."

We were the only engine company for an entire city of 60,000 people, which needed at least five engines companies, two ladder companies, and one squad.

"Is the ladder company available?" Cap asked.

The Chief decided to comment from wherever he sat. "You won't need one."

"Noted," said Cap who smelled a dereliction trap. "Dispatch. Fire under control at Cheney Dorm. No extension. Picking up and responding to the admin building."

"Engine 10, received."

Cap didn't know if the fire went into the walls or up into the ceiling or not. He knew an illegal pot grow lamp ignited the curtains and that they'd soaked down the room. Cap tossed the lamp on the lawn when he hurried out of the dorm and grabbed the ax from the door and the Halligan from Kim. She and Dicky fast drained and repacked the pre-connect after I shut down the pump and jogged to the hydrant, disconnected, and hauled the dry line back to the engine. Cap and I repacked in record times, then we four were aboard and blasting students out of the way with the air horn for the three blocks up the street to the five story admin building, a fully sprinklered glass tower. At least if the dorm re-ignited, we didn't have far to go.

Well, the Chief decided to show up for this one, most likely for the same reason he showed up at the library. The admin building housed the university president's office on the top floor. "Bring the can," the Chief radioed as I pulled up to the front of the building and set the air brake. "Small fire confined to a garbage can in the stairwell, basement level."

And that was that. Kim doused it with the pump water extinguisher, the can, while Dicky stirred the charred contents with the short pike and Cap wonder aloud to the Chief how a trash can ended up on the stairwell and why the sprinklers hadn't triggered. "Who called it in?"

"One of the staff using the stairwell smelled the smoke."

"Noted," said Cap. "Why didn't the sprinklers start?"

"Confined fire," said the Chief.

"And how did the trash can get into the stairwell? This is a building fire escape and should have no combustibles on the stairs. None."

"I'll investigate," said the Chief.

"Will you investigate the F-U-E-G-O graffiti painted in the stairwell?"

"I'll investigate," said the Chief, as in, Don't ask me again.

"Let us know what you find out," said Cap. "Kim, Dick, pick up."

"Engine 10."

"Go ahead dispatch," answered Cap.

"Respond to Cruz Elementary School. Automatic alarm."

"Engine 10 responding," said Cap.

"Let me know what you have," said the Chief. "I need to speak with the university president and then I'll meet you at the school."

Cap paused. "And get that damned Humvee off our tail."

"Security," said the Chief. "For your protection."

Glad we didn't have any line stretched. The newly renamed Cruz School stood on the far south side of the city. Usually Engine 14 would be first due and Engine 10 second due. Usually.

Log: 1448 Friday, 18 November 2016: Working fire in preschool classroom at Cruz Elementary School. Big crowd from Hispanic community present. Teacher and Chief injured. Three fatalities. Incident ended at 1541.

Journal: The automatic alarm changed quickly to a specific incident with phone calls about a known structure fire in the kindergarten classroom. The good news? The kindergarten classroom stood apart from the main brick school building. It was a 30x75 foot double-wide mobile home or, if you wish, a modular prefab building, a so-called temporary classroom the City used to, you guessed it, save money. More effectiveness, efficiency, and economy. At least they added a wheelchair ramp to comply with federal law, but no fire protection other than one pull station right outside one of two entrances and one extinguisher on the wall behind the teacher's desk. Fifty kids shared the place in the morning, and another fifty in the afternoon. One part-time kindergarten teacher for each session to avoid paying benefits to a full-time teacher. And no assistants. Volunteer parents and university students provided the added help needed to manage fifty little bundles of energy who had fire drills only at recess, meaning line up at the door.

The inside had all walls removed but for the bathroom to provide as much open space as possible. A kitchen, counter, and storage cabinets stood on the wall opposite the two doors both built into one side at either end of the room. They opened onto a half acre grassy playing field enclosed by a chain link fence.

According to the state fire marshal report I read after the fire, one of the assistants smelled the smoke twelve minutes before the end of the afternoon session, shortly after final recess, and had to go find the teacher, who had stepped outside a moment with a parent to talk because the classroom had no real private corner for parent-teacher discussions during the sessions.

That delay allowed the wastebasket fire under the sink to get a good start; by the time the teacher opened the door to return to the classroom, smoke billowed from under the sink in that wooden counter, or more precisely, a fake wood counter; a composite board counter with a laminate countertop glued in place. Stuff that burned fast, just as everything does in those pre-fab buildings with all the glue and composite board and plastic. All enclosed like an oven in a metal skin.

The teacher didn't re-enter the room but yanked the alarm and held the door open while she pulled one child after another outside and told them to march across the grass to the far side of the schoolyard. They ran. "Stay at the fence," she yelled. "At the fence. Consuela, at the fence. En la valla! Alto en la valla!" Cruz Elementary had been Chavez Elementary, a Spanish immersion school where Spanish-speaking and English-speaking children learned in two languages and left as bilingual middle school students. The City Council wanted an English-only school, but the teachers union fought that idea until the Council refused to negotiate a new contract and moved more and more teachers to co-called contingent positions, meaning part-time with no contract, no benefits, making career teaching impossible, encouraging resignations, and making it much easier to terminate troublemakers.

Of course, leaving the door open fed air to the fire and pulled the flames out from under the sink. In the three minutes the teacher and the assistants thought they had all the kids out and safety across the yard to the fence, the sink had crashed through the counter and the cabinet crumbled into ash as the fire roared up the wall and into the plenum, the false ceiling that hung on aluminum frame a foot down below the actual ceiling. It rolled toward the one open door and the teacher had to back off before she could close it. In fact, the flames on her clothing had to be smothered after she set a good example and stopped, dropped, and rolled on the grass while an assistant used her sweater to beat out the fire that remained.

Nothing, and I mean nothing gets our adrenaline pumping like a school run. Any large occupancy building makes us move a bit faster, especially one with children or elderly or ill occupants. Schools, nursing homes, hospitals, churches, bowling alleys, malls. Kids panic and hide in deadly corners and closets or simply go rigid with panic, which is why the teacher got them moving quickly without stopping to line them up or attempt any sort of orderly departure. Get them out. Get them out. Mass death in school fires proved the rule rather than the exception until major reform to re-engineer school building fire safety after the 1958 Our Lady of Angels fire killed ninety in Chicago. Using double-wide mobile buildings as temporary classrooms defeated fire safety, turned the clock back over a half century, but that's what the City Council wanted to do--returned to a past that existed only in their warped imaginations.

We had to get there with all deliberate speed and we threw the response rulebook out the window when dispatch told us we had a working fire at the school with nobody but Engine 10 responding. All of us but Dicky boy knew the construction and knew the potential for life loss. The hell with the building; we just wanted to be damned sure the kids and their teachers had escaped, and then damned certain the fire didn't jump to the main building.

"Take Western and get around downtown traffic," Cap suggested.

I'd already made the turn, and we made as much noise as possible with the electronic siren and the mechanic siren screaming every inch of the way with the air horn adding to the cacophony of controlled panic, which is not an oxymoron. On runs like that my jaw clinched, I have the steering wheel in a death drip, and all my senses shifted to hyper-aware.

"Tighten up," Cap said, more for Dicky's benefit than the rest of us who already had our seat belts cinched in for the run.

Kim leaned over to the kid and yelled over the noise even though we all had our headsets on, "Get your seat belt as tight as you can get it." He did without a word and with a look on his young face that showed a mix of grim determination--a first--and fear. Fact is, we all had on that game face.

"Has the ladder started?" Cap asked dispatch.

"Stand by," said dispatch.

The Chief answered. "Engine 10, report on arrival and we'll determine if additional equipment is needed. That's the policy."

"Buttridge, we already have a report of a working fire, and we know that classroom building is occupied and we know the construction. Start the ladder." Cap used the Chief's last name only if really pissed off.

"Negative, Engine 10."

You see, with a working fire reported at a school and confirmed with multiple calls from adults, the standard response anywhere else in the country would be an automatic second alarm. Over response is always better than not sending enough equipment and personnel given the potential evacuation challenge and the potential for mass casualty. Always respond to potential.

Cap did not have time to argue with one block to go and a column of black smoke billowing up over the school. "Jay, park it next to that fence. Forget water. Search first."

The best laid plans of men and mice. "Cap, I can't get to the fence." Two Humvees blocked the street we needed to enter and black shirts with three foot batons acted like the parents and others gathering on the sidewalk threatened the public order.

Cap yelled out the window louder than I'd ever heard him before. He tended to be the one at an emergency who rarely raised his voice. Not this time. "Move that goddamned vehicle or we'll drive through it!"

A black shirt jumped into one of the Humvee, backed it off long enough for me to get the pumper through, then moved it back to block the street again.

"Dispatch," Cap said as we stopped at the fence. "Heavy smoke showing. Multiple casualties possible. Primary search started. Give me a second alarm."

The Chief interrupted. "Dispatch. Hold that second until I arrive to confirm."

Confirm what? The screaming and crying kids at the fence and the teacher rolling on the ground and the fire rolling out through the open door with a now useless automatic closer. Cap stopped long enough to check on the teacher and ask if they'd done a head count of the kids. The teacher gasped and couldn't answer.

"No," said one of the assistants.

"Is everyone out?" asked Cap.

"We don't know," said another assistant about ready to collapse in horror with the thought of a child still inside.

Cap turned to us. "Kim, irons. Everyone in the left door."

The door had to be unlocked during school hours, and but it wasn't. Kim jammed the crowbar end of the Kelly into the door frame, and she and I shoved it toward the building and thanked God or somebody for cheap construction, at that point anyway. The door popped like a Pepsi can and we ducked under the smoke. Cap and Kim went in low and followed the front wall between the doors as far as they could go toward the other end of the room where the fire roared out of control. Richard got down, having learned his lesson about smoke inhalation, and crawled left along the wall that led to the back wall, then a right turn along the back wall with me right behind him. "Fire department," I yelled, "Anybody here?" Kim and Cap yelled from the other side of the room. Then I looked up. "Cap! Ceiling!"

"I see it," he said just as Kim felt the body. "I got one." She scooped the unconscious girl up with her right arm, sucked in a breath, held it, then stood and headed back for the door we entered, feeling her way along the wall. None of us could go any deeper into the room.

"Cap!"

"Get out. Everyone back out," Cap ordered.

"Take a breath and hold it Rich," I said as I grabbed him by the collar of his turnout coat, yanked him to his feet, and reversed direction along the wall as quickly I could to the door where Cap waited until we dove outside. He jumped clear just behind us a second before the flame roared out both doors. Flashover. We would not be able to get back inside until we had the fire knocked down.

I stopped to cough up black spit while Dicky boy did the same. Out of the corner of my eye I could see Kim, who somehow got air, using CPR in an attempt to revive the child. I could hear Cap coughing and calling dispatch for the medics, if you could call them that, and heard the screams of the girl's mother and other mothers and the shouts of the black shirted goons pretending to impose order on chaos. But the crowd pushed through to the schoolyard.

That's when the Chief walked up to Cap and said, "Report." Cap stood up and smash Buttridge in the face, split his lip wide open. "You should probably go the the hospital if and when the ambulance gets here and get that looked at," said Cap without an ounce of sarcasm in his voice. He'd just taken command.

The Chief had been working with Cap for decades and knew damned well that if any battalion chief stood in line next to head the department, it was Cap. Buttridge had political hack stamped on his forehead, and Buttridge knew it. The Peter Principle. He'd risen to his level of incompetence, and also knew, even though he stood four inches taller and forty pounds heavier (mostly flab) that he would not get up if Cap hit him again. Arrest him for assault? Hell no. Buttridge knew that the volunteers weren't trained, and knew, just as Cap did, that we were it. The four of us, if you could count Dicky (with two weeks experience and OJT), were all that stood between the city and a conflagration, especially with an arsonist or two on the loose. We could see the letters F and U and E spray painted on the outside of the kindergarten classroom. The rest had already burned off. You know the report. The investigators concluded that the torch came in during recess dressed as a school district maintenance guy, and lit the fire in the trash can under the sink. He had keys to lock that one door, and he had spray paint.

And Dicky boy was beginning to understand, or seemed to. He really wasn't as dumb as he looked. Without being ordered to do so, he grabbed the five inch hydrant line and hauled it down to the corner, made the connection, and stood ready with the wrench when I yelled "Water!"

"Jay, use the monitor," Cap ordered over his handset.

"Will do." In case you forgot, the monitor is the big stationary nozzle attached to the top of the pumper behind the cab with hard plumbing directly to the pump. It's also called a deck gun or deluge gun because it blasts 500 gallons a minute at 150 psi nozzle pressure at a fire. With limited personnel, we couldn't be polite. We had to hit the fire hard with the big gun to knock it down fast. Besides, with the flashover, not much remained of the kindergarten classroom, which was now definitely temporary.

Cap took the ground ladder off the engine and set it up against the main building of the school, then hauled a preconnect off the engine and climbed the ladder with it. "Charge the line."

I did, and Cap went to work wetting down the flat roof of the main building, appearing in and out of the smoke as I charged the monitor.

The Chief drove the unconscious child and her distraught mother to the hospital after Kim got a pulse and respiration to return.

The teacher, who also had to be taken to the ER for smoke inhalation, never recovered enough to conduct a head count and roll call before the other children left for home with their parents. So we heard. The Chief brought in the volunteer ladder company for overhaul and dismissed us about 90 minutes after the initial alarm before we could get into the burned out building wreckage to get a closer look.

Kim and Richard climbed to the roof to relieve Cap, who descended and stopped by the pumper long enough to say to me, "I may kill that bastard before the day is over."

I didn't ask him which bastard he had in mind and handed him a soaked bandana to wash the soot and sweat from his face.

Log: 1633 Friday, 18 November 2016: Chief stops by the station and tells Cap and crew four things: 1) The child died and the teacher is hospitalized. 2) Fatalities found in the ruins of the kindergarten classroom. 3) The City Council declared a curfew from sundown to sunrise. 4) The Chief resigned effective Monday morning, but was leaving town over the weekend. He left instructions with the Emergency Dispatch Center that Cap was acting chief until 8 a.m. the following morning. He also informed the City Council and the volunteer companies.

Journal: We actually did have time to return to the firehouse after the kindergarten fire. We actually had time to get cleaned up, get something to eat, and to drink a lot of water. We'd never make it through the night to the end of our shift at 8 a.m. Saturday morning if we didn't stay hydrated.

"Days like this are like long distance hiking," Kim reminded us as if we needed it. Or maybe Dicky boy needed it. "We need four liters a day. Keep drinking."

Days like that also took a psychological toll, but those who survived in fire/ems each had a way of staying sane. We all sat around in the kitchen without saying much at first, then Cap told us all we did the best we could with what we had. Nobody answered, but Cap actually turned to the kid and asked: "You okay, Richard?"

He started calling him Richard after the dorm fire, and I had to ask. "Richard?"

"Rich, if you don't mind," said Richard. Maybe Cap decided to use a little reverse psychology and bring Rich into the team rather than having him along as a hostage to keep the City Council and the Chief off our backs for the night. We'd probably all be arrested or fired or both the next day for insubordination, but that had to be the Council's plan anyway, the reason the Chief held back resources we needed at fires until he arrived hoping we'd become overwhelmed and walk off the job or screw up completely.

"Rich," I finally had to ask after two weeks of calling him "Kid" or "Dicky" or "Dicky boy," even though I knew the answer. "What the hell are you doing here?"

He stared back at me a moment, but we all stared back at him, too tired of the game any longer. "What are you doing here?" Kim asked him again.

Rich got up and brought the note pad over from the phone on the counter right by the kitchen entrance to the apparatus floor. With the pencil next to the pad, he wrote first: "More bugs." Then he wrote: "I want to be here now."

Cap took the paper and pencil and wrote: "Where?" And then: "Good. We need your help." The kid had done his part at the school fire, but we still couldn't be sure where he stood. He may have been too frightened to run after we pulled a gun on him and I threaten to hit him.

Rich pointed to the lining of our turnout coats and we each cut the stitching away from a bug, and another in our turnout pants. Another in our helmets. Another in the kitchen. Another in the kitchen phone. Another on the carriage floor. Another in the bathroom. Another in the bunkroom. He also had us remove GPS tracking from our boots and from Engine 10.

Again, after he wrote: "That's all of them, or all I know about." I asked the obvious question: "Why?

"You're being set up," said Rich.

We all laughed at the same time, Cap, Kim, and me. Rich seemed surprised. "We know," Kim said. "It's all been obvious for two years since the Council elections, but we think they didn't move against us because we're minorities, and they did not want to deal with a big fat federal legal action over and above unfair labor practice complaints. Or have any federal people sniffing around town while the changes took place."

"That's right," said Rich.

"We think," I said, "They waited until the national election and the radical right wing of the Republican Party got the White House and the entire congress to start the nonsense they've started right here in river city. Same thing that happened after Reagan's election."

"Right," said Rich, "They planted me as a witness."

"As a snitch who would lie under oath," I said. "You were set up too, kid,"

He looked puzzled still.

"The Council wants you to give the Council's version of what happened today. The Council wants to purify the town by removing anyone the Council doesn't think is white enough or right enough. How they plan to do that, I don't know. We're all Americans sitting in this room and living in this little city."

"But--"

"But your dad listens to too much Fox news and Limbaugh."

He nodded in agreement and half smiled. "My dad told me I had to drop out of college because it was a bad influence. He told me to drive that truck."

"What was your major?" I asked.

"It was going to be journalism."

"Christ," I said and laughed again. "No wonder your dad worried. You'd have to read more than propaganda."

"How do you get over it?" the kid asked out of nowhere.
"Over what?" asked Kim.

"I still hear those kids screaming," Rich said.

"You don't," I said. "PTSD comes with the job. Just don't start drinking like I did."

"Exercise," said Kim. "Sweat it out off duty. You can't let it get to you or you can't do the job. And get your nuts checked once a year." She smiled.

"What?"

"Firefighters have a 100 percent greater chance of getting testicular cancer and other cancers because of all the crap they breath, especially if they don't wear air masks, and you've been sucking it in all day, Richard."

Cap smiled and got up to open the door for the public next to the big apparatus overhead door at the front of the firehouse; he heard someone try to turn the knob. Usually we locked it at 11 p.m. when we tried to get some sleep, but Cap had locked it when he returned from the school. Our security concerns were higher than usual that night. But the Chief had already used his key by the time Cap got to the front of the carriage floor--the Chief and two of the burly black shirts.

The moment we heard the Chief, all of us without a word went out to stand behind Cap.

"You're still here," said the Chief. It was a comment and not a question. Maybe even a compliment.

"Until 8 a.m. tomorrow I have a sworn duty to protect this city no matter who is in office," said Cap. "You here to arrest me?"

Chief Calvin Buttridge paused a second, then turned and nodded to the rent-a-cops who'd walked in with full paramilitary gear from mace to assault rifles. "Wait right outside the door." They did, and the Chief got right to business. "You're in command."

Cap didn't react, but Kim asked about Pilar, the kindergartener she'd revived.

The Chief looked down, then right, then finally meet Kim's eyes. He knew she had two small children at home. He knew we all had kids. He had five kids himself with three still at home. Maybe that made him the no-prisoners career climber he'd always been. He had mouths to feed. Maybe. We all had mouths to feed.

"They worked on her for an hour, but the damage to her lungs . . ."

Kim's eyes glistened with tears for a moment, and I clenched my jaw and got a little misty myself, and I know Cap must have been resisting the urge to pop Buttridge in the face again. "What about the teacher?"

"She's hospitalized with smoke inhalation, but she'll be okay, Joe," said the Chief, addressing the man he'd worked with for decades by his first name for the first time all day.

"Can you tell us what the hell is going on?" Cap asked bluntly.

"No," said the Chief, "I can't. But I can tell you that the City Council has declared a curfew from sunset to sunrise, and that they've doubled the patrols on the streets to stop and arrest anyone who violates the curfew."

"Curfew for what?" I asked.

"Terrorism."

"You mean arson." said Cap.

"The mayor used the word 'terrorism' and declared a state of emergency with suspended habeas corpus."

"Jesus," I said, invoking once again the name of a deity. "The oldest tyrant's trick in the book."

"Richard," said the Chief, "Your father told me to bring you home."

"With all due respect, sir, I'm on duty until 8 a.m. tomorrow morning."

"But, I thought--"

"I'm here of my own free will, sir," said Richard and he moved up to stand right between Kim and me. Well, I'm not sure I trusted little Richard, but he had told us where all the bugs were, all that he knew of. But, no, he still had to work a while longer to earn my complete trust. Still, his gesture proved useful. His father would keep his distance.

"He's with us," said Cap. Kim and I nodded in agreement.

"Okay," said the Chief. "Good luck young man." And he turned as if to leave, then stopped to look back. "Joseph, I'm resigning Monday morning. What's going on here is far beyond anything I'd support, even as a Republican. Far beyond. And I'll be out of town for the weekend. So you're acting chief, as I mentioned. You're in command. I've told the mayor, the City Council, the chief of police, emergency dispatch, and all the volunteer fire companies."

"Given that we're in a state of emergency," said Cap, smiling slightly, "That means, by state law, that my authority at fire and ems incidents supersedes all other authority."

"By state law," said the Chief, and he extended his hand to Cap. "And I'm sorry. I thought I was doing the right thing."

"Apology accepted, Cal," said Cap, and then, "Is the ladder in service? Are Engines 12 and 14 in service?"

"Yes, but no guarantee on personnel with hunting season starting," said the Chief, and "Good luck" as he walked out the door.

The alarm tone drowned out any chance I would have to ask Cap if he trusted the Chief or smelled another setup. We all scrambled to pull on turnout gear and grab helmets and gloves.

"Engine 10 respond to Chevron station at 2nd and Van Buren for a car fire."

Rich pushed the overhead door button and waited until I pulled Engine 10 out onto the ramp, then he pushed the button again to drop the door and hustled to get into the cab. Standard procedure for response at dusk and after dark to make certain no one walked into the firehouse while we were out and stole anything not nailed down.

Or torched the firehouse.

Log: 1745 Friday, 18 November 2016: Car fire, Chevron. Used booster. Ended 1801.

Journal: The car fire turned out to be a fire bomb, a Molotov cocktail thrown at the gas station by a passing car. It landed near one car, but the car moved, and we doused the flames quickly with the booster line.

Log: 1801 Friday, 18 November 2016: Fire bomb, City Hall Used booster. Ended 1811.

Journal: And it seemed the bombers wanted us facing in the wrong direction, north on a one way street with heavy traffic apparently ignoring the curfew, leading to a delayed response while we drove around the block after they headed south and struck again at City Hall at 5th and Madison, tossing a fire bomb against the red brick of the building from a passing car within sight of one of those black shirt Humvees parked at the curb. Or more accurately, they most likely stopped, stepped out of the car, lit the rag stuffed into a wine bottle full gasoline, then tossed it. Lighting a Molotov inside a moving car would be a challenge, not to mention a fire hazard, especially if the car hit a bump when the bomber attempted a toss. Nothing spray painted at City Hall. No stealth arson, but a wide open public fire bombing. We now seemed to have multiple arsonists driving around town.

The black shirts took off lights and siren after the car that bombed City Hall, and we could see them racing down 5th, the one downtown two-way street and thought we heard the pop of gunshots. Cap had me stop the pumper in the middle of the street, and Kim pulled the booster and sprayed what little fire still burned on the sidewalk when dispatch called again, a third time since the Chief decided to leave town.

Log: 1811 Friday, 18 November 2016: Car fire, police assist South 3rd. Ended 1831.

Journal: Just south of downtown across the Marys River word of the dead children seemed to have ignited social fuel and the Hispanics joined forces with the local anarchists still in town who hung out at the south side ramshackle health food co-op that remained open in spite of various attempts to shut it down for bogus health code violations. They'd built a barrier across the four lane South 3rd with cars and vans, but did not close it until the car that tossed the Molotovs downtown zoomed over the bridge onto South 3rd with the Humvee close behind. As soon as the Humvee passed the parked vehicles, they were all moved into the middle of the road, three deep and set on fire. The car being chased, an old maroon Taurus, suddenly stopped and all four young men inside jumped out. Two fired pistols point blank at the Humvee while the other two lit Molotovs and lobbed them right at the hood where they smashed and flared and blocked the driver's view. The Humvee tried to back away but quickly discovered the wall of fire behind and more Molotovs being tossed from the left and right and that's when they called for us as well as a troop of blackshirt backup.

The war had started. For every political force, an opposite and eventually equal opposition emerges, a fact of public life that dictators forget again and again throughout history. Given the level of opposition organization at the South 3rd barricade, it looked like the tea partyiers running City Hall had gotten a revolution, but not the one they wanted.

We saw the barrier and Cap had me stop Engine 10 out of range of Molotovs, and with gunfire popping, we needed to stay back anyway until the rent-a-cops could secure the situation, which might have taken a while once reinforcements arrived. The only other approach to South 3rd, the main drag on the south side of the city was driving through the university campus west of downtown and then south through Avery Park, a green space large enough to offer dozens of additional guerrilla ambush opportunities.

"Dispatch, Engine 10."

"Dispatch."

"Is Engine 14 still out of service?"

"Out of service and will remain so due to mechanical problems."

"Be advised that we can't respond to south side with the 3rd Street blocked."

"Understood."

"Strongly suggest . . . No, this is an order from the acting chief to request mutual aid response from Philomath and Monroe."

"Chief, the city no longer has mutual aid agreements with any adjacent fire districts."

"Well," said Cap, setting the mike back on the dash, "I was hoping she'd forget that. We're on our own. Take the hydrant just over the bridge and, yes, use the monitor."

We stopped at the hydrant and Rich made the connection like a pro, and once again, I opened up with the heavy stream monitor at 500 gpm and blew down the flames right to left. A group of men at the fire yelled at us to shut off the water and, when we didn't, charged at the pumper, Cap had Kim and Rich ready with the inch and a half from the front bumper normally used for car fires. That drove them back. We didn't give a damn about politics and had to stay in operation, which meant defending ourselves.

Log: 1831 Friday, 18 November 2016: MVA, double fatality. Victim recovery using Hurst from ladder truck. Booster line from Engine 10 used for washdown of leaking gasoline. Ended 1912.

Journal: "Engine 10, MVA on 9th at Circle. Possible entrapment."

"Responding," said Cap using his portable. "We've got it knocked down. Pick up." I shut the gun down, shut the pump down, Kim repacked the inch and a half, Rich shutdown the hydrant, repacked the short hydrant line, then we all jumped back in the cab.

I made a u-turn on 3rd in front of the smoldering cars and we took a couple of hits from rocks, then headed back over the bridge into downtown with lights and siren and airhorn blasting through traffic for a long run to the busiest intersection on the north side along 9th Street, a commercial strip that grew up after World War II as the city spread north away from river banks--north, west, and south. You name it, four-lane 9th Street had it. Banks, clothing stores, shoe stores, grocery stores, pharmacies, gas stations, restaurants, fast food, motels, hardware stores, coffee shops, card shops, fitness centers, and lots of traffic.

But we could avoid the mess by blasting our way back through downtown on 3rd northbound. Just north of downtown, 3rd and 4th merged into US 99W for a mile long run parallel to 9th until we reached four-lane Circle Boulevard and took a left. I mention all these route details to remind you that the wisdom of the City Council left one fire engine to cover fourteen square miles, and a run from one side of town to the other could not be done to meet the minimum five minutes or under standard for emergency response. You know, that golden five minutes to stop a fire before it takes off or to start CPR on a heart attack victim before brain damage begins. That five minutes. We did it in seven minutes from time of dispatch to arrival at the intersection of 9th and Circle where a Humvee had broadsided-- deliberately--a Toyota pickup with sufficient force to roll it, which caused the cab to collapse around the driver and passenger. Oh, and the gas tank ruptured.

"Engine 10, on scene. Two vehicle MVA. Two victims pinned. We need the medics." Meaning the bread van ambulance. "And start the ladder company." Even if the untrained volunteers were useless, if one of them could drive the ladder truck to the accident, we'd have access to its extrication tools, especially the Hurst.

"Engine 10, be advised that the ambulance is in service in route to the hospital with two wounded police officers." Most likely the two from South 3rd.

Well, maybe the Humvee that caused the accident would transport once we had the victims out of the wreckage. "Ray, charge the booster and wash that gasoline away while we try to open the can." Meaning pry open the crushed pickup cab.

"They're both under arrest for arson," said the black shirt who walked over to Cap as he walked up to the overturned pickup.

"Good," said Cap without looking up. "You can take them to the hospital and arrest them there after we have them out." And then he dropped to one knee and flashed his light into the truck. Dead. The driver's head had been crushed against the steering wheel by the front bumper of the Humvee, and the passenger's head had bounced off the door window and the pavement. Two dead young men.

But we still had to remove the bodies.

Dispatch called to tell us the ladder had left its station. "Thank you," said Cap, "Tell them to proceed at normal speed. This is a recovery, not a rescue."

"Understood."

"What happened?" Cap asked the black shirt who had the requisite paunch. The City seemed to have recruited their rent-a-cops from truck stops and donut shops.

"This is a police matter."

"At any emergency incident, the fire chief is the ranking officer by state law. I'm the acting fire chief per order of Chief Buttridge. Did you get that order?"

"Yes," said the black shirt, but then corrected himself, reluctantly, "Yes, sir."

"What happened." Not a question. An order.

"We were in pursuit of a suspect vehicle, and they attempted to ram us."

"Looks like you rammed them."

"Before they could ram us."

"With a two-wheel drive unloaded half ton Toyota?"

"Sir, we suspected they had intent to commit arson."

"Why is that? Did they thrown a Molotov?"

"No sir."

"Did you find a Molotov in the vehicle?"

"Sir, they're known associates of the people who threw firebombs downtown."

"They're Hispanic."

"Correct," said the black shirt, thinking that Cap understood.

"I need your name for the run report," said Cap as the ladder pulled up.

Cap turned to the two volunteers who showed up with the ladder truck, one of whom smelled like an open six pack, and asked: "Either of you two have training with the Hurst?"

"With the what?" said beer boy.

"That's what I thought. You can help us roll the truck back over." And all the firefighters and pot-bellied police rocked the truck until it rolled and bounced back down right side up.

Cap turned to Kim. "Get the Hurst and cut that cab apart. Rich can help you. I'll keep the gasoline away from you. Jay," he yelled over to me, "Let's talk."

"Officer," said Cap, talking again to the black shirt. "I want a field sobriety test on both firefighters who arrived with the ladder truck."

The Hurst tool, Mr. Lawyer, used to be called jaws, as in the Jaws of Life when it first entered the fire and rescue services back in the 1970s, because it has two pincers on the business end that either force metal apart or cut through door posts and roof supports to disassemble a crumpled vehicle from around its trapped occupants. It's powerful and it does not throw sparks like the saw would if we cut into the truck.

Kim and Rich had the bodies free by the time the black shirt completed the field sobriety tests. The firefighter who smelled of beer failed, as you might have guessed. The other passed. Cap walked over to the volunteers and keyed his mike to include dispatch in the conversation.

"What's your name?" Cap asked the drunk firefighter.

"Rupert."

"Rupert what?"

"Mudrock."

"Rupert Mudrock, you're relieved of duty for being drunk on duty. Kim Nguyen is now acting lieutenant on the ladder company." Cap faced the sober volunteer. "Understood?"

"But I--"

"Understood" It wasn't a question, especially when Kim and I walked over and stood next to Cap.

"Yes."

"Son," said Cap, "When I served, officers were addressed as 'sir', and I am acting chief of this department. Understood."
"Yes, sir."

"You," said Cap, turning back to the drunk firefighter, "are not to get back on that apparatus."

"Or . . ." said the drunk, a momentary lapse into defiance.

"I will take your scalp," said Cap.

I added, "And he will. He's Nez Perce, butthead. In fact, his last name is Pierce. And he will take your scalp."

Well, if that drunk were dumb enough to take a swing at Cap, dispatch interrupted his stupidity by announcing a structure fire. The co-op. The anarchists apparently had become frustrated with trying to rekindle their burnt vehicles and torched the co-op building right there at the corner of South 3rd and Chapman.

"Engine 10, respond to reported structure fire on South 3rd at Chapman. Commercial building. Visible fire reported."
"You, what's your name?" Cap barked at the sober volunteer.

"Conroy."

Cap didn't wait to ask if that were Conroy's first or last name. "Conroy, you're appointed a full-time firefighter until 8 a.m. tomorrow. You will be paid. Kim, respond with Conroy behind Engine 10."

"Let's pick up," Cap yelled.

The drunk tried to climb into the ladder truck cab after we had all the gear stowed and hose back aboard. Cap grabbed him by the collar, pulled him back, spun him around, and dropped him to the pavement with a left hook that hit like a brick. The drunk didn't get up and the black shirts didn't interfere, being a bit confused now about where their authority stood with minorities in command.

"Engine 10 responding," Acting Chief Joseph Ollokut Pierce

said.

"Ladder 10 responding," said Lieutenant Kim Son Nyugen Douglass.

Log: 1912 Friday, 18 November 2016: Structure fire at co-op on South 3rd. Well involved on arrival. Exterior attack only with 1000 GPM ladder pipe and 500 GPM engine deck gun. Also extinguished rekindle of car fires on South 3rd. Used two hydrants. Job done at 1958.

Journal: The quint is not your father's ladder truck, Mr. Lawyer, and you need a little more technical knowledge about the quint to understand what Cap did to rebuild the CFD throughout the night and, at the same time, stop the City from turning to ash.

I used the term "quint" because our fire department, before the tea party coup, had to replace two aging ladder trucks and also had a pumper nearing the end of its service life, and the quint replaced all three. A quint is a ladder truck built on top of a pumper. The machine is a three-axle big dog that combines the functions of each of five old 19th century wagons. And that's literal. Nineteenth-century fire departments responded in horse drawn wagons: one wagon with the hose, one with the pump, one with the ladder, one with the crew, which is four. The quint combines all four of those wagons and adds a tank of water just as a pumper does. Not to mention a ton of other forcible entry, extrication, and rescue equipment from the Hurst to the Halligan.

And the modern quint has hard plumbing. No more hauling hose up the ladder by a firefighter. A large bore nozzle is attached permanently to the top of the ladder and metal piping runs up the ladder to the nozzle, piping that connects directly to the pump. So the firefighter's job is climbing the ladder with a safety belt to direct the flow of water from the nozzle, although with some ladders, that can be done remotely by the operator from the turn table. But it's better at times to have a firefighter aloft for a view of the fire.

In any case, all that function and all the hydraulics and hardware needed to operate more than doubles the weight of a quint compared to a pumper. We're talking 50-80 tons on ten wheels and three axles hauled by a 500 horsepower Cummins diesel. And it does not turn on a dime, but luckily the ladder pointed in the right direction when the call toned in for the co-op structure fire. The ladder left first, driving a block up Circle to turn right on 99W toward downtown. The black shirts stopped traffic on Circle while I backed Engine 10 through a T-turn, and we followed the ladder back down 99W.

"Engine 10, Ladder 10," Cap said.

"Ladder 10," answered Lieutenant Nguyen.

"Cross the bridge downtown and take the Philomath bypass to 3rd. We can get a look at things from the overpass. If that barricade is still up, push through it and take the hydrant on Chapman. We'll take the hydrant on 3rd just over the bridge."

"Yes sir," said Kim.

"Turn the ladder in the tire store parking lot. Face the truck back out toward 3rd. I don't want you getting trapped back there if we need to respond quickly again."

"Affirm," said Kim.

"I'm sending Rich over to you to climb the stick. You're on pump and turntable. Send Conroy over to us."

"Exterior attack?"

"Most likely. We'll know for certain when we're on the overpass."

The ladder Jake brake shook downtown as Conroy slowed the beast for a left turn onto Van Buren Avenue, the street that connected to the bridge over the Willamette River and became US 34 eastbound out of town. Then it stopped.

I stopped Engine 10.

"What's blocking you," Cap asked Kim on the radio.

"Police."

Cap hopped down out of the cab and walked with extreme purpose up past the ladder where a police barricade blocked the bridge. This must have been when the City Hall powers decided that if the curfew didn't work, they'd trap everyone in the city and then start purging their trapped enemies. Of course, that meant blocking emergency vehicles crossing the bridge to use the bypass to reach the south end of town to respond to, well, the kind of event emergencies vehicles respond to. A building fire. But, of course, nobody thought through the blockade and the black shirts wouldn't make a decision to piss without an order, so Cap gave them another order to move the barricade. They looked confused and didn't move.

Kim looked down and smiled. Cap looked up and smiled. "Drive through."

The ladder flattened the wooden barricades and crossed the bridge all rumble and roar and siren and airhorn followed by Engine 10. Cap called dispatch. "Tell the police that we plan to drive through any barricade if it blocks us from doing our job. They need to get them out of our way before we arrive."

"Will pass the message along, Chief."

"Thank you."

We had a short run of a couple of hundred yards once over the bridge, then a right turn onto the bypass, which was limited access for a couple of miles, meaning we ran flat out to climb the grade leading up to the 3rd Street exit, and we could see the glow by the time we drove onto the off ramp.

"Exterior attack," Cap said calmly on the mike to Kim.

"Acknowledged," she answered, and you could hear the tension in her voice. But for Richard, we'd all been trained as generalist in a small city department, meaning able to operate as part of an engine crew or a ladder company, so Kim knew what to do, but she could not be certain of Conroy and Richard. Time would tell.

The ladder slowed to exit the ramp onto 3rd and made the left turn onto Chapman. Rioters had disappeared into the night, wreckers had started to haul away some of the blackened hulks leaving enough room for the ladder to drive through and turn left onto Chapman. Conroy managed the T-turn in the tire store parking lot across the street from the co-op and faced the ladder back toward 3rd, and Kim had him position the truck in the middle of the street to allow plenty of room to deploy the outriggers, those stabilizer legs that extend out from the body of a ladder truck to keep it from tipping over once the ladder is extended from the back up to a 100 feet with weight at the top and water flowing. While we positioned the pumper at the hydrant on 3rd we'd used before, Kim sent Conroy to us and she and Rich connected the hydrant on Chapman.

"Full extension," said Cap on the radio. "And watch the wires."

"Understood," said Kim.

"Conroy," I half yelled, half ordered as he approached. "Open the hydrant when I tell you to." He didn't say a word but went right to the hydrant wrench and waited. Well, I thought, I hope he knows which way to turn it.

Cap walked over to the pump panel where I connected the hydrant line to the 5 inch intake port. "Jay, soak those vehicles first. I still see a little fire, and we want them so wet we won't have to return tonight."

"Understood, sir," I said.

"Knock it off, Jay."

"Okay Cap. Can we get a pizza on the way back?"

"Sure, if we get back to the station tonight."

"You think it's that bad?"

"I do."

I signaled down to Conroy and damned if he didn't pull the hydrant wrench in the correct direction. Water soon ballooned the hose, and I cranked the pump up to build pressure, then yelled back at

Conroy. "We need you back here." I showed him how to operate the deck gun even after he said he knew how to do it, and told him to soak the cars first right to left, then aim over at the building where flames now rumbled and rippled red and yellow up 30 feet above the roof at the front of the co-op.

Kim had the ladder pipe in action with Rich clipped in with a ladder belt at the top, directing the stream right down dead center into the fire.

"What about primary search?" I asked Cap.

"The store closed an hour ago, if it didn't close before that when the riot started. And we can't risk putting people inside."

Nothing to do then but watch the water pour onto the store, and because the fire had ventilated itself through the roof at the front of the building, we made quick work of it. At times when you can't get into a building to get at the seat of the fire, meaning put water directly on the flames, a siege can go on for hours as heavy streams are thrown into the smoke with hope of reaching the flames. Not this time. Ladder 10 dropped water practically right on top of the fire and we tossed a long arc onto the roof of the building to prevent spread and embers from flying around the neighborhood.

Usually at this time, ten to fifteen minutes into a working fire, under normal circumstances without censorship, a reporter would show up and maybe bring a camera along, just after we'd secured the water supply and seemed to be doing nothing but standing around. Well, we were. Nothing left to do but keep an eye on pump pressure and take a break, especially nearly 12 hours into a 24 hour shift when we'd been going almost nonstop. In fact, I said, "Cap I hope we can take a break after this one. We need to eat and drink plenty of water, and I have to take a piss. Can you watch the gauges?"

"Go ahead," Cap said. I walked over to the curb and just started to piss when guess who showed up. Not a reporter, but hizzonor himself, the mayor of our fair city, Wallace Theophilus Acklee, whose close friends called him Wally, the same Wally who'd paid us a visit downtown early in the day during the car fire at City Hall. His parents had named their son after George "segregation now, segregation forever" Wallace, once governor of Alabama who stood in the schoolhouse door to block integration. The mayor's middle name is the same given as a first name to Theophilus "Bull" Connor, the infamous Birmingham, Alabama commissioner of public safety who kept the white public safe by using dogs and fire hoses on black civil rights demonstrators who wanted to end the separate and unequal laws. Wally's parents had left the South for Oregon to get away from "the colored." They figured they'd find white nirvana in the land of the Cascade Mountains but for those other people like me born to parents who left the East to escape entrenched racism. None of those parents read much history and realized that Oregon, as elsewhere, had its social problems rising from the bottomless depths of human ignorance and concomitant stupidity.

Oregon had a very active KKK in the 1920s as much of the country did during a time that included reactionary politics just as any other time in American history. Nor did Mayor Wally know that Cap claimed to be a distant relative of William Clark, as in Lewis and Clark. The Corps of Discovery did not limit their observations to flora and fauna, and Lewis and Clark spent quite a while with the Nimiipuu going and returning from the soggy Pacific shore, especially in early summer of 1806 while they waited for the snow to melt out of the Idaho mountain passes before crossing them on their return trip.

The mayor did not arrive alone, of course. Along with his cigar, he brought Rich's father, Richard Spalding, Sr. and four black shirted goons, each carrying an AR-15 as visible evidence of their paranoia. I resisted the temptation to turn and piss on the mayor's shoes when he walked right up to Cap and said, "We have a problem,

Joe." They were not on a first name basis.

Cap returned the insult. "We can discuss it after this fire is out--Wally." That didn't help, but as I mentioned, Cap was a great fire officer and a lousy politician.

"You hit the chief and a firefighter today."

"Three kids died today thanks to incompetent leadership. The firefighter was drunk."

"I'm relieving you of duty."

"No you're not," said Cap, almost laughing in the mayor's face."

I zipped up and stepped over next to Cap and started my Stepin Fetchit (Lincoln Theodore Monroe Andrew Perry) act with the requisite really big grin, which always confused the hell out of them because I was high yellow and could pass on occasion. "Massa mayor, whooze you gotsa be chief if Cap be gone?"

Cap failed to see the humor and told me to knock it off but repeated the question: "Who is my replacement?"

The mayor glanced at Rich's father.

"What's your fire service education and experience, Mr. Spalding?"

Spalding didn't answer. They both knew the answer was none and both knew the Cap had no intention of turning over his responsibilities to a political hack in the middle of a structure fire without documentation or cause. It was a bluff intended to intimidate.

But Spalding did ask for his son. "Where's Rich?"

"Top of the ladder," said Cap and keyed his handset. "Rich, you're dad says hi."

"Hello dad," came the answer from the top of the ladder.

"Tell him to come down," said Spalding.

"Can't do that, sir," said Cap. "He's still on duty and needed, and he told you earlier that he intended to work to the end of his shift, which would be about twelve hours from now. So I'd suggest you and the mayor go back to City Hall and stay the hell out of my way."

"You can't--" the mayor started to say.

"I have the full backing of state statutes," said Cap, then keyed his mike again. "Lt. Nyugen, rotate the ladder this way for a moment. We seem to have a hot spot right at the engine."

What looked like a waterfall walked across the intersection toward Engine 10 while I told the mayor in my college-educated English that "Chief Pierce is the best qualified person to lead this department with his degree in fire engineering from the University of Maryland, the best school for fire engineering in the United States. . . ." But I didn't have a chance to add anything further because, well, let's do the math. 1000 gpm from a ladder pipe dropping your head is 8000 pounds of water per minute, or 133 pounds a second. Imagine being caught in one of those thunderstorm downpours that forces you to stop driving and pull to the side of the road until it lets up.

Mayor Acklee, Spalding, and their goons stood their ground as long as the mayor refused to budge and tried another bluff. "You're under arrest for assaulting . . . ," he yelled over the din of the deluge. Cap and I stood in our turnout gear complete with helmets watching them get soaked head to foot. We heard what sounded like a short laugh from behind us somewhere up near the deck gun where Conroy was stationed.

Cap yelled back from under the downpour nose to nose with hizzonor, who was having trouble staying on his feet. "The Chief left town voluntarily at the end of his shift and officially transferred authority to me and nobody else. I will not relinquish that authority, and if you threaten me again, I will call the state police and have you arrested for interfering with the sworn duty of a public safety officer during a general emergency and for allowing drunk firefighters on duty." The use of plural "firefighters" was Cap's bluff, but it worked.

The mayor and his sopping wet entourage turned and scurried away without another word.

Cap ordered the ladder pipe back over the smoldering co-op. "Shut down the monitor and pick up," he told me, and I did and saw the black school bus with barred windows for the first time down on 3rd Street where black shirts were forcing male Hispanics aboard for a trip somewhere. The County jail downtown did not have room for them all, which begged the question of where they would be housed, and I could also barely make out the first two of five words in white on the side of the bus: "Free Union . . ."

Log: 2005 Friday, 18 November 2016: Car fire Fred Meyer's parking lot King's Blvd and Buchanan. Incident ended 2027. Went to Engine 12 firehouse.

Journal: "Engine 10, respond to reported car fire, parking lot of Fred Meyers at King's Boulevard and Buchanan."

"You thinking what I'm thinking?" I said after we had Engine 10 turned back toward downtown for a long crosstown run to a small shopping area just north of campus anchored by one large food/department store, Fred Meyer.

"They have a scanner," said Cap, then he keyed the mike. "Kim, we're taking this run. Do not bother with overhaul. Get picked up and back in service and return to Engine 10 quarters. Do not return the ladder to Engine 12 firehouse until notified."

"Okay, Cap," came the answer. "Want me to drive, I take it."

"Yes. You and Rich stick together. Conroy stays with us."

"Acknowledged," Kim said.

"Dispatch, copy."

"Copy," said dispatch, and "Be advised we've got multiple calls on this car fire. May be more than one vehicle involved."

"Understood," said Cap, and I offered one other observation as we rumbled through downtown and zig zagged through the grid to take 5th northbound until it took a ninety degree left turn to become Buchanan. "Traffic has gotten light."

"Guess they finally enforced the curfew." He leaned back over his left shoulder to look right at Conroy. "Headset." Cap tapped on his own earphones. Conroy put his earphones on. The driver and all other riders in fire apparatus have a set of headphones with a mike connected to an intercom so people can talk and hear each other over the noise during a run. With the diesel vibration, both sirens cranked up, and the airhorn, a responding fire engine makes extended conversation impossible otherwise.

"Okay Conroy," said Cap, "What's your story?"

"Don't follow."

"I've never seen you before, and I've been with this department for nearly two decades, and I know and knew all the career and volunteer firefighters. You're not one of them, but you seem to know what you're doing. Where are you from, and I need an honest answer. No bullshit. Are you a career firefighter?"

"Yes. They brought me in to run Engine 12."

"They?"

"The mayor and the other chief."

"Buttridge?"

"Yes."

"Brought you in from where?"

"Detroit."

Cap and I glanced at each other with what a standard "What the fuck?" look. "You're a Detroit firefighter?"

"Yes sir. Laid off."

"Cap hit the air horn to get that Humvee out of our way."

He did and we blew through the intersection, nearly clipping the Humvee that pulled over at the last second to let us by, then got in line behind us for the drive along Buchanan past the high school to Fred Meyers one stop shopping.

"This what you expected?"

"No. They lied. They told me I'd command an engine and a ladder company, and they gave me a bunch of drunk volunteers with no training. I thought you had a combination department?"

"Used to," said Cap, "And a damned good one. You're on the nozzle. Pull the 150 preconnect. Jay, stay on the street and let's use the tank so we don't have to stop at the hydrant. This is probably a distraction while they set something bigger."

"Dispatch, Engine 10 on scene. Two vehicles involved in Fred Meyers parking lot."

"Understood, Engine 10. We have a call for a structure fire at the corner of Tyler and 2nd Street."

"Ladder 10, are you available?" Cap asked without going through the dispatcher.

"Ladder 10 responding," came the answer from Rich who handled the radio while Kim negotiated downtown with the beast. And in case you're confused, Mr. Lawyer, in a fire department, an engine or ladder or any other rig is in service when they're not committed at a fire or any other emergency call. Once committed at an emergency, the rig is out of service, meaning not available for another call until the emergency clears.

"Understood," said the dispatcher.

Cap keyed his portable as he climbed down from the cab. "Ladder 10, that location is probably a boarded up derelict, single-story home. Do not enter. External attack."

"Understood," answered Rich.

Conroy pulled the preconnect like a firefighter with years of experience, meaning he hooked the loops with his arms to drop the whole load on the ground, then grabbed the nozzle and a loop and dragged the line toward a very boiling hot Honda CR-V with someone's groceries cooking inside and the shrub burning on the street side. That shrub looked like a second vehicle from a distance.

Cap helped stretch the dry line to avoid any kinks, then yelled back at me, "Charge it!" And I opened the valve. Motor City man, Conroy, read the fire correctly, noticing, even in the dark, that the origin lay under the front of the Honda, and not the engine compartment or the gas tank. Someone had dumped fuel on the ground and lit it off. Arson again. He knocked down the shrub flames, and changed the spray pattern to fog and aimed the water down under the front bumper and pushed into the smoke with Cap right behind him. Smother fuel fires. They had it knocked down in five minutes, working from the seat of the fire up and back to the rear of the vehicle.

"Ladder 10 on scene," said Kim on the radio.

"Report," said Cap.

"You're correct. Abandoned single-story home corner of Tyler and 2nd. Heavy fire. External attack with ladder pipe from top then right through the front door. One hand line to douse hot spots, embers. Second due protect exposures on arrival." Translation: Kim would set the ladder up in the middle of the street to allow room for full extension of the outriggers, connect to the closest hydrant, then raise the ladder without extension above the house high enough to knock down the flames with the ladder pipe at full volume of 1000 gpm, then drop the ladder to horizontal to the ground or low enough to point the nozzle right into the house, right into the front door, and if the door had not burned away or remained closed, it would be blown off its hinges by the force of the water. Rich would not need to be on the ladder, which meant he could pull the preconnect and knock down embers or douse spot fires, especially any that floated into the power substation across the street. The arsonists, the group that painted LIBERTAD on the street in front of the power station, knew we'd bring everything to knock down the old house with the real concern being protection of the power grid on the north side of town. The second due rig, Engine 10, would take a second hydrant and operate a second handline to wet down the occupied homes to the right and behind the torched derelict.

"Understood," said Cap. "Pick up." All the smoke from the burning Honda had turned to white steam, a sign the fire had died, and ordinarily, we'd stand by until the stream had disappeared also and a wrecker had removed the mess, but Cap had to make a judgment call. While I shut down the pump and helped Conroy drain and repack the preconnect, Cap paid a visit to the Humvee that had shadowed us on the run and parked behind the engine. "Do you carry an extinguisher?"

The black shirts inside nodded "yes" and Cap told them to standby the Honda until it cooled. "If you follow us, I will call the mayor. And be advised that the fire chief is the top dog in town during a general emergency."

No need to turn around. With the hose back on board, we took a left onto Kings, then headed back downtown lights and siren and airhorn even though the traffic had all but disappeared.

"Did you see the sidewalk?" I asked.

"No," said Cap.

"L-I-B-E-R-T-A-D painted on it."

"What happened to F-U-E-G-O?" asked Cap.

"Freedom Unity Equality and God in Oregon," Conroy said.

"What?" said Cap, then turned back to Conroy. "The hell is that?"

"The organization that brought me here and all the other people working out at the old HP plant."

"Membership a requirement for the job you took here?"

"Not directly, but they said conservatives ran the city council."

"You're a conservative?"

"Only to get the job. I vote Republican but I'm union."
"They didn't say how far to the right, did they?"

"No sir. Should have figured it out. They made me resign from the union to take the job at half the pay I earned in Detroit."

"Just so we're straight. I don't give a damn about party affiliation. Our job tonight is to keep this town from burning to the ground."

"You think it's that serious, Chief?"

"I do. Engine 10 to Ladder 10."

Kim keyed her portable. "Ladder 10."

"Do you have that hydrant at Tyler and 2nd?"

"Correct. Ladder and one line operating. Situation in doubt." That last phrase is common in fire service communication to mean the fire is not yet under control.

"Understood. We're taking the hydrant at 3rd and Tyler. We'll use the deck gun from behind, then soak exposures."

"Blow the building down," I said.

"Yup," said Cap.

And that's what we did. The fire had the home and all the overgrown brush and bushes next to it in the overgrown yard, all of which lit up the block and sent embers flying across the street at the electrical substation, which was, did I mention, just down the street from a three-story Super 8 motel. Neither extension would have been a good thing--to either the substation causing a blackout or to the motel causing a mass evacuation problem.

But with a professional crew, we had a hydrant line charged and the heavy stream monitor in operation from a perfect position in five minutes. Cap took the hydrant knowing already that Conroy could handle a monitor and knowing enough about Detroit to trust that Conroy knew the tactic. With abandoned house fires, Detroit did a primary search if possible, but with heavy volume of fire on arrival, backed out for an external attack. No firefighter's life equalled a derelict building. Detroit, by the way, in 2011, responded to one structure fire an hour, many of them abandoned homes and buildings, many of them arson. Detroit could commit two engines and two ladders at a worker and not have to worry about having backup to cover for the companies committed at a working fire. We had one engine and one ladder and no reliable backup.

After we knocked down the bulk of the flames, Cap walked over to Kim and made certain he'd turned his handset off when he said, "We're taking a ride to Engine 12 firehouse without notifying dispatch. We think we have arsonists on both sides of this war, and both sides are listening to our radio traffic. Soak this down, forget overhaul, tell dispatch that you're on fire watch, but leave for fuel and return downtown to the Engine 10 house. If we get another call, take it, but I hope it stays quiet long enough for you and Rich to get a little water and rest."

"Understood," she said, "Do you think it's safe to use my cell phone? I need to call Mike to make sure he and the kids are okay."

"Don't use the phone. We'll stop at your house on the way. I'm scared, too."

"Thanks, Cap."

He nodded and turned to help us drain and repack the hydrant line.

"Dispatch," Cap radioed once we'd picked up. "We'll be here for a while for overhaul."

"Understood."

Log: 2101 Friday, 18 November 2016: Visit to Engine 12 station to enforce department rules on alcohol use. Two volunteer firefighters relieved of duty and removed from firehouse. Lieutenant Conroy assigned to Engine 12 as officer. Maureen Conroy assigned to Engine

12 as firefighter. Visit ended with next call at 2131.

Journal: At Kim's small house on Highland Avenue, Cap left the card key for the firehouse with Mike, who said he did not want to wake the sleeping kids and scare them and so far nobody from the city government had bothered them. Cap asked Mike if he'd heard anything new from campus. "Nope," said Mike quietly on the front lawn as we started to leave. "Same old stuff. University is in bed with the City Council and purging tenured faculty as fast as they can but for those who basically take a loyalty oath to the new regime. Otherwise their position or program is eliminated or they're given the option of working part-time with no benefits or resigning with a letter of recommendation. Most of us in English are already part-time, so we don't give a damn. People in computer science can find better paying work off campus anyway. The only new rumor I've heard is about a bunch of anarchists loosely affiliated with sociology and political science; they're the remnants of the faculty union organizers. Might be a violent fringe among them. Don't know for certain."

"Mike, if you need an escort to the firehouse at any time tonight, call me. We'll follow your Jeep downtown with the engine to make sure you're not harassed by the black shirts."

"Thanks, Cap. Take care of Kim for me," said Mike, standing there in jeans, t-shirt, beard, and wire rimmed glasses. The personification of computer geek, tech writer.

"I doubt she needs me to take care of her," said Cap.

They shook hands. Cap returned to the engine, Mike went inside and locked and bolted the front door. He'd be in the living room all night dozing and keeping an eye on the front door and the patio door to the backyard. He and Kim met in the Navy, and they both knew how to take care of themselves.

Then Cap hesitated and returned to the house and knocked lightly on the front door.

"Forget something," said Mike in a whisper when he stepped back outside again.

"Do you have a rating with communication equipment?"

"You need somebody on the radio."

"I might later. Can't be sure I can trust dispatch."

"If we can rig a relay from your firehouse, I'll do it. I need to stay with the kids."

"Understood, and thanks."

"Good night and good luck."

"Drive to Timberhill," said Cap. "We're stopping at Winco to grab a dozen sandwiches and a case of water bottles. No time for pizza."

I drove the mile to Timberhill and Cap continued to question Conroy. "What's their plan?"

"Set up what they call a 'true American' community here."

"Meaning getting rid of anybody they don't consider American."

"Right," said Conroy.

"Like Hispanics," said Cap.

"They plan to export them all to California. Bus them down there and drop them at the state line, although they call it a border."

"What about native Americans?"

"They belong on reservations," Conroy smiled, "I was told that they've had their day."

Cap laughed out loud for the first time all day.

"Blacks?"

"Back to Africa."

"Women?"

"Back to the kitchen."

"Orientals?"

"Back to the laundry."

"So what's the word 'equality' refer to?"

"Whites only."

We all laughed. Conroy had worked in Detroit.

"You got a first name Conroy?" I asked, "Or is that your first name."

"Patrick Jamal Conroy," he laughed again. "Afro-Irish. People call me 'Conroy.'"

"You pass?" I asked.

"That's how I got here."

"You're a frickin mole."

"No, we just needed a job."

After we grabbed the food, Cap kept asking questions on the drive out along Walnut to 53rd and the Engine 12 station. "Any other paid personnel at Engine 12 we can trust?"

"Nope. All of them belong to FUEGO and salute the Confederate flag and would refuse to return to work off duty anyway because they all have second jobs driving around in Humvees."

"Any sober volunteers who aren't FUEGO members?"

Cap got his answer when he walked into the Engine 12 station. Two alleged firefighters lay on the floor passed out next to a keg. "Must be the night shift," Cap said as he kicked the foot of one drunk. "Conroy, pull Engine 12 out of the station and charge the booster line." The only thing they did in response to the noise of the overhead door opening and Engine 12 being pulled out on the ramp was to turn over away from the noise without waking.

Conroy parked the pumper, engaged the pump, stepped down and chocked the rear wheel, opened the booster valve, then hauled the booster line off the reel behind the cab over to Cap. "Here you go, Chief."

"Be my guest," said Cap, and Conroy cracked the nozzle open and soaked the drunks, and that did wake them.

"What the fuck!" said the first drunk.

"What's your name?" the Chief asked in a loud voice.

"Who the hell are you?" said the second drunk.

"Chief Joseph Ollokut Pierce, as in chief of this fire department. Get the hell out of my firehouse."

"This ain't your goddamned firehouse," said drunk number one. Cap nodded toward Conroy and stepped back. Conroy soaked them again.

"God damn," said drunk number two as he jumped up, stumbled into a wall, bounced off, and took a step toward Conroy with his fist cocked. Conroy hit him again and he stumbled back into the wall a bit confused after finally recognizing who had the hose. "Lieutenant Conroy?"

Conroy smiled. "That's right. And you're drunk on duty, a violation of department rules that leads to immediate suspension from duty and termination from employment. Like the chief said, get the hell out of here."

"What happened to Buttridge," asked drunk number one.

"Didn't you get the memo?" said Cap. "Wait, I'm assuming you assholes can read. Jay, be my guest."

I grabbed drunk number two by the back of his pants and lifted him up onto his tiptoes for a quick walk out through the kitchen and out the backdoor . "Sleep it off in your truck, bubba."

"You're a nigg--" drunk number one started to say before he squealed when I grabbed him by the seat of his pants and escorted him out the same door where he somehow tripped and fell right into drunk number two. "It's against department policy to discuss personal politics or religion on duty, butthead. Respect each other; protect each other." I walked back in and tore the stars and bars Confederate battle flag off the wall, and folded it neatly before dropping it in the dumpster right outside the back door of the kitchen. In plain view of the good ole boys, of course.

Conroy took the nearly empty keg off the carriage floor and dumped it with a bang into the back of a pickup parked out back, which belonged to either drunk number one or drunk number two. Back inside he told Cap about the AR-15 in the cab gun rack.

"That's okay," said Cap, "Odds are we're not staying long. You mentioned 'we' a couple of minutes ago. Anybody else here from Detroit who could help, Lieutenant Conroy?"

"My wife. Maureen Patricia Conroy. Irish firefighter."

Well, I thought to myself, that is one solution to the clichéd movie scene wherein the wife asks her firefighter husband to find another job selling used cars or teaching college writing so she doesn't have to worry everyday about him coming home alive or not. Like my wife did. Maybe it's not that clichéd.

Conroy called Maureen on his cell. "They hire women now," he said. "Meet us at Engine 12 quarters."

"Engine 10, respond to a medical call at 29th and Bunting."

"Nature of call?" answered Cap.

"Chest pains. Shortness of breath."

"Responding. Be advised that Engine 12 is back in service."

"Understood."

"Lieutenant Conroy is the officer. No one else."

"Understood."

"Cap," I said and pointed at drunk number two weaving across the parking lot with his AR-15 at port arms. Drunk number one sat in the driver's seat of the pickup with his head out the window, puking. "If you want to take my rifle away from me, you'll have to pry it from my cold, dead--"

"Blam!"

Cap shot once in the air with the Glock fully loaded this time, and I disarmed Mr. Second Amendment and popped the clip out after exercising my Second Amendment right to shoot out all but the driver's side rear tire of the pick up to eliminate the possibility of driving under the influence. We took the rifle with us on the run to eliminate the possibility of being shot in the back if he had another clip in the truck.

Log: 2133 Friday, 18 November 2016: Medical call 29th at Bunting. Chest pains and difficulty breathing. Fire department services not needed. Symptoms abated by arrival. Caller refused treatment or transport. Went directly to the next call.

Journal: The delay in responding because of the drunks did not leave Cap in a good mood on the way up 29th Street to a top of the hill in the northwest corner of town. 29th dead ended but for a left turn onto Bunting next to a trailhead into a "natural area," meaning a city park that bordered the state forest north of town, a big reason I liked living there. Not all black men play football or basketball. Some like to hike.

But we made up time responding because by now the deserted streets had only an occasional Humvee parked at an intersection like a checkpoint on the way back in. In fact, we used nothing but our lights. No need for a siren at all, which is usually not recommended in any case for a cardiac call.

The old sociology axiom held true in Cruz City, Oregon, that the higher your elevation, the higher your income, the bigger your house. Three 4000 square foot, two-story homes with three-car garages sat on big lots on Bunting, each with a panoramic back patio view of the city. At the end of Bunting, a woman waved at us in front of the last house. "He's inside," she said when we pulled up, although her voice didn't have that urgency usually heard on arrival when someone is having a heart attack.

"I'll head in," said Cap, suspicious. "Turn to face out, leave it running, lock it, and follow me inside. "Engine 10 on scene. Report to follow."

Dispatch confirmed receiving the transmission.

After Cap climbed down, I used the driveway for a T-turn and faced the pumper back out toward 29th, parked in the middle of the street, locked the air brakes, and locked the cab doors before walking in.

Cap stood listening and still not happy as I walked in. It turned out to be the home of Arnold "Arnie" Fleischmann, a retired local attorney and former member of the city council. His daughter, also an attorney and state senator for the 8th District, Michelle "Micki" Fleischmann, elected before the coup, apologized a second time for the false call. "My father is fine, but we needed to talk to you urgently and had no other way to do it."

Cap's handset answered for him. "Any available unit respond to Moreland Hall, university campus, Jefferson Way at 26th. Sprinkler alarm. Campus security on scene report fire showing."

Cap answered. "Ladder 10 are you available?"

"Affirm, Chief," said Rich. "Responding."

"Engine 12, available?" asked Cap.

"Engine 12 responding second due," came the answer from Maureen Conroy, firefighter.

"Chief," said Senator Fleischmann, not fully appreciating the radio traffic.

"Who are you?" asked Cap.

"For the second time, Senator Fleischmann. I represent this city in the state senate. The one in Salem."

I politely motioned for her to move away from Cap to the sectional where her cigar smoking father sat in perfect health. "Senator, I know who you are. The Chief cannot answer you right now. What do you need to know, and, if you'll excuse my bluntness, make it quick. We have to respond."

"What the hell is going on? We've been hearing sirens all day and night. My father tried to get through to the City Hall, but nobody will take his call. There's nothing on radio or television or online. I saw these black uniformed paramilitary types all over town when I drove in this afternoon."

"Here's your brief, Senator," I answered, sensing an opportunity. "The mayor and the council have gone nuts. They're changing the city into a military compound, imposed a curfew, arrested Hispanics for deportation, and set fires to create an excuse to impose martial law. In the meantime, before all this, the morons in charge downtown cut the fire department down to one career engine company and the rest untrained volunteers until Captain Pierce took charge today as acting chief after the sudden resignation of Chief Buttridge. Pierce has us back to two pumpers and one ladder with six firefighters total, but that's not even close to what the city needs. The body count today so far is one university journalism faculty member, three Hispanic children, and two Hispanic males."

"You have evidence?" said the senator, practiced at never being shocked and always considering her options.

"Eye witnesses."

"Can't you call for help from Albany and other fire departments?" old man Fleischmann asked.

"The City Council cancelled all mutual aide agreements."

"That's a violation of state law," said the old man.

"Mudrock money is behind this," said the senator.

We all paused as Cap spoke: "Kim, have you been on a Moreland Hall inspection?"

"Once."

"Good. Everybody else listen up. Keep this channel clear. Moreland Hall is fire trap. Half story ground level, two full stories. Cockloft. Brick facade with all else wood. Broad, open central stairwell basement to third floor. Hidden spaces in walls, ceilings, floor. Sprinklered, but ancient piping. Attached fire escapes on the B and D sides of the building. Fire department connection in the front. Copy?"

"Copy," said Rich and Maureen.

"Ladder 10 report on arrival and place the truck in the middle of the intersection at Jefferson and 26th. You have a hydrant on that corner away from the collapse zone."

"Ladder 10, affirm."

"Engine 12?" said Cap, "Location?"

"Harrison approaching 35th."

"Take 35th south, left on Washington, approach up Jefferson. Take the hydrant just down the hill in front of the Dixon Recreation building. Drop from there up to the Native American Longhouse on C side of Moreland. Copy."

"Engine 12, affirm."

"Chief, are you responding?" asked Rich.

"In two minutes, third due," said Cap.

"Senator," I asked, "Do you have any way to make contact outside of town?"

"Well, I'm not sure."

"Good, give us your cell number and the number for the land line at this address," said Cap. "Strongly suggest you remain indoors until contacted."

"Chief, we're quite capable of --" the senator started.

"Senator," said Cap, taking a step in her direction. "By state law, I have full authority as fire chief during a general emergency. Stay inside. You are hereby appointed a member of the fire department. You will remain here for further instructions. Do you understand." That was not a question.

She didn't answer, but glared at him.

"Senator," I said in a more conciliatory tone, "You're familiar with the background of our current mayor? We took down a Confederate flag at the Engine 12 firehouse, and we've been seeing those flags all day. But they haven't burned the synagogue yet. "

She looked toward me and nodded slightly, still angry, and said, "We're Unitarian."

"They haven't burned down the fellowship hall, yet."

"Jay, we have to go," said Cap.

Log: 2141: Friday, 19 November 2016: Structure fire, Moreland Hall, Jefferson Way and 26th Street. Sprinkler system malfunction. Fully involved on east end of building on arrival. One victim recovered DOA. Declared under control at 2301. Went directly to next call.

Journal: Back in Engine 10, headed down the hill, we could see the glow from campus.

"Ladder 10 on scene. Heavy fire second floor A/B corner. Out the windows."

"Understood," said dispatch.

Cap keyed the mike. "Search has priority. Ladder 10 you have the third floor. Enter from the D side using the fire escape."

"Affirm."

"Engine 12, you have the first floor, the half floor. Enter from the C side opposite the Long House."

"Affirm."

"Engine 10 will approach up Jefferson and feed the sprinkler connection, search the second floor, charge an interior attack line."

Again, we encountered little traffic on the run across town north to south this time along 29th, then a clockwise loop around campus to approach from the east up Jefferson Way. Moreland Hall sat a couple of blocks to the west of the library, directly across from the student union building. We had an exposure problem on the B side where Moreland faced Langton Hall, another old brick relic four times the size of 150x150 Moreland. Same ordinary construction of wood and more varnished wood inside with a brick facade. And nobody enforced the rules on keeping Moreland interior fire doors closed, half-assed fire doors anyway, and only on one side of the building, the west side corridor on the third floor. The other side, the east corridor, stood wide open to smoke and fire that would easily roll up the central wooden staircase as well as the elevator shaft. Two large, natural chimneys.

"Sprinklers failed?" I asked.

"They ran sprinkler pipe down the hallways but not into the offices. Sounds like a corner office involved. Take that hydrant just up the hill and drop to Moreland. Feed the sprinklers and feed the monitor if we need it to knock down fire on the A/B corner if we can't get it inside."

Translation, Mr. Lawyer: Cap's tactic was to surround Moreland to both extinguish the fire and confine it, to keep it from spreading to other buildings. He positioned apparatus to do that. The term "exposure" means a building adjacent to the fire building that could catch fire from flying embers or, if close enough, from radiant heat. A fire building (assuming four sides) is referred to by A, B, C, and D sides, with A being the front of the building and the other three sides labeled clockwise around the building.

"Ladder 10. Heavy fire out two windows on A/B corner."

"Understood," said Cap. "Stick with the plan."

"Affirm. Positioning at intersection."

"Engine 12 on scene."

"Stick with the plan," said Cap again, and added, "That Native American longhouse is a new building and the closest exposure besides Langton. It has priority after you complete your search. Set up a water curtain near the B/C corner."

"Engine 12. Affirm. Dropping line from Dixon."

I turned Engine 10 right onto Jefferson Way and usually on a Friday night on campus I'd have to blast up the slight hill with the air horn to clear pedestrian traffic, but, like the rest of the city, the campus streets, but for Humvees parked at intersections, held no students. Or anybody.

At the hydrant, I stopped and Cap climbed down to pull the big five inch hydrant line, then he waited with the wrench as I drove up along the middle of the street to keep the pumper away from the Moreland collapse zone. Old brick buildings have a tendency to fall over once the wood frames and floors holding them up burn out. Or sometimes they drop the roof down to the basement and blow out the wall on the way down.

Air brakes locked, pump PTO set, transmission in fourth, ready to pump. Climb down, wheel chocks in place, connect the five inch hydrant line, key my portable mike. "Open it." Cap did so and then hiked with the wrench up the street to Moreland that had fire rolling up to the third floor windows now.

He stopped on the sidewalk near the main entrance. "Kim, report."

"Third floor clear east, but windows on the A/B corner starting to crack. Floor spongy. Checking third floor west."

"Conroy, report."

"Basement flooded." Well, the best laid plans of men and mice.

"Conroy, force that sprinkler room door and tell me what you find."

Cap crossed the street to Engine 10. "Let's connect anyway, but don't charge the siamese. Then we go in through the main entrance."

I nodded and helped drag and connect two 2.5 lines to the outside sprinkler system siamese feed, then I jogged back and grabbed the irons--an ax and the Halligan. Cap grabbed a light and the 200 foot preconnect and we smashed our way through the locked front door into the main floor, the second floor really, above the half floor below. "Kim, you clear on the third? We need backup on the second."

"Clear. On the way down the fire escape."

"Stop at Engine 10 and charge the preconnect we stretched. Then follow us inside through the main entrance.

"Affirm."

Cap and I left the nozzle at the top of the stairs just inside the second floor, then did a quick check of offices in the west wing away from the fire, looking for lights, banging on doors, but deciding against busting in locked offices unless we suspected occupation. Same across the wide foyer to the east side into smoke thick enough to force us down to the floor. Kim and Rich had followed the charged hose inside by then. "Cap? What's the plan?"

"Chief," radioed Conroy from the basement before Cap could answer. "The main sprinkler feed and standpipe are both cut and dumped water into the basement. No pressure in the system."

"Understood," said Cap. "Back out and set up the water curtain on the C/D corner. Charge your monitor to protect the Long House if needed."

"Affirm."

"Rich, you're on the nozzle," said Cap. "Time for a little OJT. Five minutes, then we rotate. Kim you're behind Rich. Jay and I will pull hose. Aim through that door at the end of the hall. Go."

We left the foyer on our knees down a short hallway that connected to one faculty office and the department chair's office at the A/B corner of the building. We noticed no flame in the faculty office through a glass window in the door, so Rich pushed in toward the chair's office.

"Put the nozzle right through the window," Cap instructed, "And open it."

Rich did so and we all ducked as flame shot out and crawled the ceiling.

"Swing the nozzle left and right at the ceiling and bring it down to the door."

Rich did so and started to collapse. Smoke inhalation, yes, but without a doubt reaction to a dose of pure adrenalin from having fire blown out at his face for the first time.

Cap grabbed him by the collar. "Get outside and get some good air. Understood?"

Rich waved his right hand without speaking as he handed the nozzle over to Kim and crawled back down the hall past me. "Stay low and along the wall," I said.

Kim pushed in on her knees a foot or two closer to the door. Cap ordered me to bust out the lower wooden panel with the Halligan and I obliged, then ducked back as flame shot out. "What the hell is that stench?"

Kim hit low with the water, and pushed the fire back just enough so we could see a body just inside the door.

"Conroy," Cap keyed his mike.

"Chief."

"We need one more preconnect charged from Engine 10 and pulled in right behind us. We have a victim."

"Mo is on the way."

"Maureen?"

"Correct."

"Kim," said Cap, "Can you reach the body if we soak you good?"

"I'll give it a try." And she did, and we did, putting the water right on top of her as she punched out the rest of the wooden panel on the bottom half of the door with her boot and turned to lay forward, prone, to get a hand on the collar of the body, but his sport coat and shirt had been burned through and offered nothing. Kim grabbed him under the armpits instead and pulled back into the hallway next to us and collapsed. "You okay?" Cap yelled. Kim gave him a thumbs up while I handed the nozzle to Cap and grabbed one of the victim's arms as best I could without pulling skin off, and hoisted him over my shoulders for a fireman's carry.

"You got him, old man?" Kim asked crouched in behind Cap to hold the line.

"Very funny."

Cap held the flames away long enough for me to feel my way outside along the wall and down the stairs out through the front entrance, then across the street. "Rich, grab the stokes."

"The stokes?"

"That basket stretcher on the ladder. Bring it over behind Engine 10 with the medical bag. Kim," I called over my handset, "I have no vitals. Third degree on his back, arms, and legs. Looks like a job for a paramedic."

Cap answered. "Do what you can. We're backing out. Looks like extension into the main office. We can't hold here. Mo, stay outside and aim that second line into the window until we get the monitor charged."

"Understood," said Mo.

The victim had been face down, so he still had a face for me to use to start CPR, or try. Since he could feel nothing, I rolled him over onto his back and tried to insert an airway without any luck. Something blocked his trachea. Only after I pulled off my turnout coat and rolled it up to put under his shoulders to get his head to drop back- -standard procedure to straightened the trachea for airway insertion-- did I notice it.

Kim walked over just then with Cap's light, took one look, and told me to cease. "He's gone. No big loss.

"Looks like garden tool." Somebody had shoved one of those round, six inch long root pullers with a wooden handle right into the base of his skull, which explained why the airway was blocked.

"You know him?"

"Mike's boss. A turd blossom. The English chair. The guy who busted the union, turned all jobs into part-time positions, then fired the part-timers who stuck around."

"He looks like Putin. You make the call."

Kim keyed her mike. "Dispatch, this is Lieutenant Douglass, Ladder 10. Patch me through to the hospital ER."
"Stand by."

While we waited, Cap went to the Engine 10 cab and returned with an arm full of sandwiches and water. "Eat what you can while you can. Kim--"

"ER, Ladder 10."

"We have a DOA. I need an MD to confirm the call."

"Stand by."

"Kim, after you confirm, back the ladder down here in front of Engine 10, but leave a clear path for Engine 10's monitor, and connect your hydrant line."

Kim nodded, then answered Dr. Bailey. "Male in his 50s. No vitals. 50 percent third degree burns back, arms, legs. Stab wound at base of skull. Spine most likely severed at cervical vertebrae. Weapon still in place up to the handle. Cyanosis present."

"Confirm DOA."

"Dispatch," Kim added, "Call police. Tell them to bring a body bag."

Cap keyed his mike before dispatch could answer. "This is a crime scene."

Dispatch affirmed and we went back to work. "Engine 10. aim your monitor to the roof. Ladder 10, when you're positioned, extend horizontally to the office window. I'll handle the nozzle personally. Rich, get something to eat and rest. Mo, come on back to get your sandwich. When I'm at the window, return to the nozzle and soak me down."

Show time. Kim backed the ladder away from the intersection down in front of Moreland in the middle of the street, positioning right in front of Engine 10. I charged the monitor and shot water up and onto the roof. Kim didn't have to ask for help with the outrigger setup. Maureen and Rich jumped to it, then went back to their sandwiches. Cap wolfed his down while he waited for the ladder and took a moment to show the black shirts where to find the body; they'd been parked down the street the whole time keeping an eye on us. But they didn't investigate a thing; they just rolled the dead prof into a black body bag, zipped it, then hauled it away to their Humvee. I heard Cap yell, "What the fuck are you doing?" and followed them as he waved at me to climb the ladder.

"Rich, you're on the monitor. Just keep it positioned where it is. Now for a little fun." With the ladder belt strapped around my waist after I pulled my turnout coat back on, I climbed up to the ladder turn table and climbed out onto the ladder toward the nozzle that hung off the end. "Put me right next to that window."

Kim didn't answer, but slowly moved the ladder away from the street toward the A/B corner without raising it until she had me right below the fire. "Mo, you ready?"

Mo opened her inch and a half nozzle and soaked me as the ladder raised. "Show time," I said and turned on the flood light and opened up from twenty feet away, aiming 1000 gallons a minute at 50 pounds per square inch through flames up to the ceiling inside the dead chair's office and lowered the nozzle slowly as the ladder raised me level with the window sill. Then I shot the stream straight into the room, blew out the fire, aimed through the smoke at the door leading to the secretary's office, blew it open, shot water through it into the main office, and let it soak for a while until the smoke turned to white steam. "Mo, put your water through the window. I'm going to the third floor."

Kim raised the ladder up and I repeated the recipe for extinguishment, but this time I turned the nozzle right into the sheetrock and blasted it away from the studs. Overhaul with limited personnel, and I wanted to be sure to get water inside the walls to stop the fire from climbing. If it got into the cockloft, we'd lose the building.

"Soak it good," said Cap, walking away from the cops to back up to Mo on the hand line.

"Will do," I said.

Dispatch: "Any unit respond to Madison and 5th. Smoke investigation."

"Send Engine 14," answered Cap. All units committed at Moreland Hall fire."

"Engine 14 is out of service."

Get it back in service. Or get Engine 16 in service."

Log: 2301 Friday, 18 November 2016: Smoke investigation at City Hall. Delayed response. Working fire on arrival. Building evacuated. Exterior attack only. Emergency communications moved to Engine 10 quarters. Returned to quarters 2315.

Journal: Well, shit went downhill from there on. Cap tried to reach dispatch again, but got no response, which struck him as odd, because City Hall stood at the address given, and nobody would try to . . . "Jay, you're in command here," he told me, and then left to hike back down to his "command car."

"Your what?"

"The cops donated their Hummer to the fire service."

"Donated?"

"That's right. They're assigned to guarding the corpse until the ME gets here. You can reach me on the fire frequency. Get picked up here and send everyone downtown." And he left.

We shut down the hydrants, disconnected the hose, and started to drain and repack it wet after putting the tools away when Cap radioed from downtown. "Engine 10."

"Engine 10, Chief."

"Smoke showing at City Hall. Investigating. Respond with Engine 10 as soon as possible. Note to dispatch. The word ¡LIBERTAD! spray painted on the D side of the building."

And that I did five minutes later. "Engine 10 responding."

"Engine 10, divert to quarters. Repeat. Return to quarters."

"Understood. Engine 10 returning to quarters."

"Engine 12, Ladder 10, return to Engine 10 quarters when ready."

I did not want to ask over the air why he found smoke and then told me to drive away from City Hall, but figured Cap would tell me at quarters, so I drove back to the firehouse and backed into the bay as I would have after any other run. Cap did not show up immediately, but did arrive just after Engine 12 and Ladder 10 pulled up by 2331.

"Everyone inside," Cap ordered.

"Cap, we saw fire at City Hall on the way back. What the hell are we doing here?" Kim took the words right out of my mouth.

Then Kim saw Mike and their sleepy kids. She stopped to give him and the kids a big hug and told them she'd be up to the bunkroom in a minute to say good-night. Mike, with sleeping bags under his arms, followed the kids to the stairs.

"Everyone," Cap said, "That was Mike Douglass, Kim's husband and now director of emergency communications for the city. He's got orders to activate the backup radio, radio, email, Internet, and phone system upstairs. Dispatch thought they were moving from City Hall to here, but they're not. I've ordered them shutdown, although, as you can guess, the mayor will not be happy. But we need to assure reliable communications and make contact outside the city."

"Cap?" I said, about to ask about assignments and using the bathroom.

Cap read my mind. "City Hall has fire in the basement spreading rapidly due to the age of the building. We could confine it like we did Moreland, but our problems have gotten bigger. When I pulled up into the parking lot behind City Hall, I noticed people on the fire escape at the Benson Hotel."

"Any smoke?"

"Couldn't tell in the dark, but smoke from City Hall indicates wind out of the north and west, meaning any fire downtown will move toward the commercial blocks."

"Shit," said the Conroys together.

"Exactly," said Cap. "Arson from all sides, now. We're beyond any single-building tactical response now. We're letting City Hall burn so we can use the limited equipment we have to set up a fire break pumping from the rivers with every monitor we can put into service. We also need to get Engine 14 and 16 down here."

"What about the rest of the city," Kim asked the obvious.

"Outside help as soon as Mike has the radio and phones operational."

"What's the plan?" asked Maureen Conroy.

"The Hummer is mine for mobile command. Jay stays with Engine 10. The Conroys stay with Engine 12. Kim and Rich Ladder 10. For now. I may need Pat later to bring Engine 14 into service as a stationary pump station, and the same with Engine 16 if and until we find competent help. Engine 10 head for City Hall. Dump your monitor through the third floor windows on the C side from the back parking lot. Maybe soaking the third floor will stop spread to the cockloft and the roof and we don't have a big exposure problem there. Do not pull any hose off other than short soft suction to fill the tank. Be ready to move on short notice. Engine 12, Ladder 10, Benson Hotel. Find out why people are leaving."

Cap then keyed his portable. "Dispatch. Test."

Mike responded. "Test received."

"Thanks Mike, "Engine 10, 12, Ladder 10, chief responding to City Hall and Benson Hotel."

"Understood."

"But before you go," Cap told us, "Use the toilet if you need to. Stuff your pockets with all the food we have left in the kitchen. Kim, tell you kids goodnight for all of us. This is the safest place in the city for them tonight. Engine 12 delay your response for fuel. We'll stagger fuel runs. Engine 10, fuel after City Hall. Ladder 10 fuel after Engine 10."

I need to stop here, Mr. Lawyer, because, as you know, the mayor and his minions went after Cap for not responding directly to the City Hall fire. But Cap knew what they didn't know or refused to remember about urban fire history. Like a lot of American cities, large and small in the 19th and early 20th centuries, The Cruz City downtown had been laid out and built in the same flammable grid pattern that led to urban conflagrations elsewhere. The buildings on a block had no separation or stood close together across a narrow alley. The wood construction burned quickly, no large fire break existed but for the rivers east and south of downtown. And, of course, the fire protection budget had been gutted over the last two years following the bad examples of Scott Walker, Chris Christie, Michael Nutter and every other petty governor and mayor of any party who used to Great Recession to attack public service unions. Exceptions like Newark's Cory Booker and Chicago's Rahm Emanuel supported the fire service, but too many spouted the cynical rhetoric of the Haverhill, Massachusetts mayor who said that the city couldn't afford a fire station on every block as an excuse for layoffs. Dumb. But nothing new.

For instance. In 1872, the Great Boston Fire burned for 12 hours, destroyed 776 buildings over 65 acres, and killed 30 people for the following reasons, among others:

- Boston's building codes were not enforced because no authority existed to stop faulty construction practices.
- Buildings owners over-insured and insurance-related arson was common.
- Wooden mansard roofs allowed fire to spread quickly on a block or jump across narrow streets onto other buildings.
- Flying embers and cinders started fires on even more roofs not immediately adjacent to burning buildings.
- Boston locked fire alarm boxes to prevent false alarms, which delayed BFD by 20 minutes on the initial alarm.
- Merchants were not taxed for inventory in their attics, so they stuffed their wood attics with wool, textiles, paper stocks, and other flammable stock.
- Most of the downtown area had old water pipes with low water pressure.
- Fire hydrant couplings were not standardized.
- The number of fire hydrants and cisterns was insufficient for a commercial district.
- Gas supply lines connected to street lamps and used for lighting in buildings could not be shut off promptly. Gas lines exploded and fed the flames.

In April 1908 Chelsea, Massachusetts, just north of Boston all but burned to the ground from a conflagration that started in the rag district and destroyed 1500 buildings. But Chelsea ignored the fire, rebuilt, and expanded its rag recycling businesses to include paper and other highly flammable salvage, a business only encouraged by the raw material shortages during World War II. Business boomed until the war ended, which made the daily rag district fires tolerable. But, of course, when the war ended and business slacked off, tax revenues dropped, and the city leaders in Chelsea cut back on public services, including fire protection, while still having no serious fire codes to place prevention responsibility on business owners.

By the 1960s, Chelsea had become blighted and a disaster waiting to happen--again. Some action started albeit slowly. A 1962 commission recommended removing 302 buildings in the rag district because they all stood condemned. By 1971 Chelsea redevelopment had been approved, but it proved too little too late, because in October 1973, before they could be removed or renovated, the condemned buildings burned in the second great Chelsea fire. The Chelsea fire department and 67 out of town fire companies had to retreat again and again as a firestorm generated winds gusting to 100 miles an hour (a cat two hurricane), as cool air roared in at the base of the flames to replace superheated air exploding upwards. Fact is, the radiant heat dried out buildings ahead of the flames until the buildings literally exploded into fire (see the National Fire Protection Association video on the 1973 fire on YouTube). Water had little effect, and Chelsea had to resort to a tried and true tactic for stopping a firestorm. Find a wide firebreak directly in front of the flame wall and point every gallon of water available at the fire. If necessary, dynamite buildings to create a break as they did during the 1906 San Francisco conflagration following the earthquake. Fortunately Chelsea did have one broad boulevard to make a stand, but several blocks had to be sacrificed to buy time to set up enough heavy streams to confront the fire and finally contain it after five hours from first alarm. Three days later all the flames had been extinguished.

Nine months earlier, the Board of Fire Underwriters issued a warning that Chelsea had the highest potential in the nation for a conflagration. And the weather had been dry. Wildland firefighters would call October 1973 in Chelsea a red flag month, a month with the highest fire danger. Tactics shifted from stopping building fires to containment, to limiting the damage even if it meant sacrificing buildings, or in Chelsea, whole blocks.

That's why. Cap made a judgment call that if he committed his small fire department, which barely had a first alarm capacity, to another building fire like Moreland, then the arsonists would be free to light off buildings all over downtown and we would not be able to react fast enough and the fire would move from commercial to residential buildings. So far, we'd been damned lucky no rekindle had occurred given our nonexistent or superficial overhaul after single-building stops. Besides, Cap had six firefighters who had not had a decent meal, not enough water, and no rest for almost 16 hours straight. When I drove off alone in Engine 10 to City Hall, I had that feeling I'd get sometimes when I knew our response would be to a bad situation. A touch of fatalism. I didn't want to go, but I knew somebody had to go, and besides, my paycheck said I went. So I did.

"Cap," I radioed on arrival. "Fire throughout. Need assistance."

"Engine 10, understood. Dump your monitor, but do not commit. Repeat. Do not commit," Cap responded.

"Ladder 10 at Benson Hotel. Fire showing fifth floor A side on Monroe Avenue."

"Dispatch. Log a working fire at the Benson Hotel. Ladder 10, pull all interior alarms and evacuate that building, but do not commit without checking with me first."

"Understood, Chief," said Kim, and she and Rich started to do what they could. Two people evacuating a seven story hotel is an exercise in absurdity. About all they could do would be to yank alarms and run door to door on each floor, knock loudly, and yell, "Fire department. Evacuate the building" and hope people listened and obeyed.

"Engine 10, what can you see on the hotel from your side?"

The hotel stood two blocks from City Hall, and I could barely see the upper floors illuminated by street lights. "Cap, fire showing on fifth floor, C/D corner facing 5th and Monroe."

Log: 2359 Friday, 18 November 2016: Fire reported at Benson Hotel, Fourth and Monroe . Fire reported at Lanahan's Furniture, 2nd and Jefferson. Initial response by Engine 12. General emergency declared by Chief Pierce with request for mutual aid. Never returned to quarters.

Journal: "Dispatch to any company. Police report fire at Lanahan's Furniture, 2nd and Jefferson."

Cap answered. "I'll respond and report. Engine 10, leave your location and get fuel, then respond to Lanahan's." The arsonist (assuming just one, but we had to think more were involved by then) had built a front east across downtown from City Hall to the Benson

Hotel to the furniture store. Five blocks of densely packed old wood frame buildings. Somebody was really pissed off. "Engine 12, can you respond?"

"Engine 12 fueled and responding."

"Ladder 10, report."

"Chief, we have floors one, two, and three evacuated. Headed for the fourth."

"Understood. When you're done, put the ladder pipe into the fire rooms, then leave the building, and report to Lanahan's. Tell civilians evacuating to move north, upwind, to the courthouse or west to the park and the library. Chief to dispatch."

"Dispatch."

"Dispatch. Contact the head librarian and have the downtown library opened for emergency shelter. Start calls to Philomath, Monroe, Albany, and Junction City. Tell them to send one pumper each with two monitors per engine. Ask Salem to send two ladders; quints if they have them. Staging area is Southeast 3rd Street at Chapman. Tell all responding companies to avoid downtown. Repeat. Do not enter downtown."

"Understood."

"Notify me when they are in route."

"Will do. And Chief, the mayor keeps calling and banging on the door. He's not alone. Also received one call from a state senator."

"As soon as I visit Lanahan's, I'll return and chat with the mayor. Did you give my message to the state senator?"

"Yes sir. Getting more calls about embers flying around downtown."

"Understood. What's the current wind speed and direction?

"Out of the northwest at 12 mph, gusting to 20."

"Temperature?"

"48 and dropping fast."

"When is the front due to arrive from the coast?"

"About 4 a.m.."

"Tell any caller to evacuate downtown. Call the police and tell them to leave people alone who are evacuating downtown. In fact, tell the cops to start moving door to door to tell people to leave downtown and move north or west. We also need help evacuating the hotel."

"Will do."

"Then notify the university president about the death of the English department chair. Low priority."

"Understood."

And I should mention before moving on with this report, Mr. Lawyer, that Chelsea had another little fire in 1974 that took out two city blocks. The City Hotel in what the mayor now calls Cruz City,

Oregon burned to the ground on March 29, 1873, and burned so fast people had time to evacuate in middle of the night in only their night clothes and nothing more. One died. In 1875, the city hall burned down.

"Dispatch, Engine 12."

"Engine 12."

"On scene at Lanahan Furniture. Heavy fire A side and through the roof. May have more than one building involved. Report to follow."

"Understood."

Log: 0021 Saturday, 19 November 2016: Benson Hotel fire controlled. Lanahan's Furniture fire spread to block and retreat to river required. Chief invoked the Oregon Conflagration Act to get resources needed. All companies remained in service. Dispatch remained at Engine 10 quarters.

Journal: I admit that I took a thirty-second nap while refueling Engine 10. After I put the nozzle in the tank fill and clicked it open, I leaned forward to rest my head against the truck and dozed off, and hell, I might have slept through the rest of the night standing there if Cap's transmission hadn't snapped me awake.

"All companies, keep this channel open." And he locked his mike open while he met with the mayor outside in front of the firehouse to be damned sure the conversation, like all other radio transmissions, stayed on tape for the record.

"You let City Hall burn."

"Correct. We have two other major fires in progress. Lose City Hall to save the rest."

"You don't have the authority."

"We already discussed this. Find and read a copy of the Oregon Emergency Conflagration Act."

"I've heard nothing from the governor."

"State Senator Fleischmann assisted with communications. You'll hear from the governor shortly. Suggest you also prepare to welcome the Oregon National Guard."

"When are they arriving?"

"Sometime today."

Apparently the mayor decided to change the subject. After he spewed considerable foul language, we heard: "We need the fire department for riot control at the deportation detention center."

"You mean the old HP property."

"The deportation center."

Cap couldn't resist. "Are you leaving my country?"

"Your what?"

"The fire department is committed to saving this city and

protecting its residents. We have a fire in the Benson Hotel. We have a fire in Lanahan Furniture. We have at least one arsonist lose in the city. We will not participate in police work. The police will assist us under the Conflagration Act."

"The City is not paying for it."

"Chief," Kim broke in. "We have jumpers and people on the roof. Deploying ladder."

"Mr. Mayor," said Cap, uncharacteristically polite, "Excuse me, I have to get back to work, and no one, even you, is authorized to enter the firehouse without my permission, and you do not have my permission."

I thought I would check in, fueling completed, as was the meeting between hizzoner and Cap. "Chief, Engine 10 available and responding to Lanahan Furniture."

"Jay," Cap responded, "Stop by Benson Hotel first. Mr. Mayor, get an ambulance to Benson Hotel. Put the medic unit sitting in Engine 16 quarters back in service."

We heard nothing over the radio from the mayor.

"Dispatch, Chief and Engine 10 responding to Benson Hotel."

With normal resources, Mr. Lawyer, the first due company, truck or pumper, starts rescue. Second due truck company usually ventilates, meaning they're the people you see smashing out windows and cutting holes in the roof of a building to let the smoke and heat out so firefighters and victims inside can get good air. Letting smoke up and out also improves visibility. In the meantime, the second and third due engine companies secure water from a hydrant and get hoses deployed into the building to douse the flames. Now, that's assuming at least four people ride on each arriving apparatus, ladder truck and pumper.

But why do you need four people on a ladder truck, asked an ignorant and profoundly stupid member of the Cincinnati city council during the Great Recession when political leaders gladly slashed public emergency services using the Russian roulette theory of fire protection. Play the odds. Hell, one person on a ladder truck could do the job. Or two, as in Cruz City. You can see the problem. While Kim and Rich tried to evacuate a seven story hotel, people in the hotel did what people do. Those above and below the fire floor found a way out down interior stairs or down the outside fire escape. Or up to the roof. People thinking the whole building below them burned climbed up instead of down the fire escape or climbed up the interior stairwell and smashed their way through a locked door to the roof.

Those in the west end of the 5th floor in a room not on fire may have stayed put, blocked smoke with wet towels on the floor at the door and listened to Mike when he told them on the phone to stay put. But those in the rooms on fire had nowhere to go but out, and given the choice between burning to death or jumping, people jump. They jump hoping or (if religious) praying for a miracle, but few if any survive landing on concrete sidewalks above the third floor. When the human body hits the cement, the bones explode, shatter into scrapnel that slice and dice muscle and organs, but that agony rarely has to be endured into death. The blow to the head kills, and even landing feet first knocks a jumper cold because of the shock wave smashing from heel to head. But it beats, if you'll pardon the morbid pun, burning to death.

I responded directly up 4th Street with lights, siren, and air horn this time not so much to let people know more help headed in their direction, but to make sure none of them stood in the street. The hydrant at the corner of 4th and Monroe looked good, so I stopped and connected, but the fire on the fifth floor looked worse, of course,

because Kim and Rich had to focus on evacuation and rescue first, fire suppression second. Kim had the ladder up to the roof where Rich had climbed to guide people off and down. One elderly woman he had to assist, which slowed the operation, but he didn't have any choice.
 While they descended, another body hit the pavement with that horrid thud, and I could hear screaming, not from victims, but from people on the courthouse lawn who saw the jumper.

Another hotel guest hung out his window in the room to the left of the fire rooms. Heavy smoke pushed out over him, which meant the air in his room had heated as flames found entry somehow through a plenum, a utility opening, a weakened wall--and he had no other way out. Who the hell knew why the sprinklers didn't kick in. At any second, he could not stand the heat any longer or the smoke would flashover into fire and he'd burn in the window or jump or fall out. I didn't have time to watch or save him.

I dropped supply line the half block to the front entrance, broke the line at the back of the engine, meaning disconnected the coupling at the hose bed so I could connect the line to the pump panel, and then ran back to the hydrant to open it when Cap pulled up in the Hummer to help. "I'll charge it. You connect to the siamese and jack the pressure to 150. Take the high rise pack to the fifth floor west and a light. I'll follow with the irons."

Did a pivot and followed his orders, connected the siamese, charged the double two and a half from pumper to building when the hydrant line jumped solid, then followed orders, hoping like hell as I humped the high rise pack up five flights inside that the standpipe worked, that nobody had spiked it, that the stairwell fire door had been closed at the fifth floor landing, that I didn't have a frickin heart attack.

"Right behind you," said Cap, calmly but loud enough to be heard.

"The door's hot," I said, having checked it with the back of my hand. And somebody had propped the other door, the one leading outside to the fire escape, open. That sucked smoke into the stairwell.

"Well, I'll be damned," said Cap. "Look what I brought. Stand back."

He punched a hole through the fire door with the pike on the Halligan and worked on making it bigger while I connected the hose to the standpipe, stretched it down the stairwell so it wouldn't kink when charged, then opened the standpipe valve.

"Hit it."

I put the nozzle right up against the hole in the closed door and opened up while Cap and I both leaned in against the back pressure to make sure the full force of the stream shot through the door and into the fire.

"Ever read about the 1911 Triangle fire?"

"Yup," said Cap. "Drop to the floor. I'll open."

In New York City before firefighters had air masks, they pushed in against the smoke to get close enough to the fire to put it out (wetting smoke does nothing) until the nozzle man passed out; they had enough personnel then to both replace the nozzle man with someone else until he passed out and to drag the overcome firefighter down a flight of stairs to good air. We had no backup. When Cap passed out from all the thick black junk from burning synthetic carpet filling the stairwell, I had to kick the door shut, close the nozzle, and carry him down to the street. If I left him a floor below and tried to attack on my own, I'd be dead. Hell, I even left the hose rather than risk climbing back to the landing and having the door blast open on me. We'd have to attack from the east end of the building or wait for the ladder and let people die like the man hanging out the window when I pulled up. Fireground cost/benefit analysis.

I thought for a minute that I'd have to use CPR on Cap, but when I started to position his head back down on the sidewalk, he regained consciousness and shoved me away. "I'm not dead yet." Then he rolled over coughed once, and puked before he got back on his feet.

Kim controlled the ladder pipe from the turntable after Rich had everyone down to the ground. Cap told Rich to take a breather and get water and get water to Kim on the turntable while she knocked the fire down remotely with the ladder pipe aimed into the three rooms now involved.

"Kim, keep it there. We're going back up from the east end to get fire in the hallway," said Cap. "Break time is over," he told us with a half smile. "Pull the 150 preconnect, break it down, and each of us will carry a length. Fifth floor."

"Dispatch. Engine 12."

"Engine 12."

"Heavy fire in Lanahan's Furniture main floor throughout and through the roof. May have fire in the plenum between buildings. Have one monitor and one 2.5 line in service. Exterior attack only. No primary search possible. Situation doubtful."

"Shit," said Cap, then keyed his portable. "Engine 12, backdraft potential if the fire has moved north in the plenum to other buildings."

"Chief, the window on both floors of the shop next door just blew out. Heavy fire."

"Engine 12, get off that street, go refuel, and then reposition south to the river."

"Understood. Firefighter down. But no injury."

At the fifth floor east, the door felt cold, so in we went as low as we could get below the smoke to knock down the fire on the west end of the hallway where Cap had been overcome. Kim had taken care of the rooms from outside with the ladder pipe. No time for overhaul, but we did get through to the west landing. Cap told me to pull that hose we'd left in the west stairwell into the hallway, shutdown the standpipe, and open the nozzle and let in drain on the carpet, but bring the Halligan. We picked up the other preconnect, the 150 we'd hauled up the east stairwell after shutting down the standpipe and also draining the hose on the carpet to make it too wet to allow the fire to rekindle, assuming it no longer lived in any hidden space because we didn't have time to pull walls. We kicked in or popped open doors with the Halligan next to the fire rooms and found no one. We had no time to check the other rooms on the floor. No time.

Cap keyed his handset. "Kim, drop the stick, and head south to the river at the boat landing. We'll be right behind you with Rich."

"Affirm, Chief," said Kim, sounding as bone weary as we all were. Nobody liked the thought of leaving the hotel without thorough overhaul or leaving the bodies in the street.

"Dispatch."

"Chief."

"Need weather and mutual aid updates."

"Wind out of west northwest at 15. Gusting to 25. Front still due at around 4 a.m.. All requested units responding under Conflagration Act. You will have second and third alarm capability within an hour. Philomath arrived at staging area. State fire marshal requesting update."

"Tell the marshal that we let City Hall burn, have two downtown commercial buildings fully involved and spreading, have knocked down hotel fire without time for overhaul. Report also that no thorough overhaul possible on earlier structure fires. Rekindle possible at any of them."

"Understood."

"Mike, tell him we're deploying on the river to setup drafting operations. The plan is to contain the fire to the blocks between Second and First adjacent to the river, and to place one engine in service for ember control and to handle rekindles. The rest of the city is not covered. Repeat. The rest of the city is not covered at this time. We are on fire duty only right now with no medical response capability. Acknowledge."

"Understood."

"Any problem from the mayor?"

"Nothing further."

"We'll also need one medic from Philomath and Albany and the Red Cross here. And the ME for bodies at the hotel."

Kim broke in. "Are the kids okay?"

"Yes," said Mike. "Be safe, babe."

"You too."

If the wind turned, we'd lose all of downtown and the plenum problem would look like a campfire, but Cap counted on the front coming through to blow most of the fire toward the Willamette River to the east. And with the front he hoped for rain, lots of really soaking wet cold Oregon autumn rain. Until then, we had to hold to keep the fire contained to the commercial district and keep it from jumping the river to the east or to the south into residential neighborhoods--and be ready if the wind shifted. The risk, of course, lay in high winds without rain, which sometimes happened, or high winds with nothing but squalls and no steady rain, although a good sqaull would dump tons of water in 10 minutes. Cap, though, wanted to guarantee his own squall, but we'll get to that.

Pat Conroy didn't mention or have time to mention until later than he found FUEGO spray painted on showroom windows of Lanahan's.

Kim went first for fuel, then followed us down 4th Street and east to First where we could draft from the river without having to worry about the water mains or pump cavitation, and we would not be taking pressure from the mains that could be used by other fire companies arriving who might have to set up in the city away from the river. Cap always thought two steps ahead. Hell, three steps.

I made a crack about the mayor, but nobody even chuckled as we watched the glow two blocks over on 2nd Street that lit up the night sky. Even with the engine and siren noise, we could all hear and feel the rumble of an unchecked fire. Cap once said to me to explain forest fires that the Sun tries to call the Earth back home. Guess that was an old Nez Perce folktale. Then again, just ask the people in Chelsea, Boston, New York, Baltimore, Washington DC, Chicago, San Francisco, Atlanta, and the list goes on. It's at the core of the planet. Fire.

Log: 0045 Saturday, 19 November 2016: Chief Pierce organized river draft pumping operation. Fire reported to be running the block south to north in spite of wind direction. Mutual aid apparatus arrived. Companies still working at end of shift.

Journal: We need to put the challenge in perspective, Mr. Lawyer, so bear with me for a few paragraphs while I walk you through October of 1871, the reason we now have fire prevention week each October (cancelled in Cruz City for the last two years as a waste of taxpayer's money). After a very dry summer, in three days from October 8 to10, Chicago burned, Manistee, Port Huron, and Holland, Michigan burned. Urbana, Illinois and Windsor, Ontario burned. So many structures burned that the no-longer-existent town of Singapore, Michigan turned into sand dunes after clear cutting the surrounding forest to get the lumber needed to rebuild after that incendiary autumn of 1871.

But none of those urban conflagrations seem more than yet another small example of 19th century stupidity in urban building and fire prevention standards compared to the Peshtigo fire that flared up the same day Chicago sought to blame a poor Irish Catholic woman for its 19th century nonflammable building standards. In short, there were none. Nor did the rural folk in Peshtigo on Wisconsin's Green Bay understand what we know now about the wilderness fire cycles. Each summer Oregon burns, the West burns, and planning ahead is essential, including a means of marshaling apparatus and personnel from all over the state when necessary for a fire far too big for any one department to control. Each fire district designates certain apparatus to be sent during a call up by the state fire marshal when the Conflagration Act is invoked by the governor, and it can be invoked when a city is threatened, and every city in Oregon is surrounded by or built into wild land that dries out each summer when the rains stop in late June or early July and stays bone dry into the middle of September and sometimes beyond. It's called WUI, an awkward bureaucratic acronym that means wildland urban interface.

But the irony has to be mentioned. No wildland fire led to the conflagration law. The Blast, as newspapers dubbed the 1959 Roseburg, Oregon explosion, led to the legislation and a statewide mutual aid system. In August, 1959, a parked truck loaded with two tons of dynamite and over four tons of ammonium nitrate (fertilizer) sat parked next to a building that caught fire in the middle of the night. Fourteen died, including a cop and a firefighter, 120 were injured, and 30 blocks had to be razed because buildings were flattened or damaged beyond repair.

The summer of 2016 had been dry and the usual forest and range fires burned throughout the West as Cap knew, and he'd been on Forest Service fire crews as a younger man, and he knew the effect of wind and weather on fires as well as the behavior of urban structure fires. He'd studied Peshtigo and knew the profound danger of ignorance and the equal danger of political ideologues and demagogues who howl against excess government regulation, such as burn rules during fire season. Fact is, the Cruz City Council had, claiming it would encouraging business development, suspended all fire codes, fire inspections, and burn rules during the last two years while, as the same time, shrinking the size of fire protection. Peshtigo thinking.

1871 Wisconsin had no rules for burning during forest fire season. No red flag days. No meterologists who reported on dangerously low humidity. No rangers to stop the use of burning to clear land, a common practice that October of 1871 and the cause of the fire when a cold front blew through and the clearing fires blew up to burn over a million acres before the fall rains finally doused the Peshtigo fire. Literally blew up. Wildland firefighters call it a blowup. Fuel (brush, grass, slash) had dried out all summer and into fall, the humidity had dropped, the wind picked up, and all that tender ready to burn did so suddenly and explosively when allegedly controlled fires went ballistic. Blowups still kill firefighters, like the one that killed 19 Arizona hotshots in July, 2013.

Blowups and tornadoes.

People in 1871 Chicago running from the fire front witnessed a roaring tornado as flames twisted into a funnel, as did those in small logging town of Peshtigo. The heat from the fire front rises rapidly and begins to spin, driven by the hurricane force winds pulled in at the base of the fire. You cannot run from it. When a blowup happens, wildland firefighters head for barren ground, deloy shelters, and get under. Sometimes they survive. Sometimes they don't. People in Peshtigo jumped into the river. Some survived; some didn't. An estimated 300 people died in the October 1871 Chicago fire, although only 120 bodies found could be identified. 3.3 square miles of the city with big shoulders burned. The Peshtigo fire burned 1563 square miles on both the west and east shores of Green Bay. It burned north into Michigan, destroyed a dozen towns, and killed an estimated 1200 to 2500 people--nobody knows the real number. The wind-driven fire storm moved faster than people could move. As in Chicago, the Peshtigo fire jumped a river. It grew so huge it jumped Green Bay.

Then as now, some morons like to think of fire as punishment for iniquity. Those who lived a righteous life had no fear of Hell. Firefighters such as Cap and myself tend to disagree. Those too cheap to buy decent fire prevention and protection for their community use God, the federal govenment, the communists, Mrs. O'Leary's cow, or firefighters who want pensions as an excuse . Physics and chemistry are the last thing they want to hear about, assuming they have the ability to understand physics and chemistry. Wallace T. Acklee, Cruz City mayor, did not.

And therein lies the point of this discussion. Firefighting is physics and chemistry. It's engineering, it's applied science to generate enough water power to balance the heat equation. Until the equation is balanced, water won't stop a fire. So much heat is pumped into the air ahead of a firestorm that water thrown at it will evaporate as happened in the Chelsea fire a little over a century after Chicago. A fire chief has to estimate how big the fire will get and how fast it will move to place apparatus in the right place to generate sufficient water power before the fire arrives. In short fire can move a lot faster than a pumping operation can be established. It the chief is wrong and the fire arrives before the water, apparatus burns as do firefighters if they let the fire get behind them and can't escape.

Cap had to adapt, also. He knew any fire in a furniture store, given the load (the stuff that burns, such as densely packed sofas, chairs, bureaus, mattresses, carpets, wooden floors, walls, ceilings, office paper, and on and on) would generate a huge volume of fire, one that moved quickly through an old wood frame building, and he first estimated that the fire, once it tore through the second floor and roof, would not move north. The wind direction might even confine it to the Lanahan building, but walls block wind, and fires like plenums, that space between the ceiling and roof where electrical conduits and water pipes and gas lines and heating ducts are run; and in a block of old commercial buildings, the plenum often runs through several buildings along an entire block. The fire will run the plenum. Or worse, it will smolder in the plenum for hours until it gets air, and then it flashes over and even leads to a backdraft, an explosion of superheated air that shatters windows and blasts walls apart in spontaneous combustion when the missing third element, air, is suddenly added to fuel and heat.

Boom.

The shoe store next door to Lanahan's blew out the display window and knocked Pat Conroy off his feet, but he held onto the two and a half nozzle, having positioned himself before the backdraft by sitting on the hose right behind the nozzle and being certain the line stretched straight out behind him. If he'd dropped the nozzle, it would have flown around and could have hit him hard. Every action has an opposite and equal reaction. Physics, not God. The force of the water leaving the nozzle of a fire hose has an opposite and equal reaction just as the exhaust leaving a jet engine does. Thanks to instinctively ducking when the building blew, Pat suffered no more than cuts and bruises to his face and managed to shut down the nozzle. Engine 12 took a few hits that left dents, and Mo Conroy caught a pair of running shoes in her face at the Engine 12 monitor she aimed into Lanahans. Not her size, though.

That backdraft indicated fire had traveled north in the plenum in spite of the wind.

And thank you to the pragmatic city leaders who held office and built the river walkway downtown between First Street and the river, including river standpipes, meaning hydrants piped directly into the Willamette so we could pump directly from the river for a large fire. The downtown water main grid just could not handle the number of pumps headed in our direction. We'd cavitate. And the river standpipes offered a backup system should the city water mains fail because of earthquake or sabotage. Right after 9/11, the Oregon National Guard immediately moved to guard water sources, including the cistern up there in what was Chip Ross Park until renamed two years ago as the Sarah Palin Recreational Center, including a new bowling alley on park land, dirt bike trails, four-wheeler picnic parks, a shooting range, but I digress.

Cap built a wall of water around the fire that consumed seven buildings housing the furniture store, as mentioned, the shoe store, a wine shop, music/book store, micro brewery, a credit card processing firm, a galley, a jewelry store, and all the offices above before the night ended. And when the wind shifted, it jumped the river and nearly lit off the subdivision built on park land in the flood zone were it not for quick acting mutual aid companies on ember patrol.

Once strategy and tactics are set, firefighting becomes logistics. Just solid work in bringing each rig from the staging area to the big parking lot at Western Avenue and Second. From there Cap placed rigs from south to north along First Street to pull water from the river with the biggest pumps aiming monitors at the block of businesses and supplying engine companies positioned east to west along Jefferson and Madison.

Cap created a second ring of defense around the Post Office, the USPS that occupied the block just south of Lanahan's. He placed monitors on the roof and aimed them at Lanahan's.

And the really bold move placed ladders behind the fire, on the leeward side along Second. He could have played it conservatively and moved the ladders back, but he gambled correctly on the wind shift to put ladder pipes and tower ladders in the air, six total.

He never put anyone in a building. He and I walked around the entire block with good lights and spotted again and again the signs of backdraft as smoke forced itself out around window frames, and under eaves. After the walk around, Cap held an impromptu street meeting with officers who had arrived from other departments. They knew him well by reputation and listened. "I want a truck crew on each roof. Open it up and get the hell off. Nobody steps down off the ladder without a tether. We don't want to complicate matters with having to rescue our own people."

The rest is just a matter of statistics, of tonnage of water being thrown into the fire buildings from street level or from above. The engine companies on the river side facing the wind took a beating for a time, but they held, and by sunrise, Cap call dispatch to say: "Fire under control, by orders of the Chief."

"Understood," said Mike, "Fire under control."

Cap gave the message directly to the state fire marshall, who had driven into town to act as liaison with the governor's office and the media, who also flocked into Cruz City with their satellite trucks from Portland and Eugene. That stopped the arson. Too many witnesses, especially when the National Guard trucks rolled over the bridge into town. And it stopped the riot at the illegal Hispanic detention center. All those being held were released.

Under direct orders from the governor, implemented by the state fire marshal, all five firehouse in Cruz City were reopened and all apparatus, included medics were put into service at the fire and remained in service after the fire. Laid off firefighters forced to work as black shirts changed back into their fire service uniforms and returned to work that night by order of the fire marshall, who required that only certified firefighters and paramedics, whether career or volunteer, work the fire and work after the fire in the city.

Cap should have stayed on as chief of the department, but they waited, the mayor and his cronies, until the media attention left, until the attention from Salem lessened, and did what they could to get back as much control as they could, although they'd never be able to return to the ideologically driven autocratic government they ran for two years. Nope. But they did file all those trumped up charges against Cap that
you know all about, and I hope this journal helps in his defense. He needs his job back; the city needs his leadership.

I took an early retirement, and that left me free to speak my mind. But remember that Kim and the Conroys still work in the department and have to deal with Chief Spalding. If and when they get the union back, they may be able to talk to you, but not until then. Rich is your best source inside the department, and he's taking journalism courses part-time again to complete his degree. And Rich is the one who's doing the most to keep the mayor and council in check until the next election by working on a book about the city government and the fire. He and his dad don't talk much anymore other than when necessary at work. The mayor doesn't talk to anyone unless it's through his attorney. Chief Buttridge disappeared. We never heard from him again.

But yes, we're still here.

About the Author

Barry Roberts Greer edited pipenozzle dot com, where he wrote a narrative on fireground operations at the 1911 Triangle Shirtwaist Factory Fire now in the Cornell University ILR collection. He served in Connecticut fire/ems. Comments follow on Greer's fire service books: Pipe Nozzle, Seven Two, and Of Cowards and Firefighters:

"I'm glad you have described the firefighting effort in terms that will speak to members of the profession." David Von Drehle, Time Magazine

"Greer knows what he is talking about, and he tells the stories elegantly and convincingly. So, read this book." Dennis Smith, Report from Engine Co. 82

"It's all good." Mike Meyers, Chief, Battalion 9, FDNY

"Awesome." Tyree Thomas, Philadelphia firefighter

"Great read!" Tommy Hark, firefighter, Austin, Texas

"True grit narrative" Richard Ornberg, Illinois firefighter (ret.)

Made in the USA
San Bernardino, CA
22 June 2018